MW00877615

When The Time Comes To Light A Fire

When The Time Comes To Light A Fire

Gem City Book 4

Nicole Campbell

Copyright (C) 2016 Nicole Campbell
Layout design and Copyright (C) 2018 Creativia
Published 2018 by Creativia
Cover art by Cover Mint
This book is a work of fiction. Names, characters, places, and incidents
are the product of the author's imagination or are used fictitiously.
Any resemblance to actual events, locales, or persons, living or dead,
is purely coincidental.
All rights reserved. No part of this book may be reproduced or trans-
mitted in any form or by any means, electronic or mechanical, in-
cluding photocopying, recording, or by any information storage and
retrieval system, without the author's permission.

The characters and events portrayed in this book are fictitious. Any similarity to real persons, living or dead, is coincidental and not intended by the author.

Please visit NicoleCampbellBooks.com for a suggested playlist if you like to listen while you read. You may also search the book title on YouTube or Spotify.

♪ *"Girls Just Wanna Have Fun" - Cyndi Lauper*

Prologue: Summer Before 8th Grade

Minnie Mouse would get more attention in a bikini. Looking in her bedroom mirror, Vanessa tied the strings of her new bathing suit around her neck, wishing her mom had let her buy the one she'd really wanted. She sighed at the red polka-dotted boy-short bottoms reflected back at her, remembering their conversation.

"Vanessa Roberts, no thirteen year old girl has any business showing off her butt cheeks. I will not be spending money to have you looking like a street-walker."

"Oh my god, it's a swimming suit." Vanessa's eyes rolled back in her head, hard.

"Roll your eyes at me again, and you're liable to spend the summer in your room with no need for swimwear." The tone in her voice wasn't playful, and Vanessa readjusted her expression.

"Yes, Mom." She put the beautiful purple suit with the bows back on the rack and stomped slightly to the dressing room.

Her bedroom door opened, bringing her back to the present, and she glanced up in the mirror at her best friend. Courtney's dark curly hair looked wilder than normal, given the humidity, though she had tried to tame it with bobby pins into a high ponytail. Her friend assessed the bathing suit situation.

"I don't know what you're complaining about. I think it's cute."

"Ugh, don't patronize me. I look like Minnie Mouse, and Brad James is never going to look twice at me."

"I thought you were hoping to run into Luke something-or-other?"

"Yeah well, apparently he's with Elena now, so I set my sights elsewhere," Vanessa admitted begrudgingly. Courtney's ensemble was much like her own; though her short muscular build filled it out very differently than Vanessa's more slender frame. Courtney just raised her eyebrow. "Whatever, let's just go." They bounded down the stairs with their over-stuffed pool bags to let her mom know they were ready to leave.

* * *

The pool was crowded, but she supposed that was the point. The air smelled of chlorine and warm grass- it was effectively a run-of-the-mill Gem City summer. She and Courtney found a spot in the near-shade, and her eyes scoped out the boy situation.

"I hope your mom will let me come back next summer too. Then I can almost pretend we'll be going to high school together," Courtney mused with a frown.

"My mom will let you come back anytime. She loves you. You don't talk back, so she might like you better than me," she smiled. "And don't depress me. I wish we were going to high school together too. You don't think you guys will ever move back?"

"I don't think so. I miss it though." Vanessa sighed. Her other friends were *fine*, but she and Courtney had been through everything together since they were five. The Ross' moving had done a number on her. The thought of the two of them not cheering on the same team and obsessing over boys had a melancholy effect on her demeanor. She also wasn't sure who she was going to cheat off of in math.

"Well, summers it is then, friend."

"Summers it is. So, where is this Brad character?"

"Basketball court. Black shorts, blue t-shirt." She flipped her long blond ponytail over her shoulder as if he could see her.

"He's cute. But *who* is the other guy?" Vanessa had to smirk.

"That would be Luke Miller."

"Things are making much more sense now."

"Stupid Elena."

"I don't know her, but I'll second that."

"Whatever, two more years and we'll be in high school, probably cheering varsity," she added, giving Courtney a lazy fist bump at that prediction, "and most importantly, getting our licenses. I just wish we could skip freshman year. I want a *car.* I want boys to take me out on *dates.* I want to listen to my music as loud as I freaking want. And I want a super hot jealousy-causing boyfriend."

"I think I'd probably settle for a sort-of-cute mathlete at this point, but I like your ambition," Courtney confessed, looking as she always did when she went into low-self-esteem mode.

"Stop, you're adorable. Come on. Give me your perfect boyfriend checklist." Vanessa plopped her sunglasses onto her face and prepared to mentally correct her friend's choices.

"My what?"

"Shut up, your checklist. Don't lie and say you don't have one. For example: tall, cute with a good smile, football player, preferably, because you know how I feel about the uniforms, smart enough to hold a real conversation, great sense of humor-not like 'oh he laughs at amusing jokes,' but like 'oh my god he is hilarious and my sides hurt from laughing.' " Courtney was looking at her curiously, but she didn't care. "And I want a guy who can make me mad. Just a little bit."

"Um, ok? Everyone makes you mad. Except for me," Courtney retorted with a smirk.

"Ha, until now," Vanessa replied. "No, you know what I mean, like a guy who's not afraid to argue. Someone strong." She sipped her lemonade. "Your turn."

"I don't think I have quite the extensive list you are looking for, friend."

"I call bull. Tell me anyway." Courtney made a Kermit-the-Frog face at her, but she knew she'd give in.

"Fine. Also tall. Ummm nice?"

"Nice?"

"Well yeah, nice, like easy to be around. And likes to read."

"So you want to date a nice book-reader."

"Yep."

"You're hopeless."

"And I'm your best friend. What does that say about you?"

"That I need to save you from yourself and make sure you don't date a librarian." Courtney promptly threw a handful of ice from her cup of water at Vanessa and stuck out her tongue.

1: Two Years Later

Vanessa breathed in the scent of what was left of the summer sun heating the asphalt outside of the gym. It was the last cheer practice before the start of school, and she was officially one week away from having her license. *No more parent drop offs,* she thought blissfully as she watched her mom's Durango pull back out onto the street. She trotted easily into the gym to warm up.

"Ohmygod, thank you for being here early," Jessi practically yelled, placing a death grip on her forearm as soon as she made it over the threshold of the gym doors.

"I'm here, I'm here, what's the deal?" Her friend's green eyes were shining, and her dark red hair was pulled into a messy bun atop her head. She was practically vibrating with anticipation over something.

"I need a favor. Like a big favor. Flavoricious. Flavorful. Favor. Please say you'll do it."

"English. And I'm gonna need more information. Like, any information really."

"You know that guy Josh I've been wanting to go out with forever and ever and ever?"

"From Ohio State?" Vanessa raised her eyebrows suspiciously. When Jess said "forever and ever," it could have meant since yesterday. She really didn't remember the first time her friend had mentioned him.

"Yes! Well, he's in town for the weekend and asked me to go out, but he can't like, pick me up at my house, you know my parents would flip their tea kettles. And my car is kind of out-of-commission at the moment. You see why this is an emergency right?"

"Not particularly, no. And last time I checked, tea kettles didn't flip. Just borrow your mom's car."

Jessi rolled her eyes. "The whole reason my Jeep is in the shop is because I curbed it so hard I popped the tired and jacked up my alignment. My parents told me I would never sit behind the wheel of either of their cars again."

"Still unsure how this equals a flavoricious favor from me," Vanessa let out, becoming annoyed. *Always with the drama.*

"Say you'll come with me."

"I could say it, but it wouldn't be true. I am sort of missing the key components to be able to do that. Namely, a license and a car. Plus, why would I come on your date?"

"Don't be dense, he's bringing a friend. Didn't I say that?"

"Nope."

"Oh, well he is. And aren't your parents out like playing Jenga on Friday nights or something? I'll have my mom drop me at your house this afternoon, and we can take the other car; we'll be back before they're home. I'll even drive so you're not like breaking the law." Jessi tapped her foot impatiently as if Vanessa were somehow annoying *her,* and she used the phrase "breaking the law," as if she meant "breaking a nail."

"It's Bunco. And you've lost your mind."

"Did I mention his friend is *cute?* Like Leo in *Romeo and Juliet* cute. You haven't been out with anyone since Michael, come on. It'll be fun. We'll just go play pool for a while and then go home, no big deal. Your parents will never even know we were gone."

It was a low blow mentioning Leo. *Not good enough*, she argued in her head.

"You literally just told me your own parents won't let you take their cars because you're an awful driver, but you want me to give you the okay to drive the car of one of my unsuspecting parents?" Vanessa side-stepped the red-headed devil to get to the mat and begin stretching. The conversation was getting more ludicrous by the moment, and the mention of Michael annoyed her.

"I would do it for you, but whatever. Be afraid to have any fun." Jessi stomped past her, pouting as she warmed up her scorpion. Vanessa sighed, wishing her friend hadn't helped her out of rather sticky situations that past year. She would probably still be grounded if it weren't for Jess's ability to spin a story at the drop of a hat. It wasn't a lie; she *would* do it for her.

"You swear to god we'll be home before eleven?" Jessi's expression turned from glowering to elated immediately, lighting up her full lips and wide emerald eyes.

"Cross my heart. Eeeeee!!!! I love you!" Vanessa almost lost her balance with the force of Jess's hug.

* * *

There was still sweat dripping down the curve of her spine from a particularly brutal conditioning session after practice. She had headed out the door of the locker room and was rummaging in her bag for her phone when she ran face first into a wall. A human wall.

"Jesus, look where you're going," she relayed, annoyed. She tried to fight the redness she knew was spreading over her cheeks when she realized it was a very cute, broad shouldered, grinning human wall.

"I am so very sorry for letting you run me over. How rude of me," he retorted with amusement. From the looks of him, he was headed to the weight room. She realized, horrified, that her hand was still resting on his arm where she'd placed it trying to catch her balance. Her horror deepened when she recognized who said arm belonged to, which was the new starting wide-receiver of their football team.

"I, um, well. It's possible I wasn't paying attention. I'm sorry for almost tackling you," she managed evenly, regaining some of her composure and trying to salvage the situation. She took in his dark wavy hair and bright blue eyes. He was still smiling at her, and it didn't help her focus.

"I think I might be all right being tackled by you." His grin widened, and she realized he was flirting with her. It also struck her that she was in gym clothes, and there was literally no part of her that wasn't sweaty. She bit her lip in uncertainty of how to react. "Just to make sure the rest of the students are safe, I think I'll walk you to the parking lot. I wouldn't want you to run over anyone else." He changed his initial trajectory and fell in step with her in the direction of the junior lot.

"How safety-conscious of you."

"Just looking out for my fellow man," he smirked, glancing sideways at her. She tried to flip her long blond ponytail over her shoulder and failed miserably. It just sort of flopped there, a sticky sweaty mess. *Seriously. Could this not have happened any other day?* "So, should I just call you blondie? Or do you have an actual name?"

"Vanessa. Roberts," she replied tentatively.

"Good to know, Vanessa Roberts. I'm Zack. Roads," he stated, mimicking her structure. "And tell me, why haven't I seen you around?"

"I don't know. Have you been looking?" she asked flirta-tiously, not particularly wanting to say it was because she was a freshman last year. He was only a year older, but he seemed moreso. Everyone knew who he was... high school football was sort of a religion in Gem City.

"Well, I'm looking now," he replied without missing a beat. "Will you be at Vader's bonfire next weekend?"

"Is that an invitation?" It was taking everything she had not to clap her hands and jump up and down. Vader's parties were legendary, but she had never been invited.

"It is. I'll see you there, then."

"Sounds good. Thanks for keeping the sidewalks safe," she mentioned as they walked through the gate to the parking lot.

"All in a day's work. I'll see you next weekend, Vanessa Roberts," he flashed those white teeth again and headed back towards the gym. *Oh.my.god.* She could not *wait* to see her friends' faces when she told them where they were going next Saturday.

* * *

"Are we seriously doing this?" Vanessa asked incredulously while Jessi took her hair down for the tenth time. "And just make up your mind about your hair, will you? You're stressing me out." Vanessa's own long blond hair was done in a loose fishtail braid, and she elected for a simple white t-shirt and jeans, having no expectations of anything glamorous happening that evening.

"Of course we're 'seriously doing this,' it's just playing pool, not a bank heist, V."

"Yeah, yeah. I'll feel better once my mom's SUV is back in the garage."

"Chill, we'll be back in a couple of hours." She sighed, fluffed her shiny red hair one last time, and rubbed her glossed lips together. "Let's go." Vanessa took a breath and committed to the transgression. *You're all in now.* Despite her friend's driving record, she figured letting the licensed driver operate the car was better than them getting pulled over with her behind the wheel.

"I swear to god if anything happens to this car-"

"Stop, we're driving like two inches." Vanessa shook her head.

"Who is this friend I'm supposed to be entertaining anyway? Is he actually cute or was that just a carrot you wanted me to chase?"

"Ummmm."

"Um? Jesus, Jess."

"No, I mean, I assume he's cute because Josh is cute, I just haven't actually met him," she replied, clicking the garage door to close.

"Awesome."

"It'll be fun! Come on, stop acting like Kim. If I wanted someone to be a downer, I would have asked her to come." Vanessa pursed her lips at that.

"Whatever. Kim's not bad."

"No, no, I love her. You know what I mean, she's just all mom-ish."

"Ok. I'll attempt to be more cheerful." Jessi simply smiled victoriously.

They arrived at *The Eight Ball* without incident, and Vanessa plastered on her most charming smile as they strolled in to the pool hall, the smell of old smoke flooding her nose. Dodging a precariously placed cue on the way to a table towards the back, she watched as Jessi ran up behind a broad shouldered male and threw her arms around his neck playfully.

"Hey there," he smiled, turning around.

"Hey yourself," Jess replied, her eyes shining. Vanessa stood, feeling bored already, waiting to be introduced. Not at all surprisingly, she was now invisible.

"Hi. I assume you're Josh?" she interrupted the couple's hello. He was moderately attractive, but had a weak jawline. There was nothing she could see to warrant the lengths they'd gone to in order to get there.

"Oh, yes, silly me. Vanessa, Josh, Josh, this is Vanessa, or V. Whatever," Jess giggled, flipping her hair.

"Hey, good to meet you," Josh responded, holding out his hand. She shook it, but wasn't totally fond of the way his eyes rolled over her skin. "My buddy Matt's around here somewhere, I'm sure he'll be back in a sec. You guys wanna play?"

"Sure. I'm crap at pool though. You'll help me?" Jessi asked him. *Could she be more obvious?* Vanessa thought, knowing it was going to be a long couple of hours if she was already this annoyed.

"Of course babe." Vanessa didn't really play the helpless female role very often. Being that she had a pool table in her basement, she was actually pretty decent at the game and offered to break, sinking two balls.

"Nice shot," she heard from her right. She leaned back up, away from the green felt surface of the table, and locked eyes with a completely average looking guy. She mentally calculated his stats. *Five-ten, probably one-eighty, meh hair, meh face, meh.*

"Thanks," she offered lazily. "Matt?" she asked, hoping he would say no.

"The one and only." *Charming.*

"Vanessa, nice to meet you," she said, realizing that Jess and Josh were not even pretending to play the game. "Do you feel like playing?" *One hour and forty-five minutes to go.*

"Yeah, cool," he agreed, taking the stick from Josh's hand easily, as he was otherwise engaged. They played a boring round of pool, she won, and he pretended to have let her do so.

"Sure dude, whatever you say," she retorted, watching the clock on the other side of the hall. She jumped when her gaze came back down and he was next to her. Too next to her. She took a step back but he caught her fingers and interlaced them with his. *Ummmm, no.*

"Since I let you win, I think you owe me," he smiled, leaning in to her. He smelled like stale peanuts and faint body odor, and she resisted the urge to dry heave.

"Yeah, I don't really think-" she began, but was interrupted by his hands on her back and his mouth brushing her neck. This time she stepped back much more forcefully, her hands on his chest. "Ok, *Mitt*, I get that you don't know me, but I don't like hook up in dives like this. Or with complete strangers. Sorry." *So not sorry.*

"Don't be such a tease," he responded, completely ignoring her intentional name failure, pulling her wrist back closer to him. Her heart rate picked up, and she was done. Wrenching her wrist from his hand, she walked away and ignored his almost-grab of her elbow.

"Hi, we're leaving," she stated very loudly when she found Jessi making out in some shadowy corner. *God this was such a stupid idea. Gross.*

"Ummm, why would we be leaving?" her friend questioned with a tight smile.

"Ummm, because this guy's awesome friend just assaulted me. So we're out."

"Oh my god, could you be more dramatic?" Jess's eyes were shooting killer glances at her, and she could not have cared less. She pulled her friend out of Josh's earshot.

"We are *leaving*, Jess. I am not about to let this random nobody put his hands all over me so you can make out against some wood paneling from the 70s."

"Really… you're insulting the décor of the pool hall? Whatever. I'm having fun. Leave if you want." Fireworks of feminist rage were now shooting out of Vanessa's ears.

"You know I *can't* leave without you," she hissed.

"Sure you can. Here are the keys," she quipped, plopping them into her hand. "I'll have Josh drop me around the corner from my house or something and walk home."

"You have got to be kidding me. You are unbelievable."

"Just stick it out another half hour, I swear we can leave then," Jess negotiated.

"Not a mermaid's chance in hell. See ya later, *friend.*" Vanessa turned on her black leather heel and clicked her way out of the building, a storm brewing in the back of her brain. The cooler night was a welcomed sensation. She got in the car and carefully considered the option of just waiting there until her maybe ex-friend came out and making her drive home then. *This is what you get for letting her talk you into shit,* she berated herself. Her mind also raised the worry that she could be in there a while, now that she assumed Vanessa had left. *Screw it.* She put the keys in the ignition and adjusted the mirrors, determined to make it home without getting arrested. Hands were white-knuckled at ten and two the whole way.

Her fingers visibly relaxed when her house came into view. And then the urge to vomit came- because her mother was sitting in the rocking chair on their front porch, and her expression was not jovial. A stream of expletives rolled through Vanessa's head while she tried to come up with a plausible reason that she took the car. *Someone needed help... I had to get a first aid kit... Jessi was sick and I had to take her home... dammit!* She pulled the car carefully into the garage and got out, determined to make her mother actually listen this time. *This is just so typical that I get caught when I actually did the right thing.* With fear in her eyes, she tip-toed up the stepping-stones to the front porch as if it would help.

"I cannot imagine a story good enough to get you out of this," her mom iterated, a humorless smile on her face. Her mom really was quite pretty. She had honey blond hair and warm brown eyes that just never seemed soft when looking at her daughter. Vanessa immediately launched into the half-baked story of Jessi not feeling well and needing to take her home, and her mother stopped her about thirty seconds in.

"Try the next story."

Vanessa knew she could just tell her the truth, but also knew she'd probably never be allowed to hang out with Jess again.

Despite her rage, she shouldn't have expected more, and didn't feel like losing her friend over it.

"I went to go play pool."

"And in your mind, you thought breaking the law was the best way to get there?"

"No, I-"

"It really doesn't matter, Vanessa. I thought you were taking things more seriously. I thought this year would be different... you seemed to care. But now I can see that I was wrong. You're just as self-centered and impulsive as you've always been. There will be no car for your birthday. There will be no birthday, period. Or parties, or sleepovers, or television, or phone. You are grounded until I feel like ungrounding you." Her mom rarely yelled when she was this mad. It was more of a crazy-calm. Like her head might spin around at any given moment from holding it all in. Vanessa felt tears begin to overflow.

"Mom, please just *listen* to me. I'll tell you everything that happened, I'm sorry I made up a story, this really isn't my fault."

"Of course not. Nothing's ever your fault. Do me a favor and save it. Put your phone on the counter and go to your room." Choking back an angry sob, she felt her teeth grind together and marched her way into the house, practically chucking her phone into the kitchen. *That's what I get for doing the smart thing and leaving,* she thought, furious at the fact that her sophomore year was shaping up to be a big fat disappointment. The tears came in a torrent once her door was slammed shut, the injustice of the whole night washing over her. *Whatever, she's just been waiting for a chance to bust me anyway. Nothing I could have done would have made any difference,* she argued with herself, her mom's words ringing in her ears. Makeup and pajamas forgotten, she stared at the wall with hostility until sleep finally came.

2

The weekend passed in near silence. Her house had become the tomb of her former social life. Vanessa's dad had left early Saturday morning for a fishing trip, leaving her completely alone with Mrs. Roberts, as she had taken to calling her mother when she got this way.

Slumping to the dinner table after her mother called her down Sunday night, she groaned inwardly at the flax seed infused extravaganza before her.

"This smells great," her father said cheerfully, coming out of their home office. She hadn't even heard him come home due to the volume level in her ear buds playing every self-pitying song she could find on her old iPod. God, she missed her phone. Her father sat down, running his fingers through his sandy hair, apparently oblivious to the thick tension in the room. Or he was simply ignoring them; both were equally plausible.

"Thank you," her mother responded, her face in a tight smile. Vanessa chewed the earthy tasting turkey meatballs with as much malice as she could muster.

"Ok, so when are the two of you going to get over this?" The question came after ten straight minutes of silence mixed with the scraping of silverware on their dishes. He sighed, his face losing all of the relaxation it gained while fishing.

"When your daughter learns how to think before she acts," her mother shot back without looking up.

"Are you freaking serious? You don't even know the whole story because you wouldn't listen to me!" Vanessa finally exploded.

"Do not speak to me in that tone." Her voice was icy. "And if you'll recall, I gave you the opportunity to speak, and you lied." Her father raised an eyebrow as if to say *"Really, Vanessa?"* but she didn't care.

"I already said I was sorry," she grumbled, hating that her former self for coming up with such a stupid story.

"Well, let's hear the real one," her father interjected calmly. Vanessa's mom threw her napkin on the table and got up wordlessly. She heard her mutter "typical," in a passive aggressive manner as she strode towards the stairs. She thought she perceived a slight eye-roll from her dad, but couldn't be sure. He said nothing about her mother's departure, but it still stung that her mom refused to hear her out. His gaze rested on her expectantly, and words began to tumble out. She went with as much of the truth as she could contemplate sharing, concern clouding her father's gray eyes when she told him about Matt and his unwanted attention. The story concluded with her begging him not to call Jessi's parents and apologizing with tears dripping down her chin. Her father took another bite of flax-ball and looked pensive.

"I'm really not happy with your decision to go along on Jessica's little adventure, Vanessa, but I am glad that you had the fortitude to walk away when you needed to. Obviously I wish that hadn't included breaking the law. You realize you could have been pulled over, or you could have been in an accident."

"I know." She really did feel remorse after making her dad look at her with that much intensity.

"I also remember taking my brother's motorcycle without asking, the day after I got my license, and laying it down in the middle of Rural Route One. I had to limp home. I went to bed that night hoping to god nothing was broken, I and let my brother think someone stole it the next morning." Vanessa's eyebrows furrowed, not believing that her straight-laced father had been a rebel. She was also having a problem picturing her slightly over-weight and balding uncle riding a motorcycle. "Unfortunately for me, I lived in an even smaller town than this, and a neighbor came over the following day to ask my mother if I was all right, having seen the whole debacle from her front porch."

Vanessa couldn't help but crack a smile, envisioning her tough-as-nails grandmother learning of this information. "That sort of sucks," she admitted.

Her dad let out a laugh at the memory. "Yeah, it sort of did." He looked at her for a long moment before continuing. "Point is, Vanessa, I get making stupid mistakes. It could have ended worse than it did, and I sincerely hope you've learned something." She nodded. "I will speak to your mother about the situation." Vanessa's heart lifted, visions of a little red sports car dancing in her head. "Don't look that excited. I tend to agree with her that perhaps you're not ready for complete freedom yet, but I don't see any reason you can't take the driving test and get your license. And I think, given the situation, that an endless term of being grounded might not be appropriate. Don't make me sorry about going to bat for you on this one though, ok?"

"I promise. I really do." She hugged her dad lightly, glad she felt like she had an ally in her own home. She anticipated a very *lively* discussion between her parents to follow and promptly went to her room to put on her headphones. She didn't fail to miss the words "princess," "spoiled," and "unbelievable," in-between songs. Her focus remained on getting her backpack organized and making sure she had her schedule for the next morning. She didn't want to give them any reason to doubt her maturity again.

* * *

When Vanessa awoke, her cell phone was on her nightstand with a note in her father's handwriting that read:

> *You're still grounded until Friday, and your mother and I will be taking you to dinner for your birthday. Maybe be on your best behavior until then. –Dad*

She practically squealed with glee at the sight of her phone. She had twenty-two missed calls and thirty-seven texts. At least she felt popular on the first day of sophomore year. Even though she knew it probably wasn't cool, the anticipation of the first day of school had her up and out of bed without even hitting the snooze button on her alarm. After running the flat iron over her hair and spending more time than usual on her make-up, she crept out of her room, several items of clothing in hand, with the intention of making some sort of peace with her mother. She came to find her sipping coffee out of her favorite rooster mug in the kitchen. Their eyes met through the steam rising out of the cup.

"Good morning, Vanessa."

"Good morning. I, um. I was wondering if you could help me decide what to wear?" she asked, holding up as many pieces as she could without dropping any. Her mom bit the inside of her cheek, clearly seeing through Vanessa's ploy, but she acquiesced anyway.

"The blue ruffled top with the white sweater and skirt. It brings out your eyes." Vanessa let out a breath of relief at the unspoken forgiveness held in that advice.

"Thanks, that will be cute." She turned and left the room quietly, unwilling to disturb the fragile understanding that had just been created. After sliding on a pair of white woven wedges, she didn't even complain about the fact that her mom was dropping her off at school. *Best behavior,* she repeated in her head.

* * *

She heard the telltale flip-flop sound before she felt Jessi's presence next to her new locker. "So, scale of one to ten, how pissed are you? You didn't answer any of my texts." When Vanessa turned, her friend's expression held a genuine worry.

"Last night? Eleven. Today? Four. My parents were home when I pulled up Friday night. My mom took my phone, hence the not responding to your texts."

"Oh my god, are you serious? I thought you were just ignoring me. Are you... is everything ok?" Vanessa's instinct was to make her friend feel as terrible as possible, but she was also in too good of a mood after her dad's note that morning to let that kind of negativity bring her down. Her yoga instructor would be impressed.

"Not entirely, but it's better than it was. I'm just going to be bumming rides from you for a while longer. No car for my birthday. The good news is, however, that I will be ungrounded on Friday, and Zack Roads invited me, and by me I mean us, to Vader's bonfire on Saturday." Her grin peaked out despite her immense effort to appear nonchalant.

"Shut.the.falafel.up"

"Ohhhh, shut the falafel up what?" Kim inquired as she pranced up to them, acting as if this were a normal phrase to hear. "Has it anything to do with you being completely MIA this weekend?" Her short brown hair was blown out straight, and she looked very "teen catalog model" in a denim skirt with a purple barrette in her bangs. Vanessa relayed the story again. Kim looked more anxious than excited about the party, but her words were more positive than her expression.

"Wow, ok. That really is a shut the falafel up occasion."

"Right?!" Jessi emphasized. Vanessa just allowed her glee to shine out of her eyes.

"What are you all so giddy about this morning? Did the new Bieber album drop or something?" Luke Miller interrupted their girly moment with an arrogant smile.

"No *Lucas*, just happy to be here on this glorious morning." His eyes narrowed slightly at her using his full name. "Plus I know you'll download it before me anyway." Vanessa gave him a grin to match his own.

"Ah V, you know me so well." He reached out to pat her head and she smacked his arm rather forcefully.

"Feisty this year. I like it," he smirked, his cheerful demeanor returning. "I will see you ladies around," he called as he continued down the hallway.

"How can someone that hot be so annoying?" Vanessa mused.

"He's only that way towards you, you know," Kim observed as they made their way to first period.

"Lucky me."

* * *

The day was mostly uneventful, though Zack did make a point of saying hi at lunch.

"Are you practicing safe-walking strategies?" he asked, sitting down on the orange plastic chair next to her.

"As well as I can wearing these shoes, yes."

"The plight of being a female, I guess," he replied, letting his eyes move down her legs to her heels. "If you decide you need any assistance, you just let me know," he stated, his hand grazing her shoulder as he stood up to leave.

"Well, I am on my way to the C building, in case you'd like to ensure my safe arrival." She almost hated that his line worked so well, but she did not hate the envious looks of her fellow classmates at his attention.

"I like this look," he mentioned while they walked to her next class. "Maybe even more than the sweaty after-practice thing you had going for you last time we met."

"I think that's a compliment," she stated, biting her lip slightly.

"It is. I liked you both ways," he grinned with those ridiculous lips. "I'll see you later, yeah?"

"Sure. Thanks for walking with me." She almost tripped turning around and was grateful the wall was there to catch her. And that Zack was already headed in the opposite direction. *Smooth.* Even with the near faux pas, it was turning out to be a *very* solid first day.

* * *

Her first week of school went by quickly, and she was thankful, being that she was under house arrest other than attending cheer practice. Embarrassingly, she may have walked extra slowly to the parking lot everyday, hoping to run into Zack, but she only saw him briefly in the hall mid-week. When Friday arrived, she welcomed the freedom that was her un-grounding and her 16th birthday. Courtney was the first to text her.

> C: The happiest of birthdays to you! I wish we could celebrate together… old school style.
>
> V: As in Kool-Aid and Sour Patch Kids and a piñata?
>
> C: I still genuinely like all of those things. So yes.
>
> V: You're a nerd, but I wish we could too. I haven't even told you the latest drama. I'll call you this weekend and fill you in.
>
> C: Yes, do! Good luck on your drivers' test and have a sparkle-mermaid sort of day. <3 you.
>
> V: Lol, <3 you too.

Vanessa's stomach tightened momentarily at the mention of her drivers' test, but she felt ready. More ready than she was for that afternoon's biology quiz. *Who gives a quiz the first week of school anyway?* she thought angrily. Searching the closet, her eyes finally landed on the dress she'd been saving for that day, tags still dangling from the back. The thin cotton was soft as she slipped it over her head. The purple and red floral print made her blonde hair stand out, and the hem brushed her thighs just below dress-code level. Tying the bow at the back of the dress, she slipped on a pair of sandals and finished making up her face. She flitted down the stairs to the scent of pancakes and coffee and the sight of her parents already at the table.

"Good morning, birthday girl," her father smiled warmly.

"Pancakes?" her mom asked with a lighter tone than she'd found all week.

"Good morning and yes. Are there chocolate chips?"

"Of course, what kind of pancakes would they be otherwise?" her mom responded. *The whole wheat and fruit filled kind you usually try to make me eat,* Vanessa replied silently, grateful her mom put her newest health-food kick aside for her birthday. She sat down and a small box appeared in front of her with a shiny purple ribbon on top.

"Para mi?" she asked, practicing her Spanish.

"I don't know what that means, but this is just something I thought you might want now instead of tonight," her mom answered expectantly. Vanessa appreciated the effort she was putting forth to leave their conflict behind. She pulled off the ribbon quickly and pried open the white box. Tears pricked at her eyes when she ran her thumb over the hand-stamped lines pressed into a circular charm at the end of a silver chain.

I Am
A Real
Mermaid

Next to it hung a sterling mermaid figure along with a shining clear crystal. With shining eyes, she looked at her mother with as much gratitude as she had felt since perhaps her 8th Christmas when she received a Barbie Dream House. This was a gesture of acceptance from her mom that she couldn't ignore.

"I love it," she almost whispered, taking off the butterfly necklace she had originally chosen for her new outfit and immediately clasping the statement piece around her neck.

"I thought you might," her mom said back, her tone satisfied. "Happy Birthday." Her father just gave a relieved look over his coffee cup before asking Vanessa to pass the butter.

3

Both compliments and "happy birthdays" abounded during school, and few of her friends even showed up with cupcakes and cards for her at lunch. Gravity had nothing on her that day; she just wanted to get her driving test over with after school and look forward to taking full advantage of her freedom that weekend.

"Happy birthday," Luke announced cheerfully, surprisingly serious for the moment as he sat down next to her in bio. She was frantically looking over her notes, wishing she'd done it the night before.

"Thank you?" she questioned, not sure how to take him without sarcasm. She fingered her necklace tentatively as she flipped through the pages.

"What's this?" he asked, pointing to the jewelry.

"Hmm?" she asked, not quite paying attention.

"This-" he gestured to the charms.

"Oh! My mom gave it to me this morning," she explained, moving her hand. He read the stamped message and she saw a softened look cross his face as he looked away smiling. "What?"

"You just *would* have a necklace that says you're a mermaid. That's all." She shot him a look, uncertain if he was being genuine or facetious, but he was looking over his own notes by then.

The fact that she most likely bombed her science quiz almost dampened her spirits, until she saw a particular handsome junior waiting at her locker.

"Hey there. How's it goin'?"

"Pretty well, yourself?" she asked, trying to put in her locker combination calmly after the smile he was giving her went to her head.

"Good. Just thought I'd see if you were gonna make it to Vader's tomorrow night."

"Yeah, I think so. You'll save me a spot?" she pressed, wanting to know they'd be hanging out together.

"Of course. I wouldn't-"

"Happy birthday, V!" an acquaintance called in passing.

"Thank you, Jeremy!" she offered back, a look of surprise coming over Zack's face.

"It's your birthday?"

"That it is."

"Well, happy birthday then. I'm sorry, I didn't know."

"No worries, you don't have to apologize. And thank you," she grinned, tossing her hair.

He smiled back and placed his hand on her arm. "Well, I'm glad I'll see you tomorrow, I gotta run for now."

"Sounds good, I'll see you then," she breathed, still able to feel where his hand rested even after he was many steps down the hall. Despite its unfortunate beginning, her sophomore year was shaping up exactly how she'd pictured it.

* * *

A steaming plate of braised short ribs was placed in front of her, making Vanessa's mouth water. Though she knew it was probably futile, she held on to a glimmer of hope throughout her birthday dinner that her parents would present a set of shiny car keys in a box, regardless of her indiscretion. The ribs melted in her mouth, and she chatted animatedly about the ease of her driving test, cheer, school, and anything else that came to mind while her parents- even her mother- listened attentively like they genuinely cared about the successful ground-up scorpion her stunting group had mastered that week.

"Do you want your present now or after dessert?" her father asked, already knowing the answer. She shot him a pointed look, not needing words. Her mother's tight smile conveyed that she might not completely approve of whatever was coming, amplifying Vanessa's fantasy of the jingling keys. Her father took a small manila envelope out of his jacket pocket and presented it to her, eyes sparkling. *Maybe it's the title to the car?* she questioned internally, refusing to give up on her dream. Cautiously, she opened the envelope and unfolded a rather large piece of what looked like graph paper. Her blue eyes crossed in confusion as she looked up; her parents exchanging a knowing look.

"Am I missing something?" she asked, looking at the outlines around the edge of the graph paper.

"It's a blank floor plan."

"Yeah, still not helping," she explained, absently running her fingers over the thick black lines.

"Of our basement," her mom added. Vanessa's patience was running thin, and while she was trying not to let her disappointment show about the lack of car, she knew her facial expression was not under her control. "Perhaps this will help." Her mom picked up the purple gift bag she'd carried into the restaurant earlier and handed it over. It was heavier than it looked. She pulled out issue after issue of assorted design magazines, their covers glossy and shiny and beautiful. At the bottom of the pile was a hand-written note with a number on it. A number with many more zeroes than she was accustomed to seeing on anything.

"We've decided to remodel the downstairs. Well, we've decided to let you remodel the downstairs," her dad finally conveyed. All previous thoughts of automobiles were promptly forgotten, and her chest suddenly felt full of too much air.

"Is this a joke?" she asked, afraid to believe she was going to get her own version of a reality design show with a budget to match.

"It's not," her mom said gently. "We've been meaning to do it forever- things just tend to get put on the back burner. So while we will have final approval, you may take the lead and work with the contractor- under our supervision," she threw in hastily. Vanessa's brain wasn't even registering anything past the confirmation that she was being allowed to do this. She devoured dozens of design magazines on a monthly basis and had ripped-out-pages stashed in every imaginable space in her room.

"I..." She decided to forego the word portion of her "thank you" to get up out of her chair and flit to the other side of the table, throwing her arms around both of her parents without hesitation. Lost in her own world of color and fabric and ambience, she hardly looked up with the servers came with a song and a cake. Quickly, she blew out the candle and resumed her perusal of the gifted magazines. It no longer mattered how she traveled to and from her house- just that she got to walk into her own personal haven while there.

♪ *"Supermodel" - Jill Sobule*
"Heart Attack" - Demi Lovado
"Wake Me Up" - Avicii
(Performed by: Boyce Avenue ft. Jennel Garcia)

4

Vanessa surveyed her room with an increasing feeling of dismay, frowning at her sweatpants-clad self in the mirror. She'd picked out a light blue sundress that morning, but now decided it wasn't nearly striking enough for the bonfire. Everything from her closet currently resided elsewhere, ranging from the floor to hanging over the door, and yet nothing was quite right. Her friends pulled up outside, and she knew they were going to lose their shit over her not being ready. *Oh well,* she thought indignantly. They let themselves in, as usual, voices growing exponentially louder as they giggled their way up the stairs.

"Holy hurricane, what-" Jess started to insult her wardrobe curating process, but after the look Vanessa shot her, she shut up, pressing her pink glossy lips together and flopping on the unmade bed.

"I take it we're not leaving yet," Kim stated obviously, her shoulder length brown hair done up in curls, making her resemble a member of a musical ensemble. Vanessa wished she would let her perform a makeover right then and there. Kim was cute in a girl-next-door way; her tiny features sprinkled with freckles and her hair the color of a scarecrow. But she looked how she acted- a little uptight.

"I know the right outfit is here... I'm just not seeing it," Vanessa contemplated, more to herself than to her friends. *Nothing too slutty, nothing too juvenile, nothing too casual... that leaves what?* she thought. The pieces finally came together in her mind, as they always did if she gave her brain long enough to work it out. She grabbed a hot pink lace cami from the floor and a flowing black sleeveless top from the closet door handle. She partnered them with the tightest skinny jeans she owned and a pair of four-inch black wedges. She double-checked her make-up, brushed out her long blond hair once more, and grabbed a black clutch off of the crowded dresser while her friends looked on in awe.

"You realize you were in sweats five minute ago, right? How did you do that?" Jessi asked. Her friend always looked hot, as was frequently recognized by the male population, but typically spent hours getting ready. Her deep red hair was curled perfectly at the ends, and meticulous eye make-up complemented her green irises. She sort of looked like Ariel from *The Little Mermaid,* and there was a distinct possibility that was why Vanessa had made it a point to invite her to sit at her lunch table when Jess moved to town freshman year.

"Practice, my friend, practice."

"Ok, well let's *go.* I don't want to be late," Kim complained. "And won't you be cold?" *Always the voice of reason*, thought Vanessa.

"Of course I'll be cold, until I get some adorable junior to lend me his jacket," she smiled, leading the way down the stairs. "And yes we do want to be late. How horrific would it be to arrive there before anyone else?" Their driver agreed with her on that point, so Kim resigned herself to their lollygagging and driving the long way to Vader's house in Jess's Jeep. Gem City wasn't exactly an expansive metropolis, so even "the long way" would take only ten minutes.

"Hey… what's Vader's real name?" Kim mused. "Like, we don't know him that well… is it okay to call him that?" Vanessa had been wondering the same thing, but she wasn't about to admit it.

"Eh, I figure you can call a guy just about anything as long as you say it the right way," Jessi responded, shimmying a bit in her seat. "You worry too much. Ohmygod I LOVE this song!" she exclaimed without missing a beat, apparently ending that conversation with music blaring through her speakers. Vanessa was more than a little jealous of the Wrangler. Although she had just gotten her license, it wasn't quite the same milestone as it would have been with wheels. Originally, Vanessa had envisioned great things for her freshman year of high school- parties, cheerleading, boys, and having fun with her friends. She soon found out, however, that without a ride, it wasn't much different than junior high. *This year will be different,* she thought determinedly.

They pulled up to a house on the outskirts of town, vehicles already lining the gravel road stretched out in front of it. The smell of bonfire air surrounded her as soon as she was free of the car. They had to walk down a pretty serious hill to get to the party, and Vanessa was instantly regretting her shoe choice. *If you fall and roll down this hill at the first party of the year, that will be the end of you.* She sincerely didn't want Zack to regret asking her to come.

While there were a few familiar faces in the glow of the fire, the party was mostly made up of juniors and seniors, giving her an incredible sense of satisfaction. Jess and Kim followed her over to the coolers.

"And what can I get for you ladies this evening?" a senior boy with a devastating smile asked when they reached their destination. Everyone called him Vader, and he was apparently taking his job as host to heart.

"I can think of a couple of things," Jess responded, fluttering her long lashes at him. She'd only been in Gem City for a year, but had made sort of a reputation for herself. Vanessa didn't think all of it was true; her friend was just overly flirtatious, but she worried about her sometimes. Compared to Jessi, V looked level-headed and responsible, and that wasn't necessarily a compliment to the red head taking a wine cooler from boy with the *Star Wars* namesake.

"I guess I'll be driving home," Kim muttered from behind her.

"Thanks Kimmy, you're the best," Jessi replied, clearly having heard every word. Vanessa took a berry flavored drink as well, not sure what to expect. The three of them walked over to an empty log around the fire, and she twisted off the top to put the cool bottle to her lips. It smelled like a liquid SweeTart.

"Yeah, I would definitely not drink that," an amused male voice chuckled very close behind her. She lowered the drink and turned around slowly to find Zack Roads looking like he stepped out of *Friday Night Lights* in his black and red letterman jacket.

"Because...?" she asked with a forced casualness. He was looking at her with a relaxed expression, and she was determined to hold her own as if she went to parties like this all the time. Jessi had turned to join their not-quite-conversation and defiantly took a long sip of her beverage.

"Because the sugar in that is going to make you feel like crap long before you have a buzz. Lemme get you a beer," he offered directly to Vanessa, and she felt a rush of smugness come over her with his blatant disregard for her flirty friend. "Bring your friends if you like."

"Nah, we're good here, you two go," Jessi insisted, practically holding Kim down by her wrist and giving Vanessa a no-so-subtle stare. She let Zack help her up, taking in his tousled dark hair and full lips. He didn't drop her hand as they walked toward what she assumed was a keg, though she'd never seen one in person before. His palm was warm against hers, and she wanted to memorize the anticipation she felt as he pulled her along. He handed her a cup, and she stood awkwardly, fear rising in her chest along with the realization that she had no idea how to use the contraption in front of them.

"Will you pour mine? I just did my nails," she smiled sweetly at the boy with the perfect white teeth. He grinned back and did as she asked.

"I'm glad you came out," he stated, looking her over.

"Yeah well, small town, not a whole lot going on, ya know?" she asked, desperately wanting to make it sound like she hadn't done a happy dance in her mom's car after he'd told her about the shindig.

"I hear ya. We kind of have to make our own fun around here." He nudged her playfully, and she felt her confidence grow. She took a sip of the beer he'd poured and managed to let it roll down her throat without a reaction. *Why would anyone choose to drink this?* she wondered seriously, wishing she had the pretty pink drink back. Her experience with alcohol up until that moment consisted of sneaking Arbor Mist and leftover margaritas from her parents' gatherings, and downing a couple of bottles of Hooch at the park with some random boys at the pool that summer.

Quite a few people had shown up since she and her friends arrived, and a couple of seniors had backed a truck down the hill to add a beat to the party. The music was not her style, a little too rap-tastic, but she liked that Zack now needed to lean in closer to speak. He was tall, but not too tall, and she imagined his arms would fit around her nicely. He introduced her to some friends as they walked by, and eventually they sat down on the uneven stumps around the bonfire to roast some hot dogs. The waves of heat from the flames warmed her skin, but she couldn't help but shiver from the cold creeping up her back.

"You're cold. Here, take my jacket, I'm gonna go grab something else to drink, you want anything?"

"Just some water, thanks," she relayed, not liking the residual taste of beer on her tongue. She slid her arms into the too-big coat and relished the envious glances from several other females. Kim made her way over and plopped down on the log to her left.

"Oh my god, he is so cute," she whispered, not nearly quietly enough. Vanessa shot her a look and she lowered her voice.

"Where's Jess?" she asked, mildly concerned. When her friend disappeared, it usually wasn't innocent. Kim just tilted her head to the left, and sure enough, there was Jessi sitting on some guy's lap, her lips to his ear, giggling away. "She wastes no time," Vanessa said, shaking her head. The sound of crunching gravel alerted her to Zack's presence.

"Don't tell me I picked the wrong sophomore to flirt with," he smirked, staring at Jess. Vanessa felt her stomach clench, thinking there was no way she'd heard him right.

"Um, what?" she asked, tentative anger behind the words.

His blue eyes flashed with a challenging glint. "Just a joke, babe, dial back the tone a little. I'm kidding with you," he explained, sitting down next to her and rubbing her knee. *Not a super funny joke*, she thought. "I'm sorry, it takes people a while to get used to my sense of humor. I wasn't trying to be a dick, honestly." Vanessa willed the knot in her stomach to untangle, forcing herself to move the conversation forward. Kim just pressed her lips together in silence, looking uncomfortable. Vanessa introduced him to Kimmy, and some of the tension left the air around them. He placed a wine cooler in her hand, rather than the requested water. "So do you guys wanna head upstairs? That's where the real party is anyway," he let out, finishing what was left of his new drink.

"Sure," Vanessa answered, though she could feel Kim's eyes burning a hole into the back of her head. They stood and traipsed through the crowd and up the outdoor staircase to the main house. Zack opened a large sliding glass door to let them in. Vader's house was beautiful, and she admired the custom pine cabinets and the gold flecks in the granite. Zack tugged her along before she started opening drawers. There was a large round table in the next room with several upperclassmen around it. Upon drawing nearer, she saw that they were playing poker, and her nerves died down. *Just cards,* she realized and laughed inwardly at herself. *What did you think would be going on up here?* She wasn't exactly sure, but poker didn't scare her. Happily, she even knew how to play thanks to her dad's monthly poker nights over the years. Zack took a seat and patted his knee expectantly; she obliged and sat on his lap. Attempting to find a comfortable position, he wrapped his arm around her waist, and she no longer cared about being uncomfortable. He pulled out the chair next to him for Kim. They got a round of introductions, and Vader dealt the cards for the next hand.

"Be my good luck charm?" he asked, pressing his lips into an almost-kiss along her jaw as he asked. Her stomach flipped, and she found herself agreeing even though she kind of wanted to play her own hand. He tightened his grip, and his fingers came to rest on her stomach under the pink cami. She held her breath for a moment before she could relax.

As it turned out, he was crap at poker. She was quite good, however, and he ended up winning some money in the end. He squeezed her side and kissed her on the cheek, causing her to light up. "Not bad Vanessa. I dare say I should take these earnings and treat you to dinner."

"You can call me V," she answered, "and I think that would only be fair." He kissed her cheek again, and she glanced at the clock on the wall.

"Crap. We gotta head out," she told him reluctantly.

"At ten thirty?" he asked incredulously. She was mentally cursing her mother for her early curfew.

"I know it's ridiculous. I got caught driving my mom's car, and, well, I sort of didn't have my license yet. So, long story short, there are a few consequences I'm still suffering from," she explained, hoping she sounded like a rebel and not an idiot.

"Seriously? Okay then. Consider me intrigued." She let out the breath she'd been holding hostage. "Let me walk you guys down." Kim pushed out her chair, seeming relieved they had to go, but thanked the guy next to her for teaching her how to play. They reached the bottom of the stairs, and she sent Kim to go find their wayward friend.

"Thanks for inviting me, I had fun tonight," Vanessa told him lightly. His almost-black hair was harsh in the outdoor lighting, but those lips were inviting.

"Me too. Do you have any dinner requests?" he asked, his fingers tracing the space between hers. Annoyingly, her heart-rate increased at the thought of him asking her on an actual date, but she tried to be cool.

"Ummm, somewhere with good dessert," she decided, dreaming about the brownie sundae at Max and Erma's.

"Oh I can think of a few excellent ideas for dessert," he responded suggestively. Nervous, she giggled, not quite sure how to respond. She'd flirted with more than her fair share of guys, and made out with plenty more- having been called a tease on more than one occasion. But Zack seemed... serious, when he said that. Finally, he let out a laugh, and she relaxed. "I'll think of somewhere. Give me your number." She eagerly took his phone and entered the information, giddy at the thought of telling her friends he'd asked her out.

"I'll talk to you later, then," she concluded. Unexpectedly, he leaned in. She didn't have a chance to appreciate the moment, but his beautiful soft lips were on hers and she was so grateful for the stick of gum she'd had while they were playing poker. He tasted like beer and chips, but she didn't care. He was Zack freaking Roads, and he was kissing her. Intensely. His hands were making their way to other destinations when Kim and Jessi strolled up. He let go of her slowly and said goodnight to her friends.

"I'll call you," he promised before disappearing up the stairs. She was still catching her breath when Kim started to speak.

"Not a word until we get to the car," Vanessa insisted. They walked in an anticipatory silence.

"Evening ladies," they heard a cheerful voice call out as they made their way to the top of the hill. "V, good to see you," Luke Miller grinned, shoving his hands in his pockets, and she was certain he was flexing under that shirt.

"Luke," she responded in a noncommittal tone, "good to see you too. Enjoy the party."

"How can that be possible when the three of you are leaving?" he grinned, showing off a self-assured expression.

She rolled her eyes forcefully. "Do those lines ever actually work, Miller?"

"All.The.Time." He just laughed and started back down the hill.

"Jesus, do you have some sort of hot-guy perfume I should know about?" Kim asked.

"What are you talking about?"

"Luke Miller was just flirting with you."

"Luke Miller was just annoying me. He had his chance to flirt with me in junior high, and he went out with Elena instead. Too bad for him I hold a grudge," she replied stubbornly, approaching the Jeep.

"Seriously? You're pissed because he went out with Elena in the eighth grade? You're insane. He's sure as hell single now," Jessi interjected.

"Yeah, I'm not sure if you've met me, but I don't tend to let things go."

"That is a true statement if I've ever heard one," Kim agreed. She took the car keys and unlocked the Wrangler.

"Spill," Jessi demanded upon the closing of the doors.

"Spill what? There's not a lot to tell. We kissed, he asked me to dinner, that's it," Vanessa responded, giving no emotion away.

"Yeah, sure, no big deal," Jess spat facetiously. She reveled in the little bit of jealousy in her voice. "You know you're dying to talk about that kiss."

"His lips are just so pretty," she admitted. "But you're one to talk, Miss I-Make-Out-With-Random-Strangers."

"Eh, he was cute, but wayyyyyy into his car. Like I now know more than I ever wanted to about piston rings."

"Whatever, I hate you both," Kim interjected, and they tried to advise her to loosen up when they went out.

"Let me fix you up with someone," Vanessa insisted.

"Ugh, no. That's humiliating."

"It is not, not when *I* do it. I swear it won't be embarrassing at all. Plus, like half the sophomore class is afraid of me after I ripped Brent a new one last year for cheating on Megan, so no one will mess with you," she grinned, liking that particular memory. He'd had it coming.

"I do not want someone to go out with me because they're afraid of you, V. Seriously, let's just move on," Kim begged.

"Fine, fine." She turned up Demi, and they danced and sang their way back to the house.

* * *

Vanessa casually pulled out the stack of magazines her parents had given her while the girls got ready for bed. The moment they'd arrived home, she began folding corners and marking photos she liked.

"Ohhhh, new stash?" Kim asked excitedly. "Lemme see." Vanessa quietly handed over a few she had read the night before. Kim turned to one of Vanessa's favorite photos- a Moroccan themed den- and sighed dreamily. "This is so pretty. I want to have a giant house someday where I can decorate every room in a completely different theme." Vanessa rolled her eyes discreetly. *A house needs continuity of some kind*, she thought. Although, moments later she realized her hypocrisy in wanting to completely differentiate the new basement's look from that of the main house. *Whatever. This is different.*

"So, for my birthday, instead of a car, my parents are letting me re-do the whole basement. Like, with a contractor and a budget and everything." She tried to contain her geek-out from bubbling over, but did not entirely succeed.

"Seriously?" Jess asked incredulously, actually looking up from the text she was so intently studying. "That's pretty generous. They must not be that mad at you about the car." Vanessa glared at the side of her friend's head for bringing up the car incident, some residual anger surfacing to the forefront of her mind.

"We totally have to take some before and after photos or videos or something. Maybe you can submit them to HGTV and be a Design Star!" Kim gushed. The level of her enthusiasm was endearing.

"Yeah, definitely."

"No, like right now, let's do it," Jess insisted, holding out her cell phone.

"Seriously?" Vanessa looked at them both, not sure why they would want to indulge her little fantasy.

"Yes yes yes! Jessi and I will produce, or one of us can act like the desperate homeowner, begging for your design skills to save us, and then you can walk around and talk about your vision for the space, just like on TV. It'll be great practice."

"Well, I don't know about *desperate*, but yeah, I'm down to showcase mah actin' skillllz," Jess declared.

"Is that supposed to be an impressive accent?"

"*Yes*," she hissed. "I'm a meth-head actor, I have to get into character." Vanessa spit out the sip of water she'd been prepared to swallow.

"A *what* actor?!"

"A meth-head actor, you know, like the people who get really into their roles or whatever. Like they're on meth, I guess."

"It's a METHOD actor. Oh my god," Vanessa blurted out dissolving into the floor in a giggling heap with Kim. "A meth-head actor, I can't even..." Jess tried to appear less than amused, but a stray giggle or two broke through her façade.

"Whatever, are we going make this video or not, ladies?"

"Yes, yes, I just have to collect myself. You're too much," Vanessa explained, breathing through the laughing fit. "Let's make me a star."

5

Sunday dragged. Her mom insisted that they go to yoga together, that it would help her focus. Every time her mother spoke, it felt like she was trying to fix something that was broken. Vanessa's clothes, her diet, her grades. So she knew the sentence, "It will help you focus," actually meant, "You're focused on the wrong things." It was too early for this, and of course her mom had also thrown out the coffee because tea was "so much healthier."

After the longest yoga class in the history of the world, she spent the day finishing up her homework and wishing Zack would call. His reputation preceded him, and she knew he wasn't the type to fall all over himself for a girl, but it didn't stop her from daydreaming about being the envy of every female in her class. Her phone buzzed in the middle of that particular 80s-montage-style fantasy, and her heart leapt into her throat. When she looked down, however, she saw it was Courtney.

"Hey girl," she answered, calming her heart rate.

"Hey yourself, how's it going?"

"Not too shabby. I got to make out with the cutest varsity football player in the entire world last night."

"The entire world, huh?" Courtney laughed. "Elaborate." They hadn't spoken in the couple of weeks since school started, but as usual, it didn't feel that way. It just felt like talking to her best friend, and it never mattered how long it had been. Vanessa had gone on for a full five minutes about Zack's hair and his eyes and his to-die-for mouth when Courtney interjected. "And is he, I don't know, nice?"

"Sure, he's nice."

"Funny?"

"I guess."

"You're a wealth of information."

"Shut up, I didn't like, interview him."

"Don't get sassy, I'm just asking. You know I'm protective." Vanessa did know this about her friend. She was also loyal to a fault- never the girl to talk behind her friends' backs. "Most importantly, what kind of music does he listen to?"

"Ha, that I don't know. I'm more interested in whether or not he can quote all of *Empire Records*. But for you? I will find out. Happy?"

"Moderately." But Vanessa could practically hear her grinning through the phone. Courtney got her up to speed on the goings-on at her own school before they hung up. Vanessa sighed, wishing she still lived five minutes down the road.

* * *

Dressing with special care before school on Monday, she was hoping for an invite to sit with Zack and his friends at lunch. A gray belted mini-dress seemed to put off the right amount of "I don't care, but I sort of do" vibe that she was going for. When she saw Jessi pull up, she grabbed her bag and a granola bar on her way to the front door.

"Hot mama!" Jess exclaimed when she strutted out the door. "I take it Mr. Handsome called?" Vanessa tried not to let her annoyance show as she climbed into the car.

"No. But he will after he sees me in this dress," she smiled confidently.

"Decent plan."

They arrived almost late for first period, and she slid into her seat as the bell rang. She was attempting to pay attention to the notes on the board when a different kind landed on her desk. She opened it carefully, trying not to draw attention.

> Don't shoot the messenger, but I heard Jenna showed up at Vader's after we left Saturday night. She was apparently all over Zack. I don't know if anything happened, but I thought you might want to know. I'm sorry :(
>
> -Kim

Vanessa's blood pressure spiked. Jenna was Zack's ex. His large-chested, pouty-lipped, raven haired ex. She crumpled the note as quietly as possible and stuffed it into her bag. Kim was nice, but always trying to stir the pot. *She needs to get some business of her own and be less concerned with mine*, she thought angrily. With difficulty, she tried not to let the information bother her. *It was one kiss anyway, who the hell cares?* But she did… care. *Dammit.* Her note taking skills went down hill after that. She left at the bell without waiting for Kimmy, really not in the mood to hear any gossip.

Busily, she was slamming her Spanish text into her locker and looking for her history notebook when she felt a hand on her back, nearly sending her sky high. The owner of the hand didn't seem to notice.

"So, I am sincerely hoping you wore this for me, because I'm going to have a hard time accepting it if you were thinking of someone else when you got dressed this morning," Zack's voice stated in a low tone, his thumb running lightly across her back.

She broke out into goose bumps down her arms and hated her body for betraying her.

"Hmmm, that's so interesting. I would have thought you'd be more preoccupied with what Jenna had on today," she smiled sweetly as she turned around to face him. He wore an amused expression, his blue eyes sparkling annoyingly, rather than a guilty one as she'd expected. "Why are you smiling?"

"Why are *you* smiling?" he asked, calling her out on her passive aggressive statement. It did not go unnoticed that he hadn't responded to her thinly veiled accusation.

"Just having a lovely day, I suppose," she answered evenly, determined not to look at his mouth.

"Let me walk you to class," he suggested, and, without waiting for an answer, took her books and her hand. *Maybe Kim heard wrong? Why would he be walking me to class if he were back with Jenna?*

"So that's a yes on the dress then?" he confirmed to himself while she contemplated denying it. Her silence earned a satisfied smirk. "I'll stop by and see you at lunch, yeah? We can talk about dinner. And dessert," he added, making her stomach flip again.

"Yeah, ok. See you then." She walked into biology, almost late again, and groaned inwardly when she saw they were doing a lab. Jess and Kim had already partnered up, so she took the last open seat. It was currently occupied by Luke Miller's feet. She glared at him, her annoyance overriding any measure of charming vibes he was giving off. It was undeniable he was hot. He looked like he stepped out of an Abercrombie ad, but it was overshadowed by his hubris and need to push her buttons all.the.time.

"Do you mind?" she asked pointedly, gesturing to his footrest.

"Not at all. I'm quite comfy."

"Luke."

"Vanessa."

"Can you please move your feet?" she asked with as much courtesy as she could bear. She was on the verge of pushing him backwards off of the stool. That would have been much more satisfying. He moved them back and forth slowly, then quickly, like he was tap dancing in the air.

"It appears that I can indeed move them," he offered, grinning far too much for the quality of the joke, his green eyes dancing with laughter. She reached down, fully prepared to heave his feet up into the air when Mr. Lessner walked in. Luke quickly sat up straight and allowed her to sit down. She made a production out of dusting off the seat.

"Sorry I'm late, I had to grab your supplies," their teacher apologized. He dumped cups of Jell-O and various boxes of candy on the counter. "We've been studying cells for two weeks- so today? You build one. Send up one partner from each pair to get your supplies."

"Allow me," Luke stated with mock chivalry, and he hopped up to grab their lab instructions and materials.

"I sort of need an A on this assignment," she muttered upon his return, willing him to understand she couldn't be messing around that period. She hadn't done well on their first quiz, and was now in danger of a lower-than-average progress report.

"Yeah, me too," he added, suddenly serious. She wondered if he was in the same boat, and remembered that basketball wasn't too far off. *All right, well, as long as he's going to work.*

"Well, let's do it then." His grin returned, and he raised his perfectly expressive eyebrows at her. "Ugh, shut up. Let's just *complete the assignment,*" she punctuated, shoving him. He didn't even flinch, but he did refocus his attention to their cells. They worked together, cutting the Jell-O with plastic knives and constructing two pretty decent models. Mr. Lessner came by their table and looked surprised that they were furiously filling out the lab report already.

"You two actually work well together," he remarked before moving on to the next table.

"Hear that V? We're good together."

"Yeah that's not actually what he said. Keep dreaming." She hated to admit that she'd had fun collaborating with him though, even to herself. God knows she'd never say it to him, his head already in danger of not fitting through the door each day. She settled for being content that they didn't try to kill each other and fail the assignment.

"See ya tomorrow, partner," Luke stated before sauntering out of class. Her eyes rolled back out of habit even though he couldn't see her.

* * *

Without success, Vanessa attempted to keep her eyes at her own table during lunch rather than wandering around for Zack's face. *He did say he'd come by at lunch, right?* she questioned, wondering if she heard him incorrectly. By the end of the period, she had given up all hope of looking cool and searched for him in the lunchroom as well as the courtyard upon leaving the building. No sign of him anywhere. *I hope he didn't get sick or something.* She spent the rest of the afternoon alternating between worried and incredibly pissed off that he was messing with her. Somehow she'd had the forethought to hold her tongue at lunch and didn't tell her friends he'd be joining them. *Thank god.* At least she didn't have to eat her humble pie in front of anyone else. *He's just not interested. Move on.* She began making a mental list of other possible homecoming dates on her way to the locker room after school, cheer bag in hand.

"You seem to be concentrating awfully hard for someone going to cheer practice." She was fairly certain there was an insult in there somewhere about cheerleaders being stupid, and she was fully prepared to school him in the precision and difficulty of stunting and tumbling when he was suddenly sharing her personal space. "I'm glad I caught up with you though." Taking a step back, she attempted to regain her bubble, but he followed without hesitation. Startled, she moved halfheartedly to slip past him, but was enjoying the closeness a little too much. Finally, she pressed on his chest, breaking their connection.

"What the hell?"

"What the hell what?" he asked innocently, licking his bottom lip. *Don't look there. Maintain your resolve,* she coached herself.

"You ditched me at lunch. That's what the hell."

He grinned. That was becoming irritating. "I'm sorry babe, I didn't know that was like, set in stone. A bunch of us went off campus."

"I enjoy off-campus lunching," she prodded. Never in her life had she been off campus for lunch, as that was a privilege reserved for upperclassmen, but she knew plenty of people who left anyway.

"I didn't realize I was dealing with such a rebel. Stealing cars, leaving campus. What else do I need to know about you?" He asked, still grinning, still avoiding her actual question.

"That I don't deal well with people blowing me off."

"I swear I didn't blow you off," he promised, losing his smile slightly. "I honestly thought about inviting you, but Jenna was going, and I didn't think you'd be down with that based on our conversation this morning." The grin returned, if only in his eyes. *Annoying.* She ignored the fact that her stomach dropped when he mentioned going out with Jenna.

"So you had lunch with your ex, but you're stalking me outside the D building? Classy." She had all but lost the desire to get him to like her, despite the fact that her hands were still shaking after he had been that close.

"I think I like you," he stated unapologetically, running his fingers through his hair. "Let me take you out. Tonight. I'll pick you up at six-thirty, yeah?"

"Um, no?"

"Um, yes," he replied, mocking her slightly. "I didn't *have lunch* with my ex, she happened to be there. I didn't think you'd be comfortable, so I didn't ask. I'm going to take you to dinner to make up for it, so just let me." When he put it that way it made her anger feel like an overreaction. *It's not like you're actually dating,* she realized. As her hostility faded, the more fluttery feelings came back and she looked at him less sharply, sighing. "Yeah, that's what I thought," he stated smugly. He leaned in and pressed his mouth to hers, kissing her intently before continuing on his way to the locker room. She was about to be late for the third time that day. "See you at six-thirty," he called over his shoulder with a much-too-casual tone. *Jesus,* she breathed.

6

Practice was brutal. She had eaten mat throwing a back tuck. Twice. This did not appear to please her new captain.

"Maybe think about landing on your feet? That's gonna get ugly when you're out on the track," she mentioned in passing. Vanessa kept her response to herself, not needing to piss off Brooke Stanson, in all her poufy blonde glory, the second week of school. *Get it together.* She threw the next four perfectly but with no recognition. There were four weeks until the homecoming game, and the schedule handed out at the end of practice was insane.

"She can't be serious," Vanessa complained to her friends on their way out. "That's double practices for two weeks." She and Jessi commiserated until the car was idling in front of Vanessa's house. She realized she actually had a date in an hour and hadn't even told anyone about it. *Maybe wait to see that it actually happens,* she cautioned her overeager tendencies. "I'll see you tomorrow, Jess," she said, hopping out of the car, now near panic-mode. Rushing, she flew through the front door and was halfway up the stairs before her mom called her name.

"Yes, Mom, I'm home, but I have a date, can this wait?" There was a long pause. *Shouldn't have used the word 'date,'* she scolded herself.

"A date with whom?" her mom questioned, brown eyes casting a harsh gaze as her head popped around the corner of the stairs.

"Zack Roads?" Vanessa answered, not sure why she made it sound like a question.

"Roads…Natasha's son?"

"Yes," Vanessa responded cautiously, hoping that Zack's parents' status in their town would be a point towards her getting to go out.

"Where are you going?"

"We're supposed to go to dinner. I really need to get in the shower if I'm going to be ready." Her mom frowned slightly, and she began to worry in earnest that the whole thing wasn't going to happen.

"Ok, well, be home before ten. It's a school night. And all of your homework better be done."

"Yes, Mom." She didn't wait for any further conversation, turning on her heel and high-tailing it into the bathroom. The hot water did nothing for her nerves; she was continually wavering between stupidly excited and vomit-inducingly afraid that it would be awkward. By 6:20 she had on a killer outfit consisting of strappy gold sandals, a denim mini, and sheer coral halter that left just enough to the imagination. She sat down at her desk to stalk the street through her bedroom window in peace.

6:22

6:25

6:29

6:35 *He's not that late*

6:43 *If I curled my eyelashes for no reason, heads are gonna roll.*

6:52 *I.Will.Kill.Him.*

Zack's black Charger rolled up at 6:53, and Vanessa had the distinct urge to slash every tire on it. She swung the door open forcefully moments after he rang the bell to find him leaned up against the side of her house, purple tulips in hand. The only greeting he received was her raised brows and pointed stare.

"You look… hot. Like really hot," he let out appreciatively. She tried to ignore the tingling sensation in her gut and keep up her pissed off glare. "What's wrong?" He seemed genuinely confused, and her anger started to mix with relief that he hadn't stood her up. The fact that he was standing there with her second favorite flowers didn't help her cause. This was compounded by the fact that he was looking irritatingly delicious in a soft blue t-shirt and faded jeans. Even the way he smelled was distracting. Crisp and clean.

"Um…nothing, are those for me?" she asked, all but abandoning the visceral diatribe she had planned in her bedroom. *Maybe he's late because he bought you flowers. Can you really be pissed at that?*

"They are. You like them?"

"I might," she smiled hesitantly, not sure she wanted to fully commit to being nice just yet. She took the flowers inside to place in a vase and pranced back out to meet him. "So, where are we going?" she asked, some of her earlier excitement returning.

"Wherever you wanna go babe." She felt a twinge of annoyance that he didn't have more of a plan. *Boys.* She suggested they go to Max and Erma's, because well, she still really wanted that sundae.

"That's kind of far, don't you think? I was sort of hoping we'd have time to drive down by the river after dinner. Is it cool if we hit up that café on Main?" *Then why'd you say wherever I wanted?!*

"Sure, that's cool," she responded evenly, knowing full well that a trip down to the river would mean making out in his backseat. *There are worse ways to spend a Monday night,* she mused, looking again at his full lips and how they curved up into a smile when he glanced at her.

* * *

He pulled out her chair when they arrived at the rustic café, and she began to relax into the evening.

"So what do you do for fun, Vanessa Roberts?" he inquired once they'd ordered. She got the impression he was looking for a specific type of answer, and she wavered between playing along and being a smartass.

"Other than boosting cars and hustling people at poker you mean?" she grinned, her meticulously curled hair brushing against her back when she tilted her head at him.

A slow smile spread across his face. "Right, any other exciting hobbies?"

"Well, there's cheer, and that takes up a lot of time, but I just got maybe the best birthday present ever from my parents this weekend, and it will be my new project." She couldn't stop the smile from stretching over her expression. The image of the floor plan and the stacks of perfect rooms she'd ripped out of magazines made her feel like a rainbow might appear above her head at any moment. *Like a Carebear stare,* she imagined.

"Which is..." Zack asked, interrupting her daydream with a forced expression on his face.

"Oh, sorry. I kind of got lost there. They are letting me remodel our basement. I'm meeting with a contractor this weekend. Interior design is kind of... well, I like it." It felt foreign to share that information with someone new, and once the words were out of her mouth she wondered if they sounded lame, like a little girl wanting to dress up in her mother's heels.

"I totally thought you were going to say they bought you a car. That's a bummer. What all are you going to do with the basement?" His response was lackluster at best. The food arrived, and she was grateful for the interruption, needing to decide how best to convince him of the design masterpiece she had planned.

"I feel like you are not fully appreciating the awesomeness of the situation," she replied, trying to sound flirty rather than annoyed. He raised his eyebrows doubtfully, and she proceeded to tell him about her plan to create the perfect ambience in her new space. When his eyes started to focus on the décor around the room rather than her, she decided perhaps she'd gone a step too far in discussing Moroccan lanterns. "I'm sorry, I went off on a bit of a tangent, didn't I? What about you... what do you do for fun?" she smiled, biting her lip.

"Nah, that's ok. You're still pretty to look at even if I have no idea what you're talking about," he informed her, taking a sip of his soda. Confidence returning, she brushed his ankle with her foot in a juvenile attempt to flirt. "As far as fun, I think I'm a pretty open book. I like to play football, hang out with my friends, and I guess I go hunting with my dad and brothers sometimes." Images of Bambi crossed Vanessa's mind, but she let them go around the same time he reached for her hand across the small wooden table. *Why isn't anyone here to see this?* she thought giddily.

"That's cool. I can't say I've ever been, but you know, dressing in camo seems like it would be a fashion adventure. Kudos to you," she joked.

"Ah, well, I'm nothing if not adventurous. You think I can pull off the camo though, huh?" he asked, eyes lit up.

"I imagine you can. You'd probably look like an REI catalog model." He just laughed and played with one of the silver rings on her finger.

"So, I'm starting to think of a couple of other things I'd like to do for fun." His dimples showed when he smiled this time, and her heart sped up when his intent became clear. He interlaced his fingers with hers tightly before letting go of the smirk he had going on.

"Like?" she questioned. She wanted to kick herself for asking; she was really just searching for something to say that would keep her heartbeat from becoming audible to everyone in the restaurant. He just laughed again and shook his head.

"Let's get out of here, yeah?" he asked, though it was more of a statement than a question. He threw some cash onto the table with the bill and stood up, finally releasing her hand. She took a breath to steady her nerves before following him towards the exit. The cool night air caused her to shiver, and she wished Zack would offer his jacket. It seemed, at the moment however, that he was very interested in something on his phone, so she quickened her pace to keep up, her heels clicking on the pavement. Sinking into the passenger seat, she watched him open the moon roof and felt a pang of jealousy about her non-existent car. Her body shivered again as the cold air fell down around her shoulders, and this time he noticed. "Oh, sorry, I forgot you weren't wearing… well, much," he declared appreciatively, though it didn't feel like a compliment. She straightened her skirt involuntarily.

"I'm fine," she insisted, more to convince the feeling rising in her stomach than to reassure him. He turned on the heat anyway.

"I told you you looked hot, right?"

"Yeah. Thanks." At the present moment, she couldn't quite muster up as much gratitude as she thought might be appropriate for such an observation.

"You still down to head to the river for a bit?"

"Sure," she responded, determined to shake off whatever had come over her. "I just have to be home by ten," she informed him, checking the clock. He let out a breath somewhere between a sigh and a laugh before turning up some form of god awful screeching noise from the stereo speakers. She gritted her teeth, but almost smiled when she thought about how forcefully

Courtney would disapprove of this musical selection. "Interesting melody this band has going on."

"These guys are awesome. I saw them live last year, it was incredible." *Ok. Apparently not picking up on the sarcasm. Got it.* When they pulled up to one of the well-worn banks of the river, she felt curious about what it would be like to *really* kiss him. The thought made her knees shake with apprehension. It's not like she was a prude, but most people assumed she was much more…experienced than she actually was. She plugged in her phone to his sound system, effectively ending the dying cat sounds that were emanating from the speakers, and turned on her own playlist. *Better.* Her heart rate slowed, and she ignored his incredulous glance at her actions.

"Do you wanna get out and dance?" she asked when a slower song came on.

"Not particularly," he answered. She turned quickly to look at him, not loving that he shot down her idea, and was startled at how close he had leaned into her.

"How do you do that?" she asked, willing her voice to sound normal.

"Do what?" he murmured.

"Like, ninja your way closer to me."

"Practice."

"You practice being a ninja?"

"No, but I've had lots of practice doing this," he finished before closing the space left between them and pressing his lips to hers. Her initial annoyance at his cocky attitude took a backseat to the sensation of his mouth on hers and his fingers brushing her waist. She couldn't quite settle on where to put her hands, as everywhere she tried seemed awkward. His biceps seemed as good of a place as any, and she tried to focus on their interaction after that. His hands seemed to have a similar issue, though she ventured a guess that it wasn't for the same reason, and he casually familiarized himself with her bare back. "You know, there seems to be a lot more room in the back… if you'd rather…" he whispered as he kissed below her jaw. She laughed inwardly. *I guess there's really no suave way to ask a girl to climb into your back seat,* she thought, mildly amused. Nevertheless, she moved to extricate herself from his embrace to make her way to the other part of the car when she caught the time.

"Shit. I have to be home in fifteen minutes." He grabbed her waist and bit her neck lightly.

"Fifteen minutes is fine with me," he whispered against her skin. Her eyes widened at the implication, and she smacked him in the shoulder. "What the hell was that for?" he asked, seemingly surprised.

"You know exactly what that was for. I'm being serious, I can't be late. I'm already on my mom's bad side."

"Way to be a tease," he sighed, annoyed. But he did start the car and move completely back into his own seat.

"I'm sorry, what?" He shot her a sideways glance, assessing her anger.

"You're just a tease. Whatever, it's fine. I'll take you home, you won't be late. God forbid." She sat quietly for a moment, really having no frame of reference for how to deal with his comments. All that was clear was a mix of embarrassment, hostility, and self-doubt making itself known in the pit of her stomach.

"Screw you, Zack," she finally uttered.

"Interesting sense of irony you have there." He put the car in gear and started back towards the road. Tears pricked at her eyes when she deciphered what he meant, feeling lost at his change in attitude.

"You're a dick. Just take me home."

"As you wish, princess." He turned his awful music back on, but she didn't even care as long as it drowned out the replay of the last ten minutes that was going on in her head. He pulled up to her house and turned down the music as her hand reached out for the door handle. "V, wait," he let out, his tone apologetic.

"Not a chance," she retorted, but he locked the door as she grabbed the handle. "Seriously? You're going to try to *lock me in the car*? In front of my own house? Stellar plan."

"Dammit, I just... I'm sorry I called you a tease. I was excited to come out with you tonight, and you look like that, and I thought we were having a good time. I shouldn't have said what I said, I was taking out my frustration on you." He wasn't meeting her eyes, and his rapid mood swings were making her head spin.

"Um, ok?" *What the hell is going on?*

"Look. Being with Jenna. It kind of screwed with my head. She would... whatever. It doesn't matter what she did. But I'm sorry for dragging you into my issues. You didn't do anything wrong." His openness took her aback.

"Well... thank you for explaining that much to me, I guess? And, I was having a good time. I don't know..." He finally met her gaze and his blue eyes were clear.

"Can we just try this again? Can I walk you to your door and pretend the last ten minutes never happened? I wasn't lying the other day when I said I liked you." The emotional cocktail going on in her stomach took on surprise and contentment as he spoke, and she wasn't entirely sure what to do with that combination.

"I like you too," she found herself saying. He gave her a relieved look and got out of the car.

"I'm sorry tonight ended the way it did. Will you let me make it up to you?"

She sighed, not entirely ready to deal with more decisions. "Maybe don't ditch me at lunch tomorrow, ok?" she requested, giving as much consent as she could muster.

"Done. I will see you then." He kissed her cheek and sauntered back to his car.

Vanessa physically attempted to shake off the feelings from their fight, but the energy was wrapped around her like a scarf.

She couldn't have said whether she was happy or angry or hungry or tired. When she tried to replay the scene from beginning to end upon reaching her bed and falling into it, she found that there was no making sense of the whole ordeal. His comment about Jenna had piqued her interest, but she hadn't been capable of pressing him for more information. *Next time... What could she possibly have done?* It was going to drive her crazy until she knew. While she was almost at the point of giving up on analyzing her own emotional state, her phone dinged.

> J: Hey, did you do the math homework? I need help.
> Or answers. Whichever really :).
>
> V: Ya, I did it. Just call me.

Her phone rang moments later. "Hey Jess, what seems to be the problem?" This question was rhetorical of course. The problem was that Jessi never took notes, but she always seemed baffled by her lack of understanding, regardless.

"Just the triangles. Why are there so many triangles?"

Vanessa smiled, amused, but talked her friend through their homework. After the odd ending to her date, she wasn't even sure she wanted to mention it to anyone, but her mouth got the better of her. "So, I sort of had a date tonight."

"And what possible reason do you have for talking to me about geometry for thirty minutes instead of leading with this? With Zack?"

"Yeah. I saw him before practice and he asked me to dinner. I didn't want to say anything, because, I don't know, he doesn't seem to have the greatest follow through."

"I can't believe you said *nothing*. My brain would have snapped, fizzled, and cracked trying to keep that to myself. Seriously, you're like a secret agent." Vanessa just laughed and listened to her friend prattle on about how cute Zack was and fantasize about being introduced to his friends on epic double dates.

She zoned out, still not able to reach a consistent train of thought in regards to their date. He seemed to like her. He complimented her and it caused her to blush. He kissed her and it made her heart flip flop. Despite that, she couldn't shake the sense that she was supposed to be playing a part or that he wanted her to be something different. *Or maybe you're self-sabotaging because this is something you've wanted forever,* she scolded herself. It was so *like* her to get close to what she dreamt of and then do something stupid to screw it up. *Like the car.* She still frowned, thinking of how she let that blow up in her face. Desperately, she was holding onto her final judgment about his dickish behavior until she knew what really happened with Jenna. She couldn't go with her gut reaction until she had the whole story.

The was an uncharacteristic silence on the other end of the line. "Well?" Jessi questioned, apparently exasperated.

"Well what? Sorry, I was in my own world there for a minute." Vanessa could practically hear the eye roll through the phone.

"When can we go *out*? I want a homecoming date."

"Oh, um... I don't know. I'll ask Zack. He said he'd call later. You do realize, though, that we've been on a total of one date. He's not like my boyfriend. And don't you already have a homecoming date?"

"Yeah, yeah, I'll be rid of him tomorrow. Silly details. Can you just be a little more enthusiastic? I mean, if you're not into him, I would *gladly* take him off your hands, just-"

"Keep your French-manicured hands to yourself, Jessica." Vanessa grinned slightly at the jealousy in her friend's voice, no matter how masked it was by humor.

"You know how I feel about the use of my full name."

"I do," Vanessa replied, her grin getting bigger.

"Hmph. Whatever. You're lucky I love you. I'm going to go and complete this torturous homework. I want actual details tomorrow. No more of this 'we went out, it was fun,' bullshit. I wanna know what he tastes like."

"Ew, you are too much."

"Or maybe just exactly enough. It's why you keep me around. Talk to you later."

"See ya." Vanessa had to simply shake her head as he tossed her phone on the bed. Contemplating the situation, she decided to give the boy the benefit of the doubt. For now. Maybe he was just screwed up after whatever happened with his ex, but he seemed willing to try.

7

The next morning felt like fall, though several weeks of summer were still clearly visible on the calendar. Vanessa groaned, remembering why her alarm was set so early, and rolled out of bed to get dressed for her before-school-practice. *Unconstitutional,* she thought mournfully. She threw on sweats and a t-shirt while attempting to pack a reasonably cute outfit without completely opening her eyes. There was a half-eaten granola bar held between her teeth as she carried her bags outside at the sound of Jess's horn.

"I literally want to poison Brooke's lunch with cilantro today, so we can stop with this double practice bull," Jess stated emphatically upon Vanessa's arrival to the Jeep.

"Cilantro isn't poisonous. I think you mean cyanide. Either way, I'll provide you an alibi," Kim offered cheerfully from the backseat.

"Mphmt," Vanessa tried to agree with her mouth full of chocolate chips and oats.

"So entertain us with stories of your uberhot boyfriend," Jess demanded once they were on the road, and Vanessa had nowhere to run. She shot her a victorious grin.

"Don't call him that."

"Don't call who what? I'm so lost," Kim complained.

"V doesn't want to dish about her date with Zack Roads. Persuade her so I can drive."

"You went on an actual date with him? And I didn't even get in on like a group text about it? You owe me details now," Kimmy guilted her.

"Ay, guys. There's really not that much to tell. We went to the café, we ate, we chatted a bit, we drove to the river, he took me home." She bit her lip, wondering if she should divulge the argument in which they'd found themselves, but she didn't think she could handle their particular brand of advice-giving right then. She had only just decided how she wanted to proceed less than six hours ago.

"Back up. You went to the river?"

"Yes, that was my geographical location."

"And theeeeeeennnnnnn?" Kim pressed.

"And then we made out and he took me home."

"I knew it!" Jess shouted, pushing her more forcefully than was necessary while at the stop-light. "Oh my god those freaking lips of his. Are they as heavenly as I imagine?" She licked her own lips dramatically.

"They might be," V answered coyly, not hating the attention. Her blood pumped a bit faster while thinking about their encounter at the river, and she became anxious about giving him another shot, hoping some of the awkwardness from the night before would have dissipated.

"I can't decide if I hate you or want to be you right now."

"I firmly stand on the 'want to be her' side," Kim interjected as they pulled into the lot. Vanessa's head grew two sizes before she hopped out, her energy ten times higher than when she'd left the house.

"You guys ready to show your spirit?" Vanessa questioned, sarcasm dripping over her words.

"Only if murder is out of the question," Jess reiterated, and they trudged toward the gym.

* * *

Practice went better than expected, though Brooke still wasn't satisfied, and she confirmed their schedule for the rest of the week. Vanessa showered and braided her hair in a fishtail, not in the mood to try and blow-dry it successfully in a room full of cranky cheerleaders. The black hooded sweater and jeans she donned were not her usual attire, but her brain couldn't mix and match that early in the morning. Yawning, she shuffled to class, not bothering to wait for her friends. She passed her own locker on accident and had to back up to get to it. *Sleep. Want. Now,* she thought.

"Did you get lost?" an amused voice asked next to her.

"Only mentally," she responded, turning and taking in the clean scent of whatever cologne Zack was wearing. He looked as good as he smelled in a brightly washed denim and a gray and white hooded shirt.

"You do look kind of tired." *Gee, thanks,* she said to herself, holding back her grimace. "So, I guess it's a good thing I brought you coffee." He unveiled a very large latte from behind his back, and the smell of it instantly brought a smile to her face. She reached for it, but he held the liquid goodness inches from her fingertips. Her eyes narrowed at him. "Kiss first," he smiled. On her tip toes, she leaned in towards his cheek, but he caught her lips with his instead and pulled her in closer. She was surprised, but glad he seemed to be back to his charming self. She smiled against his lips, enjoying the way his free arm was strong around her waist. He tasted like spearmint. Sliding her hands down his chest, she stepped back when she realized they were in the middle of the hall at school.

"Good morning to you too," she stated, reclaiming her own personal space along with the coffee.

"I'll bring you a muffin next time too and see how that works out for me," he replied, shooting a less than innocent look her way.

"Or maybe you just bring me a muffin because you're nice. Chocolate chip please," she retorted. He laughed briefly and took her backpack.

"Want me to walk you to class?"

"Sure. It's a whole twenty five feet away, but you can ensure my arrival." She couldn't quite name the look on his face as he began the short walk down the old cracked vinyl floors. Annoyance? Apprehensiveness? She signed, wishing they were past this awkward I-don't-really-know-you-yet phase. It was tiresome.

"So, what color corsage should I order for you?" Her heart skipped. Was he asking her to homecoming? Or assuming his way into taking her to homecoming? She glanced up at him.

"Are we going somewhere that requires a corsage?" she asked, feigning confusion. He ran his fingers through his dark hair.

"You're gonna make things difficult, huh?" he smiled that delicious grin. "Would you like to go to homecoming with me, Miss Vanessa Roberts?" She shot back a matching smile at her victory.

"I think I would. And I will have to get back to you about the corsage color after I pick out my dress. There's a process, you see, you can't just skip the dress-buying," she explained playfully, brushing his arms with her fingertips.

"Can I make one request about the dress?"

"You can. I'm sort of picky about my clothing though, so I can't promise to honor it," she let out truthfully. He leaned over and whispered in her ear, making a heavy blush color her cheeks. Her heartbeat made itself known in her chest, and she looked at him with narrowed eyes. *Someone is certainly sure of himself.* She answered with only a raised brow and a long sip of her latte before the first bell rang, not sure she had a remark ready that was suitable for the situation.

"I'm excited. About homecoming. I'll text you later, enjoy the coffee," he hurried, kissing her on the cheek and handing over her backpack before making his way to class. She willed her body to calm down before walking in to math. *Numbers, triangles, area, perimeter,* she repeated while she flitted to her desk. She supposed it was no longer a question if he liked her. Her friends were going to lose it.

* * *

Luke was grinning in a less annoying manner than usual when she took her spot next to him in bio. "What?" she asked, knowing he would tell her anyway.

"Lab grades were posted last night. We aced our report. Because we're awesome," he said in an earnest tone, holding out his hand.

"Do you want to shake on it?" *He is so odd.*

"No, god, you are so uncool," he said, laughing, and he manipulated her hand into a complicated series of movements like a secret handshake. "There."

"Now I'm cool?" she questioned incredulously.

"Well, you're friends with me, so you were always cool by association, I guess." She swatted his shoulder and got out her notes.

She was almost knocked out of her seat by the force of nature that was Jess sprinting over to her. "Oh my god, is it true? Please tell me it's true. Is it? Why aren't you saying anything?"

"Um, what? And I can't say anything when you're shouting at me. And cutting off the circulation to my arm," Vanessa complained, extricating herself from her friend's vice-like grip.

"I'm sorry, but you know exactly what I'm talking about."

"Fine. Yes, it's true. But how did you even know that? It happened like a an hour ago?"

"Well, from what I understand, your PDA beforehand was eye-catching. Holy crap, V. Ok, so first, get one of his friends to ask me. Then, we shop." Jessi's well thought out plan was interrupted by the final bell and she shuffled reluctantly to her seat.

"Did I miss something?" Luke asked quietly.

"Oh, Zack asked me to homecoming this morning. It appears Jess is more excited than anyone." Luke frowned slightly at her news.

"V. Listen, I don't know if-"

"-I'm sorry, am I boring the two of you?"

"No sir," Luke answered their teacher as all eyes turned towards them.

"Great. You can gaze into each other's eyes somewhere else. Moving on…" Vanessa's cheeks burned at the implication and the negative attention. It was difficult to discern whether she was more angry or embarrassed, but the fire in her chest felt the same regardless. She kept her eyes glued to her notes and ignored Luke's attempts to catch her gaze. A piece of paper entered her peripheral vision.

> Lessner's a douche. I 'm sorry. I do wanna talk to you though… after class?

Vanessa gave him an imperceptible nod, wondering what in the world Luke Miller needed to talk to her about. Usually they just bantered- this was new. The rest of class passed without incident, and she was out of her seat the moment the bell rang, not wanting to be kept after and given a lecture about appropriate behavior.

She felt Luke walk up beside her in the hallway, and he pulled her elbow gently for her to follow him. They were walking the opposite direction from the cafeteria, which was where everyone else was headed. Irritated, she wrenched her arm out of his grasp once they were mostly alone.

"Ok, what's with the drama? You're kind of freaking me out. You're not like on drugs or anything, are you?" She watched him roll his sea green eyes and almost snort at her.

"Yes, V, I dragged you over here so I could tell you I'm on drugs and convince you to, what? Get me into rehab? Get high with me? Do you even think before words come out of your mouth?"

"I think we're done here," she shot back, not loving that he was making her feel stupid.

"No, stop. I'm sorry. You did sort of walk into that one though, come on. You've known me a long time, you know I wouldn't act like this unless I had something to say." She turned back around slowly.

"Ok then, say it."

"I, uh, don't think you should go to homecoming with Roads. Well, I don't think you should go anywhere with him, really." He spoke matter-of-factly, but she could tell his jaw was clenched as he relayed this information. Confusion set in first.

"What? Why? And how is it your business anyway?" Being offended came next. "You're not like, my keeper. I can go to homecoming with a hobo if I really want to. What's your issue with Zack? I thought you were cool with those guys."

He looked at his feet and grinned as if her response didn't surprise him at all. "Step down from your self-righteous soap box there V, this isn't an anti-feminist statement I'm making. And I am cool with those guys, insofar as I can shoot the shit with them and lift weights. I sure as hell wouldn't let any of them date my sister."

"You don't have a sister."

"You are being ridiculous."

"You are being cryptic, and it's annoying. I'm going to lunch." He caught her shoulder before she even had the chance to make a dramatic exit.

"I hear the way he talks about girls he dates, or hooks up with. Whatever. I don't want to hear him talk that way about you, or for you to get burned. That's it. Ok?"

The softness with which he spoke surprised her, but it didn't quell her exasperation at his condescension. "I'm pretty sure I can take care of myself going to a school dance with him. I'm not your little sister, and that implication is actually kind of offensive. So thanks for your concern, but I'm good."

"I hope so," he replied, letting her walk away this time. Her pace was near frantic as she let her anger burn through her. *How dare he butt in to my social life and treat me like a child.* All of her excitement about the dance was now tainted by his stupidity, and for that she was even more pissed off. She didn't even get to enjoy the high of being asked for an entire day, and now her mood was ruined. *Ass hat,* she cursed in her head. She stomped over to her regular table and tried to appear semi-normal.

"Hey?" Kim asked tentatively, assessing her mood. She was the hardest to bullshit because she'd known V the longest. Well, other than Courtney, but Courtney wasn't there. *She would totally have my back if she were, though.* Vanessa made a mental note to call her friend soon.

"Hi."

"Everything ok?" Kim asked slowly, her hazel eyes searching for an answer.

"Yeah, I'm fine. I just need to eat." The chatter around the table helped to bring her back to a middle ground, and she felt her shoulders relax. Picking absentmindedly at her salad, she was brought back to reality by the obnoxious sound of a chair scraping along the floor next to her. Thankfully, she looked up prior to making a bitchy comment to the holder of said chair and saw Zack's blue eyes looking back at her. Her posture changed automatically, and she sat up and crossed her legs towards him.

"See? Not ditching you at lunch."

"Nice to know you can follow through when you want," she chided him.

"Oh, I want," he flirted, low enough that only she could hear him. Or at least that's what she hoped. Jessi was making very awkward facial expressions at her from behind Zack's head, and she briefly wondered if her friend was suffering from a stroke. She finally got it when Jess started to dance. By herself. In the middle of the cafeteria.

"So, do you happen to feel like setting up any of your friends with my friends for the dance?" She felt like a seventh grader even asking, but it was better than enduring the wrath of Jess for the next three weeks.

"Ah, which friends?"

"Namely Jess. You can turn around and look at her if you like, she's acting like an insane person. Perhaps it will make her stop." His eyes crinkled when he smiled and he turned around, immediately causing her friend to revert to her normal human state and scurry to the other side of the table to resume conversation with Kim.

"Yeah, I remember her. I'm sure Vader or Rich would be down to go. I'll find out."

"Why does everyone call him Vader, by the way? Is he like a Star Wars fan?"

"Well, I'm sure he is, because it's *Star Wars*, but that's not why he has the nickname. His first name is Garth. His mom's a huge country music fan or something, I don't know."

"Yeah, still not getting the Vader connection."

"Well, Garth is a really terrible name, but it sounds like Darth. So. Garth Vader was born." She giggled at that, having to admit it was kind of clever. Plus, Vader was a way cooler name than Garth.

"I'm glad I asked, I never would have guessed that."

"Glad to be of service. What are you up to tonight?"

"Um, cheer practice until five, and then I'm supposed to meet with our contractor tonight for initial plans on the basement."

"Do you think I could swing by later? Or we could go for a drive?"

"Yeah, that should be fine. Just text me so I know when."

"Sure, see you later babe." He kissed her quickly and sauntered out of the cafeteria. Her mood had improved considerably, for she felt the awkwardness she'd been wishing would disappear finally had. His kiss still felt exciting but now more familiar, too. She sat back in her seat and downed the rest of her lunch with a renewed appetite while she waved Jess over to give her an update.

♪ *"Wake Up" - Hillary Duff*
"Roar" - Katy Perry
(Performed by Alex Goot and Sam Tsui)
"Burnin' Up" - The Jonas Brothers

8

Vanessa's parents had gone over the basement plans with her the night before, giving their stamp of approval on her initial notes for the contractor. Sitting at the kitchen table, she wiped her sweaty palms on her jeans while she went over the floor plan again. She was also ready with photos and swatches for flooring and paint, but wasn't sure if he would need that already. Originally, she envisioned a white-washed wide plank floor, but her parents had shut it down, citing the risk of flooding if there happened to be a strong storm. She settled instead for a warm, amber-colored concrete stain and many area rugs. Like, a multitude of area rugs- to give off a sort-of Moroccan vibe with a modern color pallet.

The bell rang, and Vanessa heard her mother come down the stairs and open the door. "Mike! Good to see you, thanks so much for being willing to work with us on our project," her mom greeted the man at the door. He was the husband of someone her parents knew through one committee or another.

"Not a problem, I'm looking forward to it." Vanessa stood and put on her best "I am not a silly teenager" face. The man who walked in the room looked as she expected him to. Mid-forties, in a flannel and jeans with a flat pencil behind his ear and a clipboard in his hand. He had a nice face, though. Non-judgmental. Her mother introduced them, and if he was surprised by the fact that she would be running the remodel plans, he didn't show it.

"All right, Vanessa, show me what you're thinking," he offered warmly, gesturing to the table. She launched into her design tentatively at first, but he was taking notes and looking at her like she knew what she was talking about, and her confidence grew.

"I'm not sure how much detail you need at this point in the process, but I just wanted to be prepared."

"No, this is all great. Most people I work with just have a general idea what they're looking for, but the more detail I have, the better. I can also get you some samples of window coverings now that I know the look you want. Could you show me around the space so I can take some of my own measurements and photos?"

"Yeah, absolutely." She was walking on cloud nine down the stairs. While he worked, he started pointing out some options they had for running electrical where she envisioned several lanterns hanging, giving off a dim glow. She almost had to close her eyes to believe she was going to get to see this project come to fruition. Vaguely aware of her mother opening their front door again, she was so lost in her vision she jumped noticeably when a pair of solid arms wrapped around her waist.

"Whoa there, sorry. I didn't mean to scare you," Zack muttered.

"You almost gave me an aneurism, I didn't think you were coming over until later," she replied, turning to face him and catching her breath.

"What can I say? I wanted to see you," he smiled broadly and bent down to kiss her. She pressed her lips to his quickly and focused her attention back to Mike, who had a question about the arrangement of the three-piece bathroom. Vanessa bounced around, wondering where the wave of confidence she'd been riding had gone. She was also acutely aware of Zack's eyes on her as she followed Mike around with her notepad.

"Well, I think I've got more than enough to go on. Let me do some mock-ups, get a total budget together, and I'll be in touch. I think this is going to look great though when all is said and done." Mike reached out to shake her hand before heading upstairs.

"Thanks so much, I can't wait to see it all come together." She turned around slowly to take in the picture of Zack Roads leaning against the wall of her basement, his dark hair falling into his face. *God he is pretty,* she thought. It seemed ridiculous that he was in her house. To see her. Her heart fluttered at the realization of it, and she half-skipped over to him. "Sorry about that, that was our first meeting. I didn't mean to ignore you or anything." She chewed on her lip, not certain the meaning of his passive expression.

"It's ok, you can make it up to me," he declared with a megawatt smile. "You look very official with your notepad and a tape measure. It's very cute." She blushed at his compliments, hoping they were genuine and he wasn't making fun of her over-preparedness.

"Yeah?" was all she could manage.

"Yeah," he confirmed, rubbing his hands up and down her arms. His presence was enough to make her dizzy, and the feeling of his skin on hers wasn't helping matters. "Do you have time to go for a drive or something?"

"Yeah, let me just tell my mom. You met her I suppose?" Vanessa asked, climbing the stairs.

"I did. I think she likes me," Zack bragged, following.

"Confident, are we?" she giggled, thinking he was probably right. His parents were the kind of people everyone in town knew- the ones who ran the fundraisers for improvements at the town park and sat on every committee imaginable. She was surprised no one had named a street after them, until she realized how ridiculous "Roads Road" would look on a sign.

"I try," he murmured. "I'll meet you outside, ok?"

"Ok." She went to find her mother, who looked like she'd been waiting in their kitchen posed like a statue- arms crossed and a curious expression on her face. "Hey, Zack and I were going to run out for a bit, maybe grab some food."

"He's cute, Vanessa," her mother stated as if it were an accusation.

"I am aware."

"Well, be careful."

"Will do."

"And be home by nine." Vanessa managed to smile over the eye-roll she was stifling. The day had been too perfect to mess it up with a fight now. She grabbed her black and silver *Pink* sweatshirt on her way out the door, the air much cooler now that the sun had set. She opened the car door, excited about being alone with him now that things seemed to have settled a bit. He was looking at something intently on his phone, but quickly put it away and made her insides twist with the intense stare he shot her way.

"Anywhere in particular you wanna go?" he asked.

"Not necessarily. I didn't eat dinner, so if you're hungry we could grab something fast."

"Sounds good to me. Rich just texted and asked me to swing by there, too. Do you care if we head to his place after? It should only take a minute."

"Not at all." She was secretly elated that he wanted her to hang out with more of his friends. Ignoring the fact that she had no interest in football, she asked him about his season and the team. He drove through Wendy's so that she could order the least healthy dinner she could dream up: chicken nuggets, and a cheeseburger, and fries, and a frosty. There was no meal from Wendy's complete without a frosty.

"You can seriously eat all of that?" he asked incredulously.

"Probably before we get to Rich's, yes," she confirmed proudly. Usually, she ate healthy, though it wasn't by choice. Her mom was a salad pusher.

"You're not worried about like, calories or fat grams or anything?"

"Not particularly, no. Why?" She was starting to feel self-conscious about her choice at the moment.

"Just different than what I'm used to, that's all. You gonna share your fries?" He stole several before she could answer, however. Her mind immediately flew to Jenna, and she wondered if that's who he was referring to. She had a body most girls would kill for. *Whatever, he's not with her anymore for a reason.* Although, she still had a morbid curiosity to know exactly what happened.

"So, I think Vader is down to take that redhead to homecoming."

"Jess?"

"Yeah. He remembered her from his bonfire."

"Awesome, she'll be so excited. Do you think we should go out before then? The four of us?"

"Yeah, sure. I was thinking of having some people over this weekend anyway, why don't you guys come, and they can hang out?"

"Sure. Do you want me to bring anything?"

"It's not a potluck, V."

"No, I know, but like snacks or something?"

"Sure. Snacks would be great," he acquiesced. "And maybe you can wear that purple dress? Not that I'm not loving this hoodie and jeans look, but I've been bragging to everyone about your legs," he grinned.

"You have?" she asked, taken aback a bit by the wardrobe request and the fact that he'd been talking to his friends about her.

"Hell yeah I have. Have you seen you?" He grabbed her thigh affectionately. A smug feeling came across her chest, reaffirming that it didn't matter what she ordered from Wendy's. She bit her lip to keep from smiling too widely.

"I might have something better than the purple dress," she admitted flirtatiously. Feeling appreciated, she slid her hand into his as he drove.

"Well this I have to see," he retorted, tracing a figure eight on her palm with his thumb. The light motion gave her goose bumps, but she didn't ask him to stop.

They pulled up outside of Rich's house in one of the nicest neighborhoods in town, complete with a two-story brick façade and a wide front porch. The door swung inward, and she had to admire the boy's shirtless look. He looked mildly surprised to see her there with Zack, but didn't seem bothered. His sandy brown hair was messy, but it didn't make his arm muscles any less impressive.

"Hey, sorry, I didn't know you had anyone with you. I'm Rich," he stated, reaching out his hand. She shook it and introduced herself. "Ah, Vanessa, of course. Zack has been talking you up a bit." Zack shot him a look, but Rich just grinned harder. "Come on in, I just gotta grab your shit Zack, I'll be right back." Zack led her down the stairs to the basement, which had clearly been upgraded when the home was built.

As with any new place, Vanessa looked around to study the décor and the architecture. Rich's house was lovely, but fairly plain- neutral textiles and wall color, beige carpet. There wasn't much there to inspire her. "Is there a bathroom down here?" she asked- partially because she had to pee, but also because she was nosy and wanted to see how the bathroom was decorated as well. As she suspected, there were only builder-grade fixtures in there as well. She still sighed happily knowing that her design plans were going to be amazing. She had picked out an over-sized arabesque wall tile in white with metallic tiles scattered throughout. Impatiently, she just wanted everything to arrive, so she could actually *see* it all.

In walking back to the main area, she could hear Rich talking to Zack, but only caught the tail end of it. "...couldn't understand why you were cherry-picking, but I get it now. I'd put in the work for that too."

"Dude, shut up," Zack replied, making Rich laugh. It clicked in her brain that he was referring to her being a virgin, which he had absolutely no way of knowing, and she felt her self-control take a hike along with her sense of propriety. She walked into the room confidently and with a smile, not wanting to let on that she'd heard them.

"Hey babe, you ready to go?" Zack asked, not seeming startled at her appearance. Rich still had the trace of a laugh on his face.

"Yeah, almost. I'm still hungry though. I could really go for some dessert. Rich, do you happen to have any fruit? Specifically cherries? I don't know why, but I'm really in the mood for cherries right now. Doesn't that sound good?"

Rich now looked unsettled. "Uh, no. No fruit unfortunately. Maybe next time."

"Yeah, you'll have to go cherry-picking. I hear it's worth the effort. So nice to meet you." She grabbed her purse off of the couch and started for the stairs. She heard Zack mutter "*Shit*," under his breath and follow her out.

"That was quite a tantrum," Zack finally said, blowing out a long breath once they were out at his car.

"I'm sorry, *what*? He was literally talking about my virginity while I was in the bathroom. How is that ok?"

"Obviously it wasn't ok, that's why I told him to shut up. Or maybe you were only eavesdropping on part of the conversation. I wouldn't let him talk shit about you, ok? It didn't have to turn into a scene though. He was just kidding around anyway, because you're younger than me, he didn't mean it as like a personal attack, Jesus."

"*Seriously*? You think *I* was the one behaving inappropriately in there? Thank god I did hear your conversation, otherwise I would have gone on thinking you genuinely liked me." She hated herself for letting tears well up in her eyes. *You are so stupid.* Zack sighed heavily.

"Come here please." His voice was low and almost apologetic.

"I'm fine where I am." Her voice wavered and she cursed silently. He shoved his hands in his pockets and took the three steps necessary to be standing in front of her.

"V. Please stop. I do genuinely like you. If I didn't, I would already be driving you home." This did not make her feel any better. "What I like about you is that you don't seem like you play games. I can't deal with more girl drama, I just can't. Being with Jenna drove me insane. I understand one hundred percent why you're pissed, I'm just saying you could have been straight with me about it rather than trying to make a passive-aggressive point and storming out. Rich will apologize to you; I guarantee it, because I will kick his ass if he doesn't. I don't know what you think of me, but I'm not the guy you are acting like I am. I need for you to give me the benefit of the doubt here. Have I done something to make you think I'm playing you?"

She paused. "Not exactly, no," she answered as honestly as possible. There were a couple of things that had bothered her, but he seemed to be more even-keeled the last couple of times she'd seen him.

"Please, tell me. Like I just want to hang out and have things be cool." She debated on whether to divulge what she was thinking. When she listed out her concerns in her head, they didn't feel like enough to justify her recent actions. She didn't like that he'd ditched her at lunch, but she knew she technically wasn't allowed off campus, and it bothered her he'd shown up late for their date, but he stopped to get her flowers, and it was confusing that he'd sort of flipped out on their last date, but again he'd offered an explanation, making all of this very *blah* for her to think about while standing in front of him. His bright eyes were searching hers for an answer, and he ran his fingers along her palms, causing her to lose her train of thought anyway.

"Can you tell me what happened with Jenna?" He looked surprised.

"Does it really matter?" He finally broke eye contact with her and looked elsewhere, his tone tired. She bit the inside of her lip to get her emotions under control. *Deep breaths.* "I'm sorry, you're right. I'll tell you; it's really not a long story." Vanessa locked eyes with him expectantly. "I liked her. I really liked her, actually. But she constantly messed with my head. She would flirt with my friends to make me jealous and make me feel stupid when it worked. She ended up cheating on me with a friend of mine from Central at a party one night. And I never would have known if I hadn't walked in on them by accident. I decked the guy and broke up with her. The end." His jaw was set firmly and his eyes were hard.

"I'm sorry," she murmured, feeling like she had nothing adequate to say.

He dropped her hands and put them behind his head, causing his shirt to lift above his waistband. "It's uh, kind of a hit to my ego to admit that she cheated on me, but I don't want you to be wondering. It's better that you know the truth." Vanessa now felt embarrassed by her display from earlier, and wanted nothing more than to touch this beautiful boy in front of her.

"Thank you. For telling me. And I'm sorry for... earlier. I should have just told you I overheard the conversation and asked for an explanation."

"Well, I kind of liked the look on Rich's face regardless," Zack grinned, showing his dimples. He pushed a stray hair behind her ear, and she couldn't take all of the not-kissing any longer. Her toes lifted her up, and she leaned into his chest until she could feel his heartbeat. He kissed her back intently, his fingertips tracing circles on the back of her neck. She found the hem of his shirt and allowed her nails to trail up his sides. His muscles contracted beautifully, but he started laughing instead of kissing and reached for her hands. "Yeah, you can't keep doing that," he admitted, playing with her hands.

"You're ticklish?" she asked playfully.

"I am. You have discovered my kryptonite."

"I kind of like that power," she continued, reaching for his sides again. He squirmed at her touch, but grabbed her wrists and held them behind her, kissing her deeply again.

"Are we ok?" he asked softly.

"We're ok." He kissed her top and bottom lips separately, then together, and then her neck, making her toes curl up into her shoes.

"How long until you have to be home?"

"Fifteen minutes," she breathed reluctantly. She never wanted him to stop kissing her like that. A low rumble emanated from his chest.

"That is upsetting."

"Yes," she agreed.

"All right, well, I'm glad we're good. I will get you home on time. I don't want you to be grounded from coming over this weekend. I want to be able to do lots more of this," he smiled before he demonstrated exactly what he meant.

"I think I can get on board with more of that," she flirted when he finally broke their connection and opened the car door for her. He proceeded to kiss her at every stoplight on the way back to her neighborhood, and by the time she walked through her front door at 8:59, she was buzzing with the anticipation of seeing him again.

V: You busy?

C: Just got home. How's your world?

The thing Vanessa loved most about Courtney was that their friendship was easy. She never worried that Courtney was mad at her for something stupid, or judging her behind her back. They could text every day or talk once every three months, and it didn't matter. They lived their lives and didn't hold that against each other.

V: Really freakin' good, actually. And yours?

C: Mine's boring. Let me live vicariously through you. I take it things are going well with Mr. I-guess-he's-nice?

V: Lol, they are. I didn't think they were. Actually I sort of flipped out on him and his friend tonight, but things turned around after that. He's just so freaking dreamy I don't even know what to do.

C: Flipped out about…

V: His friend said something stupid to me. I blew it out of proportion though, Zack will handle him.

C: Lame sauce. And I can't imagine you ever blowing anything out of proportion. So unlike you. Do you have a picture? I wanna see him :).

V: No one says lame sauce anymore. You need a new phrase. And shut up :). I don't, but I'll take one soon. He's having some people over this weekend.

C: I like lame sauce. It has a nice visual to it.

V: You are hopelessly nerdy.

C: And you're my best friend, so what does that make you?

V: :P

C: I gotta do homework, I miss you though. <3

V: I miss you too.

Finishing her homework quickly, she got ready for bed. She could still feel his lips on her neck and shivered with delight. Grinning, she pictured the perfect outfit to wear to his house that weekend to make his jaw drop to the floor.

9

When Vanessa strolled down the hallway towards the sophomore locker bay the following morning, she stopped short when she saw Rich leaning against her locker. He looked very much like Emilio Estevez in *The Breakfast Club* in his letterman jacket. *Oh this is going to be so uncomfortable*, she realized. Her mouth was a lot less bold when her brain was not boiling over in anger. Squaring her shoulders, she continued her path towards her locker with feigned confidence. She cleared her throat obviously upon arrival since he didn't appear to notice. Rich looked up and shoved his phone in his pocket.

"Hey, Vanessa. How's it goin'?"

"Oh, just fine." He ran his hand through his straw hair.

"Listen, about last night. I was being an ass. I didn't mean it as anything personal. Obviously I don't know you, so I shouldn't have said anything."

"Thank you. For the apology."

"Yeah, no problem. Are we cool?"

"Sure."

"All right, I'll see you around then."

"See ya," she nodded. He left for the junior hallway, and she could only shake her head at the surreal nature of that conversation. Rich Michaelson wasn't really known for his sincerity. More for his DUI the previous year.

"Hey, hi, hello, good morning!" Vanessa smiled even before she saw Jessi's red hair.

"Aren't you in a good mood."

"Well that remains to be seen. Or heard. What have you heard? Tell me. Like right now, I'm going to combust."

"I heard that you have a homecoming date with Vader. And we're going to Zack's this weekend so you guys can hang out."

"Shut.up.right.now." Her eyes got wide like a kid on Christmas.

"Well, if you don't wanna go with him..."

"Bite your tongue. Bite your whole mouth even. Of course I want to go with him. Oh my god, we are going to have so much fun. Can we shop now? Like tomorrow? Or right now? Let's skip and go to Fairfield."

"Yeah, the only problem with that is when my mom finds out I skipped school, there will be no homecoming. Or me. Because I'll be dead."

"Ugh, fine! This weekend then? Yes. I will pick you up."

"Ok, ok. I'll be ready." Jessi clapped excitedly and hurried to class without saying goodbye. Vanessa trailed after her, wondering if she remembered they were in the same homeroom. The day passed by blissfully quickly, but she was disappointed when Zack wasn't in the cafeteria at lunch. She speared her lettuce rather forcefully with a plastic fork, attempting to mask her disappointment. Her eyes lit up when the screen on her phone did the same.

> Z: Hey, I went off campus for lunch, but I'm bringing you back something. I didn't want you to think I ditched you. I'll see you in a bit.

She promptly threw her broccoli salad in the trash and listened to Jess and Kim go back and forth about their homecoming routine. She couldn't lie- the looks she got from her classmates when Zack sat down next to her with a cheeseburger and a frosty made her sit up a little straighter.

"Thank you! So much better than my salad," Vanessa exclaimed.

"You are welcome. You guys down to come over tomorrow night? Probably like seven?"

"Yeah we'll be there," she answered gleefully.

"I'm not sure what's going on after the game tonight, but I'll text you if it's anything fun, yeah? And I think you should cheer extra loud for me."

"You got it," she promised, taking a sip of her milkshake." He leaned in closer to whisper in her ear.

"Truth? There's something kind of sexy about watching you eat a frosty." He finished with a laugh, but she blushed anyway. He kissed her beneath her jaw and went to go sit with his teammates.

"It's not even fair how pretty he is," Jess declared rather loudly.

"Amen, sister," Kim agreed. Vanessa felt guilty that she hadn't included her friend in their weekend plans, and immediately extended an invitation. She also resolved to help find her a homecoming date as well.

* * *

The game Friday night did not go well for Gem City High, and no one was quite in the mood to go out and celebrate. Vanessa tried several cheerful messages to Zack after the loss, but he insisted he just wanted to go home and sleep. Reluctantly, she began to text her mom to come pick her up, realizing that her vehicularly blessed friends were nowhere to be found.

"Well, that was disappointing," a voice came from her left as she trudged toward the parking lot.

"Right?" she answered, turning to see Luke with his car keys swinging around his finger playfully. She supposed he could afford to be in a jolly mood since he played basketball.

"Do you need a ride?" The keys stopped swinging and he shoved them into the pocket of his dark jeans.

"Actually, yeah. Would you mind?" It struck her that this was the most civilized conversation they'd had since perhaps the sixth grade when they first met.

"For a small fee, of course," he grinned. She could see his green eyes sparkle even in the dark.

"Whatever, bite me. I'll just call my mom." He had to go and act like himself.

"Stop, you know I'm kidding. Let's go." He took her phone out of her hand and held it in the air so she couldn't reach it.

"You are a child," she complained, following him towards his car, her pleated red and black cheer skirt bouncing around her as she stomped. Jumping on his back to get her phone was not out of the question. *This is ridiculous.*

"A child? With these guns? I don't think so," he bragged, flexing his biceps casually under his Hollister shirt.

"Ugh. Can you just give me my phone back and take me home?"

"Magic words?" he asked, holding it above her hands and still wearing that stupid smile as they approached his black Chevy Silverado.

"Screw you?"

"Eh, close enough." He dropped her cell into her grasp and opened the door for her chivalrously. It was surprisingly clean inside, and it didn't even smell like gym clothes.

"Your truck is nice," she stated begrudgingly when he got in. He just looked at her for a moment, grinning like an idiot.

"Thanks. My uncle, ah, he has a dealership… so he helped, whatever. Do you wanna grab some food? Concession stand hot dogs don't really do it for me."

"Um, sure. I could eat. Just not Wendy's please." No matter how much she loved burgers and Frosties, there was only so much a girl could take.

"Pizza?" She was surprised at his suggestion, as it would mean they'd actually have to sit down together for the length of a meal. It was entirely possible one of them would end up wearing the pizza before it was over.

"Are you sure?"

"About pizza? Yeah, I'm one hundred percent sure about pizza. Do you have some sort of objection to Italy's greatest gift to America?"

"I don't think pizza actually came from Italy, but ok. Pizza it is." They mostly chatted about their bio homework, after he made her Google the origin of pizza, until he pulled into the lot at Pizza Hut.

"I can't even believe pizza isn't from Italy. I've been crediting the wrong culture with my favorite food, and now I have to start giving props to the Babylonians or something."

"I'm sorry my knowledge of food history has disrupted your world," she joked. They sat and ordered quickly once inside; the restaurant was busy after a game night. Luke ordered a Mountain Dew and a ridiculous amount of carbs. "I heard that drinking Mountain Dew can mess with the effectiveness of your, um… You know? Never mind." She couldn't believe she had just willingly entered into a conversation about the abilities of Luke Miller's manhood.

"I'm sorry, what? What are you trying to do to me here? Jesus! First pizza and now Mountain Dew? You are a cruel woman." He called the waitress back over and asked for water instead.

"For the record, I'm not worried about anything in that general vicinity, I-"

"Stop the words from coming out of your mouth immediately. We are not having this conversation." She wanted to be mad, but a laugh bubbled up from her chest anyway and she covered her face with her hands. "Moving on. Do you have a date for homecoming?" she asked, an idea forming in her head.

"Not as of yet. Why? Did you decide to take my advice and ditch Roads?"

"No," she retorted pointedly. "And even if I had, why would you assume I'd want to go with you? You would just make me want to kill you the whole night."

"Touché," he admitted.

"And I think you should take Kimmy."

"Selner?"

"Yes. Do I have another friend named Kimmy?"

"I suppose not. Why? Does she have a thing for me?" He raised his eyebrows suggestively just as the pizza arrived.

"Not everyone is in love with you, Lucas. But since neither of you are dating anyone, you could go as friends."

"Yeah, maybe. I'll think about it, she's cool." Vanessa produced a satisfied smile and dove into the pizza.

"Why is this so good?"

"That's what I'm saying!" They bantered easily as they ate, and she insisted they split the bill despite his protests.

"This is very emasculating, Vanessa."

"Define emasculating, and I'll consider letting you pay," she smiled knowingly.

"*This.* This is the definition of emasculating. Whatever, now I don't even want to pay for you."

"That's what I thought." He blew a straw wrapper at her like he was seven years old, and she rolled her eyes. They spent the ride arguing about who had worse taste in music, and she was trying to outline the incredible talent of One Direction when he finally pulled up to her house.

"I kind of had fun tonight, thanks for eating with me. It definitely beat going home and eating whatever my mom imagined up as an appropriate dinner."

"I kind of had fun too. Thanks for the ride."

"See ya, V."

"See ya."

What a random night, she thought. She texted Zack once more to try and bring him out of his mood about losing the game, but she got tired of waiting for a response. Instead, she scoured her closet for an outfit for the get together the following night that would make him forget he even played football.

10

Vanessa spent most of the next day attempting to appease her parents in the hopes that her curfew might be extended that night. The dishes were clean, her homework was completed, and the floor of her room was visible. Her phone buzzed as she was hanging up the last of her laundry.

> Z: Hey, sorry I was MIA last night, I just needed to blow off some steam. Everything cool for later?
>
> V: That's ok, I get it. Yeah, what time do you want me to come over?
>
> Z: Right now.
>
> V: I believe there are three hours before your friends will be arriving. Do you really need that much help setting up? ;)
>
> Z: Nope :).
>
> V: I will be there early, I promise. I just gotta get ready.
>
> Z: See you soon. In something better than the purple dress ;).

She was a little dizzy from his affectionate tone. Part of her wanted to race over there and continue what they'd started outside of Rich's house. *He's just so freaking delicious.* The other part of her tensed at the thought of where things would go with that much uninterrupted time. Zack did not have a reputation for being innocent or shy, but she supposed it was the opposite that attracted her in the first place. She forced a deep breath and implored her brain to think rationally. It didn't work. As a general rule, she wasn't a rational person, but she knew someone who was.

> V: Should I go over to Zack's house really early before his party thing? Or does that make it look like I'm easy? Am I over thinking it?
>
> C: How early?

This was why she texted Courtney. Logical questions.

> V: Three hours.
>
> C: That's a lot of hours.
>
> V: Yeah.
>
> C: Are you guys like together, or what exactly is the situation?
>
> V: We've only been out a couple of times. We're going to homecoming. I like him. A lot. But it's still new, so, I don't know.
>
> C: I say go a little early. I don't really have anything to compare it to, but it seems like you're still getting to know him. So do that.
>
> V: You're right. I just needed someone else to say it.
>
> C: Lemme know how it goes!
>
> V: I will :). Have a good night.

The tension had already lifted from her chest, so she knew the advice was sound. She wasn't ready to be faced with the decisions that could present themselves in a three-hour span of alone time with a boy who kissed like Zack did. Instead, Vanessa took her time getting dressed in a tight black mini and a cream colored top that just barely fell off her shoulder. Amazingly, she even took the time to curl her hair so that long blond waves fell down her back. *Yeah. Better than the purple dress,* she thought confidently.

Her parents had already left for the evening, but had agreed to let her take the Durango *and* to extend her curfew until midnight. She couldn't have been happier if she'd won the lottery. Stopping by the store, she grabbed what she thought were reasonable snacks: chips, dip, fruit, cookies, brownies, and some other pastry concoction. *Everyone likes dessert,* she justified when looking over her selection. With effort, she maintained her calm façade until she was pulling onto Zack's street. He lived in a newer build that sat on a giant lot at the back of a subdivision called Clearwater Estates. It appeared that the Durango was the first car there, and she breathed anxiously as she took the food out of the trunk. Her very tall cream peep-toes wobbled as she waltzed up the rounded gravel drive to the front door. Containers were balanced precariously on her arms when Zack appeared in front of her. Well, at least the top of his head did.

"Whoa there, you're kind of serious about your snacks," he joked, taking several items from the top so she could see.

"I know, I know, I went overboard with the sugar." She felt slightly over-dressed, but that thought became buried beneath the returning pounding of her heart upon crossing the threshold. She took in the sight of him in dark jeans and a black t-shirt that was stretched just slightly too tight across his shoulders. Following him into the kitchen to relieve herself of the food, Vanessa conducted her compulsory home-inspection. His parents' tastes were more mid-century modern than she normally saw in Gem City. The structure of the house was typical- an open floor plan from the front door into a foyer and a great room, but she appreciated the clean lines of the sofas and the mix of neutral colors that made it feel less stark. "Your house is decorated impeccably. Is that an actual Eames chair?" she asked him, now less distracted by his biceps and very interested in where his mother shopped. "Can I sit in it?"

His facial expression showed confusion. "It is a chair, so yes, you can sit in it. I don't know what an Eames is. You sound like my mother though. You'll have to come over when she's home, she'll love you." His tone was mildly disapproving which brought her attention back to him.

"Sorry, what can I do to help?" she questioned cheerfully, finding her way back to him at the massive kitchen island.

"You can come over here and let me appreciate this skirt," he replied flirtatiously. A smile spread across her face as she slid in-between him and the counter. She couldn't help but admire the dark stained butcher block that made up the island's counter-top and ran her fingers along it lightly. "If you are going to put your hands on something in this room, I'd rather it be me," he murmured, removing her hands from the counter and folding his fingers into hers. All attention was refocused on him and the way his chest felt pressed against her. He kissed her slowly while his thumbs traced circles on her palms, and she tried to control her breathing. Kissing someone new was like reading a map in an unfamiliar city, and she tried to let him navigate. He did so by making a trail down her neck with his lips and up her shirt with his hands. Heat rose in her cheeks, and her pulse could be heard for miles, she was certain. Attempting to gain a moment to collect herself, she asked breathlessly, "So you approve then?"

"Of?"

"The skirt. Better than the purple dress?"

He broke out in the wide grin that showed his dimples. "Much better than the purple dress. You look amazing. I didn't say that before."

"Well thank you," she answered, pleased. "Do you want me to put some of this food out on actual plates?"

"My friends really aren't that picky," he sighed, stepping back and chewing on his perfectly shaped bottom lip. All of the intensity and playfulness was instantly gone from the room.

"Show me the rest of the house," she offered, taking his hand back in hers and pulling him towards the stairs.

"Whatever you say, babe." He followed her with some reluctance down to the basement. It was fully finished with a massive projector screen on one wall and a pool table on the other, sandwiching in a sitting area with an oversized couch.

"This is kind of awesome down here."

"Thanks, it's kind of nice to have it to myself now that both my brothers moved out."

"Do you miss them?"

"Hell no. I mean, they're cool and whatever, but being the youngest sucks, you know?"

"Well, no, I don't actually *know*, being an only child and all, but I think I can imagine." His phone buzzed during this portion of the conversation, and he read the incoming text. She felt the energy shift. His muscles tensed and his anger was palpable. "What's up?"

"Nothing."

"Ok? You seem sort of-"

"I seem nothing. I'm fine." His tone knocked her down a bit, considering how affectionate he'd been not ten minutes earlier. "I'll be right back, I gotta make a phone call." He briskly stepped outside through the basement's walk-out feature, and she took a deep breath before sinking into the soft suede of the sofa. Zack was gone long enough for Vanessa to count all of the squares in the abstract painting hanging on the wall. Four times. She was more than a little concerned when he walked back inside with an agitated expression worn on his normally confident face.

"Hi..." she tried, standing up uncertainly.

"Hi," he responded curtly. She wasn't sure where to go from there, but thankfully he kept talking. "I'm sorry, about before. My friend Jeremy texted me to say he was bringing Jenna tonight. That since he knew you'd be here with me, he didn't think it would be a big deal. I didn't mean to... I don't know, be an ass. I just.... I called him to tell him to screw himself. I have no idea if he'll show up with her or not. So, that's that, I guess."

Her stomach dropped with his explanation. She was worried enough about how the night would play out without adding Jenna into the equation. "Oh, wow. Ok. That seems... like a really crappy thing for someone to do to his friend. I get that I'm not a guy, but if one of my friends did that to me, I would put Nair in her shampoo." Zack actually cracked a smile.

"That's not a horrible idea. Jeremy's kind of particular about his hair."

"Then I say totally do it."

"You're kind of a cool chick, you know?"

"I know," she shot back playfully, crinkling her nose. He made his way to her and found her lips again with much less control this time. With his hands securely around her waist, he sank into the couch and guided her to sit on his lap. Her earlier fear dissipated when she realized how much he was hurting. She only wanted to make him feel better, and to see his dimples come out again. The power to do so rushed through her, and she allowed him to fully demonstrate how much he valued her mini-skirt.

The doorbell rang at an inopportune time and he swore under his breath. "Do you think anyone will care if I tell them to get the hell out?"

"They might," she let out, forcing her breathing to return to its normal state. He sighed and helped her up off the couch while she hastily tried to correct her hair and makeup.

When she returned to the main area, several of Zack's friends had arrived and made themselves comfortable in front of the TV. Vanessa stood somewhat awkwardly off to the side of the couch, trying to determine how to proceed. She knew all of their names, but she didn't really *know* them. "Does anyone want anything? I can bring down some of the food."

"Yes please," Zack answered, smiling that wide dimpled grin she'd been hoping for. He turned his attention back to the game, and she started confidently for the kitchen. It felt weird to go through the kitchen cabinets, even though she admired the up-graded soft-close doors, but she needed to find plates. Feeling like a snoop, she gasped when she turned around to find Zack leaning against the island. "I thought you might need help," he grinned, clearly enjoying her start.

"Just looking for plates. Preferably not the ones from Sur La Table," she stated in her best French accent.

"From huh?"

"It's a store… where your dishes are from? I didn't think you'd want to risk breaking them."

"We're not five, I'm sure we can hold plates."

"Okay. Your house." She would never in a million years serve teenage boys anything on dinnerware that nice, but whatever.

"All right, maybe paper is better," he admitted, moving to-wards a bottom cabinet and taking out a stack of Dixie plates.

"That's more the speed I was thinkin'" They were in the process of loading up plates with all manner of chip and cookie when the front door opened. Jenna strolled in a little too com-fortably with Jeremy following behind her. Vanessa supposed all high schools had a Jenna. The girl everyone envied but no one really liked. Her black hair tumbled down to the middle of her back, and while Vanessa wished she could comment on the poor quality of her spray tan, she suspected it was real. The girl looked good in a pair of skinny jeans and flats, topped by a pur-ple t-shirt with a printed sparkly cupcake drawing attention to her chest. V would have hated her more if she didn't desperately want to know where she got that shirt.

Zack seemed to be taking in the same scene when she finally glanced over at him. His jaw was tense, but the rest of him seemed confident. "Hey Jer, Jenna. Everybody's downstairs," he said tersely. Instead of heading that way, Jenna glided over to the kitchen and surveyed the snacks. Well, she pretended to anyway, but her eyes really never left Vanessa.

"Who's this?" Jenna asked, raising a perfectly waxed eyebrow.

"Not that it's your business, but this is Vanessa. V, this is Jenna." The girls took to more staring rather than shaking hands or doing anything remotely adult-like.

"Did you hire her?"

"Hire her to what?"

"I don't know. She looks like a hooker, so I thought I'd ask." Jenna yawned as if the whole situation bored her to tears, but Vanessa was ready to rush the bitch with a pair of kitchen scissors. She paused for one breath, waiting for Zack to intervene before she had to seriously consider murder, but when she shot daggers at him, he was chuckling to himself. He continued smiling despite her shift in energy, and Jenna continued to appear quite blasé about the whole encounter.

"I love the way you look, babe," he grinned and slid across the tiled floor to wrap his arms around her, his hands finding a place they liked on her butt. Jenna finally reacted and rolled her eyes before heaving herself up off of the counter.

"I'd rather look like one than act like one," Vanessa spouted off while Jenna was still well within earshot. Jenna's midnight hair whipped around so fast it probably could have harmed someone, but Zack was already in her space before she could open her mouth.

"Walk it off Jenna, you started it." He physically turned her around and ushered her out of the kitchen. He turned back towards her and mouthed, "I'll be right back," before disappearing.

Well the rest of the evening should be interesting, Vanessa mused. The sound of clicking shoes in the entryway made her heart race, preparing her for further confrontation, so she almost leapt into Jessi's arms when her friend flew into the room- she really didn't have any other speed setting.

"So I see you're getting all Dorothy up in here this evening," Jess spit out quickly and cryptically as usual. She appeared to still be drying her nails while attempting to fluff up her mermaid hair without using them. It was almost comical.

"My Jess translator is out on vacation."

"Oh! Sorry. I just mean the wicked witch I passed on my way in. Flying monkeys and shit were following her around. *Dammit.* Why do I try to do eleven things at once?" she complained, holding up her now smudged bright green nails. "I wonder if your man-person has nail polish remover." She started looking around as if it would materialize in front of her. Thankfully, she got side-tracked from her nail polish mission by the food and the potential dirt. "What went down?" Jess pressed, her mouth now full of Cheetos.

"That crazy B called me a hooker!"

"Eck-oo meh?!" her friend responded with garbled indignation, her eyes wide and mouth still stuffed with orange crisps. Zack took this moment to re-enter the kitchen. He appraised Jessica's tight black pants and sheer green top ensemble with an approving glance.

"Good evening Jess, help yourself to some snacks," he teased her. She swallowed with difficulty and checked her face for cheese dust.

"Thanks. You're so gracious," she gave back in a similar tone. He smirked and turned his attention back towards his date for the evening.

"Do you think you'll be able to keep the claws in for the rest of the evening?"

"Me?! What about her?" Vanessa asked, seething at feeling scolded. He chuckled again which did nothing to tame her anger.

"Did I say you weren't in the right? No. I just want my friends to get to know you without any hair getting pulled," he explained, and then added quietly, "You can save all that pent-up energy for me later." Her eyes jerked up to meet his and her stomach flipped. He smiled widely at her reaction and turned back to her friend. "Jess, glad you could make it. Are you ladies going to grace us with your presence down there?"

"Do you have nail polish remover?" Jess asked, finally coming back to her original purpose. Zack just looked at her quizzically and sauntered back out of the room. "I take it that's a no then." She focused on Vanessa, perhaps really for the first time since she arrived. "You do kind of look like a hooker," she laughed. "Like in the best possible way, though. You look fierce."

"I kind of hate you right now. There is no best possible way to look like a hooker." She couldn't help but start to smile though. Jess could get away with saying the most outrageous things, and no one could get mad at her. Her delivery was too endearing.

"Of course there is. Julia Roberts in *Pretty Woman*? Come on," she argued as they gathered up as many plates of food as possible.

"Yeah, yeah. Just consider yourself on thin ice. You know Vader's down there already, right?"

"I figured. I sort of tried to forget though. Should I be nervous? I shouldn't be. It'll be fine. Do you think? I mean, these pants are pretty jaw-dropping. It'll be fine. Right?"

"You don't even need me to have a conversation. You're good all on your own." It was apparent that a snarky reply was imminent, but they entered the party before she could get it out. There were only eight or ten people gathered there, but it was sort of an intimidating crowd. Complaints started to rise up when the girls stepped in front of the TV to place food on the table, but whether it was the snacks or the addition of Jess to the mix that quelled them, Vanessa couldn't be sure.

"Since when do you have actual food at a party?" Rich asked Zack, possessively grabbing a plate and digging in.

"Don't look at me. This is V's doing."

"I love you Vanessa," Rich stated, evidently forgetting their previous quarrel. "And I might love you, mysterious red-headed friend. I'm Rich," he asserted to Jessica.

"I'm aware," she returned with a look that added *that you were mean to my friend.* Vanessa could have kissed her for her solidarity. They moved out of the way so the boys could continue playing, and Vanessa pulled up a beanbag chair for them to share. *Who has a beanbag chair anymore?* She wondered, seriously thinking there was no way she'd be able to get out of it gracefully in the skirt she had on.

"Nope, veto. You sit with me," Zack commanded, watching her with interest. "Vader, I'm sure you can make some room for Jess down there, yeah?"

"I am absolutely certain that I can," Vader answered, his lopsided grin coming out, maybe more to taunt Rich than for any other reason. He kissed her hand playfully and she giggled. *Annnnnd she owns him now.* Vanessa shook her head and leaned awkwardly on the arm of the sofa next to Zack. Without dragging his gaze away from the game she was pretty sure he was losing, he tugged her onto his lap with one arm and resumed playing. Despite how delicious he smelled, she was bored five minutes later.

"Can I play?" she asked. After a fairly blatant lack of response she asked again. "I want to play, it's boring just watching."

"I thought sitting there and looking pretty was part of your hostess duty," he finally answered. She rolled her eyes and moved to get up, deciding she would find entertainment elsewhere. He caught her by the waistband of her skirt and pulled her back to him. "I'm just kidding babe. You can play if you want." He handed over the controller willingly and she got ready to fight someone, she assumed. She had no idea what buttons to push, so she pushed them all at varying intervals. As it turned out, her strategy was kind of brilliant, and she found herself actually having fun talking crap to his friends when she beat them.

"KO!" she shouted to Rich when she did some sort of fancy spinning kick to his fighter."

"Do you even know what KO stands for?" Zack laughed in her ear. She could smell alcohol on his breath, but had no idea where it had come from, as she didn't see anyone with a drink.

"Killer...Outfit?" she guessed jokingly.

"Well, no. But yes. Meaning now that I'm undistracted by playing this game, your outfit is killing me. Please tell me you're done embarrassing my friends, and let me have you to myself." She broke out in goose bumps with his breath traveling down her neck, and handed the controller over to Jeremy, all whilst ignoring Jenna's glare. Vader looked completely enraptured by one of Jessica's dramatic stories, or perhaps overwhelmed, but he appeared happy either way as she gestured wildly about something or other. Vanessa stood, and Zack followed, his arms wrapped securely around her waist. "Upstairs or outside? I could start a fire," he offered, though the first option was clearly his favorite. Her heart raced at the thought of being in his bedroom. *No way he thinks we are doing that with a room full of people down here.*

"Ohhh, let's make s'mores!" she requested enthusiastically. He almost snorted and shook his head.

"As you wish." He led her outside to an impressive stone fire pit and got to work. The night was beautiful and clear, but also rather chilly, and she wished she had re-thought the skirt. Distracting herself, she looked around. They had a large property, and there were remnants of childhood aging a ways out into the yard. A swing set stood like a beacon of nostalgia with a trampoline nearby.

"Is that trampoline still structurally sound?"

"What? Oh, yeah, it's not that old. Why? You wanna bounce?" He wiggled his eyebrows at her.

"I'm going to pretend you're interested in my gymnastics skills and not my boobs."

"I am *very* interested in your gymnastics skills," he laughed.

"Dammit, you know that's not what I meant!" She shook her head at her own stupidity, but carefully made her way to the trampoline anyway, trying desperately not to roll an ankle in her heels. She kicked them off happily and climbed up. "Light please?" she asked, and he flipped a switch on the wall of the house, giving her the ability to see the edges better.

"Let's see what you've got." She began with perfect form, toes pointed, of course. With sincerity, she hoped she wasn't going to fly off and face plant in the grass. She couldn't help but laugh the higher she got; it was impossible not to smile on a trampoline. Like she was playing pool, she called out her tricks before she did them.

"Back tuck. Layout. Full. Front tuck." The flips continued as long as she could stand it, but she finally collapsed, out of breath.

"Dizzy?" Zack asked as he climbed up to join her.

"Very," she replied, even moreso now that he was next to her.

"I give you props for your mad gymnastics skills," he grinned, licking that lip that she found so intoxicating.

"I told you," she whispered. He leaned in to kiss her, and her breath caught in her throat, the chill in the air all but forgotten. Surprisingly, he blew in her ear, and while she honestly thought that was something only done in 80s movies, it tickled in a delightful way. His large hands wrapped around her ribcage and he kissed her neck playfully. Moving her hands to tickle his sides, he caught her wrists.

"Uh-uh, no tickling," he admonished. Her face lips pursed together, and he continued, "no pouting either." She felt his hands tickle her behind the knees, effectively breaking his own rule, but before she could comment on it those same hands were pushing her already barely-there skirt much higher.

"Zack," she murmured, really not fond of the idea of anyone wandering outside to find her quite that exposed.

"Shhhh, it's fine. We're alone."

"I just, I don't..." He kissed her more hurriedly than before, and she tried to relax. It wasn't working. "Can we just do this when you don't have a house full of people?"

"I will kick them all out right now. Just say the word." *This is what an anxiety attack feels like,* she thought, willing her lungs to take in air normally and searching for the right words not to make her sound like a prude or a tease.

"Won't your parents be home soon?" Now she was grasping at anything to slow down their encounter.

"No," he said flatly, clearly realizing that the moment was over. "Their charity events usually go until late. Whatever. Let's go make s'mores." He sighed, sliding towards the edge of the trampoline. More of the group joined them outside once she retrieved the marshmallows and skewers, and she crossed her fingers that he would let his disappointment go.

Most of the rest of the night was spent consuming large amounts of sugar, and him talking to Rich about how to win their game the next week. Feeling ignored, the sting of rejection made itself known in the pit of her stomach, and suddenly she was entirely too exposed in a completely different way than before. She pulled Jess away from her flirtation fest with Vader into the downstairs bathroom.

"Are we planning a covert operation or something?" she whispered.

"No. I need advice," Vanessa voiced miserably.

"Ok. Lay it on me." She relayed the story of what had happened outside and Zack's avoidance. Willing herself not to cry, she set her jaw in a firm grimace.

"Oh no no no no no. No. Absolutely not. There is no sex on a trampoline. What an idiot. No. I'll tell you what your problem is." Her head was shaking so dramatically it was making Vanessa worry she was going to pull a muscle in her neck.

"I'm listening, oh wise one."

"You joke, but I'm being serious. Instead of being all apologetic about not wanting to *lose your virginity* on a damned trampoline, tell him he better step it up and like rent you a unicorn or something."

"Rent me a unicorn."

"Yes. You know what I mean."

"I literally have no idea what you mean."

"Ugh. Ok. Like, don't feel bad for wanting things to be special or whatever you want them to be. And don't be passive aggressive about it."

"I wasn't going to-"

"Yes you were. You were going to say something snarky and stomp out of here. Don't lie." Vanessa glared. "Yeah, that's what I thought. Instead, make him walk you to your car and spell it out for him. If that's even what you want. You are woman, so growl. Or bark. I don't remember the saying. Just do it."

"Roar. Jesus. Fine," Vanessa answered, exasperated. Jess grinned victoriously.

"I'm gonna head out too. Playing video games and roasting marshmallows is only entertaining for so long," she yawned dramatically, fluffing up her hair again." They walked outside arm in arm, and Jess wandered up the stairs and out the door after saying goodbye to her new toy, who was looking rather longingly after her.

"Hey, walk me out," Vanessa stated confidently. She leaned over Zack's chair and let her hair fall around him.

"Sure." He followed her up the steps and out to her car. "Thanks for coming, and for making sure we were well fed," he offered in a lackluster tone.

"Can you stop with the pity party?"

"Come again?" he asked, his gaze sharper now.

"We've been on like three dates, and I didn't want to hook up on the trampoline while your basement was full of people. It is not necessary to passive-aggressively ignore me for the rest of the night."

"I didn't ignore you."

"Uh-huh." He was quiet for a long moment, assessing her statement.

"So... you want more dates?"

"Yes."

"And, like, flowers?"

"Yes." He laughed at that.

"And for me to do some work to get in your-" She unceremoniously clamped her hand over his mouth before he could continue.

"Don't ruin it!"

He chuckled again. "What? I was going to say car. You need to get your mind out of the gutter." She swatted him playfully and let him open the door to the Durango for her.

11

J: Wake up woman. We're going dress shopping.

V: Now?

J: Now. I'm on my way over.

Ugh, I really hate her sometimes. Vanessa rolled out of bed.

V: Did you ask Kimmy to come?

J: Yeah, she didn't text me back.

V: Weird, ok.

Before ten a.m., her standards were seriously different for hair and makeup. It only became a necessity to look halfway decent so that she could adequately judge dresses.

V: Going dress shopping for homecoming. Any last requests? ;)

Z: Yes, that there is no texting before noon on Sunday.

V: Jess woke me up, so you have to be up too.

Z: Tell her I hate her. And I already told you my request ;).

Vanessa was almost embarrassed to admit she was testing him to see if he still felt the same way. This information was to be downplayed.

V: Anything *else*? What's your favorite color?

Z: Nope, that should do it. I'm not five; I don't have a favorite color. Can I see you later? I feel like I need to start wooing you.

V: I'm not five, and I have a favorite color. And yes. Woo away. I'll text you when I get home.

Z: What is it? I feel like it might come in handy with the wooing.

V: Purple.

Z: Got it. Have fun.

Jess was a genius.

* * *

Loudly, Jessi let herself into Vanessa's house, greeted her mother, and ran up the stairs. "Get your ass in those skinny jeans and let's go."

"Where does your energy come from?" Vanessa grumbled, shimmying into her pants and a black lace tank top.

"Probably ADHD."

"You're so odd."

"If by odd, you mean odd-some. See what I did there?" Vanessa couldn't help but laugh.

"Ok, ok, your excitement is the tiniest bit contagious. Let's go." Her mom reminded her that her dress needed to be a "respectable length," whatever that meant, but she was flying high regardless after Zack's promise to see her later.

"Judging by the easy-breezy look on your face, I'd say my relationship tutorial worked for you."

"Yes. I bow down before the master. He's singing a whole different tune this morning."

"Told ya. I think Vader is in love with me or something."

"Oh yeah?"

"Yeah. Whatever. You know how I am. Once they get all myeh, I feel bleck, and I don't know. Why do I do that?" She raked one hand through her hair and brushed non-existent lint off of her emerald colored t-shirt.

"Again, I need a translator."

"Just, *this*," she stated emphatically, shoving her cell phone into Vanessa's face. There was a text from Vader on the screen.

> Vader: Have fun shopping. I know you'll look pretty in anything.

"That's nice!"

"Ugh."

"And that doesn't mean he's in love with you. He's just being sweet."

"Too sweet. Syrup is sweet, and I don't like that either."

"You don't like syrup?"

"No. It's weird and sticky and maple-y. Gross."

"What do you eat on pancakes?"

"Whipped cream. Chocolate chips. Butter."

"Ok then, no syrup. Got it."

"Anyway. New topic. He says he's having a sleepover at his place after homecoming. Are we going?" Vanessa crossed her eyes at her friend, annoyed that she didn't know about the party, and that she even had the nerve to ask.

"Under what planetary alignment would my mother allow me to sleep over with a bunch of upperclassmen?"

"The one where she thinks you're at my house?"

"Not even if you promised me candy and mermaids. The last time you talked me into one of your crazy schemes, I lost out on a car."

"That was unfortunate and isolated incident. We've done this a dozen times. His parents will be there anyway, it's not like it's going to be a rave. I guess they'd rather have people there than out partying at the river or something…and I bet there *will* be candy. Maybe mermaids too."

"Shut up."

"Just think about it!"

"Fine."

They drove the rest of the way to the mall to the tune of some old school Whitney and Mariah, needing to bring out their inner divas to shop properly for gowns. They waltzed into the largest department store in existence and sighed happily.

"Retail smells so good," Vanessa let out.

"Better than a Cinnabon," Jessi agreed. "Let me pick out some dresses for you, and you do the same for me. We have to try them on no matter what."

"Are you going to pick out ugly ones on purpose?"

"Maybe just one. The rest will be legit, I swear."

"Same," Vanessa grinned, ready for the challenge. They continued into the sea of formalwear, surrounded by a rainbow of chiffon and tulle. "You get one run through. Meet me in the dressing room in ten minutes."

"Deal," she called, already on her way. Vanessa searched frantically for the ugliest dress she could find, and her eyes landed on quite a beauty. It was a high-low gown in a fruit print with a bright yellow belt cinched around the middle. *She'll look like Carmen Miranda meets Fruit Ninja.* Smiling and feeling victorious, she started looking for actual dresses her friend might consider wearing. Choosing mostly jewel tones to compliment her red hair, she scurried to the dressing room. Jess was already hanging garments in a vacant room when she walked up.

"I'll take those!" she shouted, snatching the armful of gowns Vanessa had been carrying and slamming the door to her own room. "Ugly ones first!" she heard floating above the door. All Vanessa could see when she walked in the space was rainbow. Rainbow tulle. Rainbow sequins. Rainbow ribbons. It was terrifying. Reluctantly, she slipped into what would be a leprechaun's wet dream and zipped it up the back. To her horror, it even had a short train on the back.

"I concede. You win the ugly dress contest," she admitted, barely fitting through the door opening.

Jess gave an evil laugh and pressed her fingers together like the villainess she was. She didn't even look that bad in the stupid fruit dress. "Ok, next!" she grinned, flying back into her dressing room. Vanessa let her fingers run through the rest of the dresses after discarding the vomitus multi-colored abomination on the floor, and her eyes lit up at one in particular. *Please fit please fit please fit*, she chanted as she slid it over her head. She was almost afraid to glance in the mirror, wanting so badly for it to look how it did in her mind, but her fears were unfounded. *Ariel herself would be jealous,* Vanessa concluded, twirling maybe more times than needed to get a glimpse of her reflection from all angles.

* * *

The bed called her name when she finally made it through the door to her room. While Vanessa had found her dress, jewelry, and shoes within forty-five minutes, Jessi tried on eight thousand-seven hundred and sixty-four gowns before buying two because she couldn't decide. The girl was a shopping robot. She groaned when her phone vibrated in her pocket, but she convinced herself to roll over and fish it out.

Z: You can't seriously still be shopping.

V: I'm not. I think I'm dying though.

Z: Because?

V: Because Jess is a super human, and I think she's single-handedly trying to save the economy. And I can no longer feel my feet. Come and make me feel better.

Z: Done ;).

Must get up and put on makeup, she warned her brain in an attempt to wake up.

"Rise and shine, beautiful," she heard while someone was shaking her shoulders. It took all of four point nine seconds for her to realize that she should not be sleeping, and possibly drooling, and that Zack was standing in her bedroom. A bedroom that was covered in both clean and dirty clothes from her rushed awakening that morning, though it would have been impossible to differentiate between the two.

"Oh my god, you have to get out of my room."

"Not quite the reception I was hoping for-"

"No, I'm sorry. Ugh," she shook her head. "Let's go downstairs and start again. Please." Hoping that she could keep him from looking around by sheer force of will, she prayed she looked halfway decent and began to push him out the door.

"You're kind of messy," he commented, looking thoroughly amused at her humiliation. Of course he looked like the poster child for golden boys of America in jeans and a white button down. *Why the hell did the woman who calls herself my mother let him up here?!*

"Shut up, I'm just... busy," she huffed as they came down to the main floor. Her mother looked positively victorious.

"Maybe now you will find time to keep your floor visible. It hasn't even been twenty-four hours since you 'cleaned' it," she admonished with a passing look before disappearing into the kitchen. *Unbelievable.* She led Zack down to the basement because even if it was half torn apart from construction, it was still a better option than sitting in a room under the watchful eyes of Mrs. Crazy Pants.

"Hi!" she began, trying to re-set the whole visit.

"Hi," he chuckled, smirking adorably as he fell comfortably into their brown suede sofa. She couldn't wait until her new furniture arrived. "Come here." She slinked over to him, still feeling self-conscious at the exposure of her less-than-charming side.

"I'm here," she announced, standing in front of him more confidently than she felt.

"I can see that," he joked. His hands reached out and gripped her waist, pulling her onto his lap.

"Hi again," she breathed, taken aback by their sudden closeness.

"I brought you a present." She finally took notice of the small white paper bag sitting next to him.

"I like presents."

"I thought you might," he ascertained, and he placed the bag in her open hands. It was heavier than she'd anticipated, and she opened the top of it eagerly. The smell of sugary goodness hit her in the most delightful way before she even realized that everything in the bag was a shade of purple.

"You brought me purple sugar! Like enough to give me diabetes," she declared, unable to keep a giant grin off of her face.

"I didn't know what kind of candy you liked, so I just told the lady at Butler's to put everything purple they had in there."

"You're so sweet. Like this candy," she smiled, the corny nature of her comment intended. She leaned in slightly so their noses were touching. "Thank you. For the present and for not running away after seeing me drooling on my pillow in my pigsty of a bedroom."

He snickered slightly at her admission. "You weren't drooling. You looked kind of cute, actually. And I'll pretend I didn't see your room. You can show it to me another time, and I'll act really surprised." He wrapped his arms around her snugly so she was pressed against his chest. She hoped to god he couldn't feel her heart pounding.

"Deal." She murmured before kissing him.

They spent the majority of their afternoon that way She even convinced him to watch *St. Elmo's Fire*, but only after she promised not to tell anyone. He seemed more relaxed than he had on their previous dates, and she definitely was. *Maybe this can be an actual thing,* she contemplated as he kissed her shoulders lightly during the movie. Her body wiggled as close to him as possible, and she enjoyed the way she fit just right under his shoulder. There may have been happy sighing involved.

12

Two hours after he went home, her room was spotless. Promptly, she took a photo and sent it to Zack.

> V: Since you've never seen my room, I thought I'd send you a picture.
>
> Z: That is one good-looking bedroom. I'd like to find myself in it sometime ;).
>
> V: I'm sure Mama Roberts would totally be okay with that.
>
> Z: Buzz kill :).
>
> V: Lol sorry. I'll call you later, I gotta do some homework.
>
> Z: Later

Though her homework made an appearance, she was far too excited about homecoming to think straight about anything else.

* * *

Kimmy collapsed next to Vanessa at their lunch table, words flying out of her mouth before her butt even hit the chair.

"Have you *seen* him?! Ohmygod he is the most beautiful... I don't even know what to call him. He's in my English class third period and I don't even know what to do with myself," she blurted.

"Context please?"

"The new guy. Ethan Fisher. Please tell me Jess hasn't met him yet."

"There's a new guy?"

"Your brain must be elsewhere, because he's all anyone has been talking about since eight a.m. this morning."

"Well, did you talk to him?"

"Define talk."

"Utter syllables that make up words in the English language."

"Not exactly, no. I gave him a pencil."

"Great! You're like twenty-seven steps away from going steady then," Vanessa grinned.

"Please don't toy with my emotions!"

"I'm sorry, I'm sorry! Geez. I gotta see this guy. Want me to talk to him for you?"

"No!" Kim shrieked, her hands pulling at her soft brown hair.

"Why not? I could just invite him out with a bunch of us. He's new, he'd probably be delighted by an invitation."

"Do you swear on King Triton's trident you won't embarrass me?"

"That's a new one."

"I figured he meant more to you than any holy text."

"You might be right," Vanessa mused. "Yes, I swear on King Triton's trident I will not embarrass you."

"Ok. Well, he's coming out of the lunch line now. *Don't* be obvious in looking at him!" Vanessa's eyes traveled the length of the cafeteria, and she spotted an unfamiliar, uncommonly tall male with uncommonly shiny hair. She sized him up. He *was* good looking. Not entirely her type, a little too shaggy and a little too thin, but she got the hype. He was sitting with a group of notorious stoners, but Vanessa had known them all forever, so what did she care?

"I'll be back," she declared with an overly dramatic tone and eyebrows to match. Striding across the multi-purpose room, she came to notice a majority of the female population directing their attention his way. She approached their table with ease and pulled out a chair where Tyler Webb was currently resting his feet. He scowled at her, and she was certain he thought he looked intimidating with his newly pierced eyebrow and random maroon hair, but she still remembered him wearing a vest in his second grade class picture. Intimidating he was not. "Thank you so much for saving me a seat, Ty. *So* sweet of you," she offered graciously, batting her eyelashes at him. He looked completely baffled. Plopping into the now empty seat, she turned her focus towards this Ethan character. He really was striking… something about his cheekbones and those dark eyes.

"You're Ethan," she asserted.

"I am. Most people call me Fisher. But you can call me anything you want," he flirted, giving her a smirk she assumed would melt most girls on the spot. She let out a brief laugh.

"Oh, you are very smooth. I totally get it now. Why all of the girls running around here like there's a Jonas brother on campus. I'm Vanessa."

"Should I be offended, Vanessa, that you're comparing me to a Jonas brother?"

"Not at all," she smiled, holding back another laugh. "Just save your super awesome lines for someone available. I came to see if you wanna go to the movies or something with a group of us, maybe this weekend? Oh! Except homecoming is this weekend. Damn. We'd have to schedule around that. Unless you're looking for a date? I know this awesome girl-"

"I'm certain that you do. I don't really do set-ups, though," he interrupted her, seeing through her fake airhead moment.

"I do," Jared interjected. She rolled her eyes.

"Yes, Jared. We all know. You're far too fickle to be deemed a respectable homecoming date." She watched his green eyes dance with laughter as he stuffed another French fry into his mouth. He wasn't bad to look at either, but he had total attention deficit when it came to girls. He'd charmed almost every female on her cheer squad freshman year. Some of them twice.

"Don't hate, V."

"Just being honest. Anyhow, if you change your mind, *Fisher*, let me know. I sincerely think you're missing out. It was lovely to meet you, though, I'll see you around."

"I won't. But nice to meet you too. Let me know if your, ah, *availability* changes." She just shook her head, preparing to head back to her table to deliver the unfortunate news to her friend when Zack appeared, his hand roughly clamped around her wrist. He pulled her back into her chair and pulled up his own.

"Don't leave on my account," he spit out, his eyes fierce. "Introduce me."

"Um, ok? Zack, this is Ethan. He's new."

"Hey man," Ethan started, seemingly unsure of how to take Zack's demeanor. He wasn't the only one. Fisher reached out a hand in a friendly gesture and Zack shoved his arm out of the way.

"Yeah, I really only came over here to tell you to mind your own effing business."

"Zack, I came over here to ask him about Kim, I didn't-"

"Shut up." His tone was razor sharp. Ethan only looked mildly pensive.

"Yeah, I'm not really wanting to throw down with some guy I don't know over some girl I don't know, and get suspended my first day here, so whaddya say we all just calm down, mad dog?" The guy was surprisingly chill for someone being threatened on his first day of school.

"Pansy," Zack muttered loud enough for the table next to them to hear.

"I said I didn't want to. Not that I wouldn't." Ethan stood up with a tight smile and towered about four inches over Zack. Though he was thin, she was not about to find out who would win in a fight. About *nothing*.

"I'm sorry, we're leaving-"

"Do not apologize to this asshole," Zack interrupted again. "But you're one hundred percent right that we are leaving." He grabbed her hand and squeezed it as he led her into the deserted locker bay. She tried to pretend the entire room hadn't heard their quarrel, and that they were staring for some completely unrelated reason. "What the hell is wrong with you?" he sputtered, finally releasing her hand once alone.

"Are you insane? I went to ask the guy if he wanted to go to homecoming with Kim, and you freaking attacked him. So what is wrong with *you*?" She took on her signature bitch pose- arms crossed, hip cocked, foot pointed, and gave him the best glare she could muster. Zack whipped around and punched a locker, the sound reverberating down the hall. She bit the inside of her lip, sincerely wishing he would calm down, or that they were back in the cafeteria.

"You know exactly what is wrong with me. I spilled my guts to you about Jenna, and you're in there making me look like a complete ass by sitting and flirting with that stoner. I actually skipped lunch with my friends to be with you, and that's what I walk into. It's the exact same bullshit as with her." Her breathing became as shallow as his while she tried to figure out what to say.

"Zack, I didn't mean to make you look like anything. Kim asked me to talk to him for her; that was the extent of it. I told him right away I wasn't available-"

"He hit on you?"

"Stop it, please. I'm telling you the whole thing was innocent. I'm sorry if it looked otherwise, but I feel like you're making it out to be something it absolutely was not. And you're being mean." The last words had her voice shaking, and she hated it. She was not the girl who cried in the hall about a fight with her boyfriend. She was the girl who judged other girls for doing so. And he wasn't even her boyfriend.

"Am I being *mean*, Vanessa? Seriously, is this third grade? I'm still waiting for an actual apology for blatantly-"

"'Scuse me friends... I just need to squeeze right in here and grab my Spanish notes. Pretend I'm not even here. Go right on yelling. Seriously, not a bother at all," Luke interjected cheerfully into their argument. She hadn't even heard him walk up.

"Luke, we're sort of in the middle of something," she got out in an exasperated tone.

"Yeah, so I gathered. I'm just sort of in the middle of needing not to fail my Spanish quiz later though? So I'm gonna do that. Then I'll be out of your hair, no worries." He took his sweet time and whistled as he put in his locker combination, making quite a production of searching through his folders before he pulled out one labeled "Spanish." "Finally, here it is. Thanks so much guys for pressing pause there, I appreciate your commitment to my academic excellence. See you in weight training, Roads. Later V." Zack only glared at him. He whistled and ambled slowly back towards the cafeteria.

Vanessa's emotions had settled down during the brief inter-mission, and it appeared Zack's had too. Or at least he had un-crossed his arms. "So I guess you're going to tell me I'm being a jackass," he mumbled.

"I might? I really don't even know. Can you explain why you are *so* angry? I mean, I get walking up and wondering what was going on, maybe I shouldn't have gone over there alone, or something. I don't... but you can't just yell at me and tell me to shut up."

He paused, and she wasn't quite sure where he was going to go with things. "I just saw you over there with those guys, and I felt all of the same rage as when I walked in on Jenna at that party. I know that has nothing to do with you, I just… I'm an ass I guess." He wouldn't look at her, his hands clenching and unclenching at his sides.

"You're not an ass. Well, not right now anyway," she chided, attempting to lighten the mood. He finally glanced at her, his blue eyes much softer now. "I'm really not playing games with you. I like you." She tried to impart a sense of sincerity with her words, needing him to know she meant it.

"I like you too." They stood in an awkward space between hugging and walking away for a few torturous moments. "Um, do you think we can just erase the last fifteen minutes?"

"If you'll promise just to talk to me next time instead of flying off the handle, yeah, we can forget it."

"I promise."

"Let's eat some lunch then." He held her hand again, but much more gently this time, and she finally relaxed on their way back to the general populous.

"Everything cool?" Jessi asked, her eyebrows scrunched together in an exaggerated manner.

"Yep," Vanessa answered quickly, wanting to move on from the embarrassing display. She plopped down in the open chair, expecting Zack to follow.

"I'm gonna grab some food, I'll catch up with you later ok?" he asked, continuing with a concerned "We're good?" in a lower tone.

"We're fine. I'll talk to you later." He kissed her cheek and wandered to the now empty lunch line.

"Is everything really ok?" Kim questioned softly, concern swimming in her eyes.

"Yeah, it's fine, seriously. Just a misunderstanding." Vanessa then remembered the reason for her rendezvous with the four-twenty club in the first place. "Bad news though about the new kid. While he's actually pretty amusing, he's sort of incredibly full of himself. He didn't really say if he'd come out in a group or not; I'll work on him."

"Really, it's fine. He's outta my league anyway."

"Stop it, he's only out of your league if you think about it like that. Buck up, buttercup," Jessi chimed in.

"I'll try," Kim replied meekly. "Anyway, when are we going dress shopping?"

"Huh?" Vanessa replied, confused.

"Homecoming? Dresses? Usually you wear one? I don't even have a date yet, but I figure putting those vibes into the universe can't hurt. Plus, I can always return it," Kim added glumly.

"No, I mean, we invited you to come shopping this weekend, and you didn't respond," Vanessa explained. "Right Jess?"

"Yeah, I texted you and *nada.*"

"You didn't text me."

"Yes I did. I can show you if you like." Jess pulled out her phone and clicked through a few new messages. Then her hand stilled. "Ohmygod, I'm so sorry. I typed out the message and I thought I hit send, but it's still here in the response box. I swear to god I thought I sent it to you, I'm sorry Kimmy, please don't be mad at me." Jessi looked worried, and Kim only responded with frustration.

"Sure, whatever. It's fine, I probably won't need a dress anyway."

"Quit it right now. You know I'll shop with you anyway, like I've ever needed an excuse. Let's go after practice tomorrow."

"Are you sure?"

"Never been more sure of anything in my entire life. Yes. We'll go; it'll be great." Vanessa kept waiting for Jess to jump in and offer to come, but it never came to pass. *Maybe she thinks Kim doesn't want her there? Weird.* At least the focus was off of her spat with Zack, and hopefully the rest of the student body would forget it as well by the following period.

* * *

No such luck was in her cards, nor did people forget by the next day. She sat down in bio, attempting to stare back at each of the eyes currently boring into her, many of them sharing a face with a whispering mouth. *So obnoxious.* She smoothed the purple dress that she'd worn with a purpose that day, hoping to solidify the stable ground between her and Zack.

"Hey, you all right?" Luke questioned softly when he sat down next to her.

"I would be if people stopped asking me that," she snapped.

"Well, for what it's worth, I'm sorry."

"For what? Interrupting us?"

"No, that you guys broke up or whatever."

"Why would you think we broke up?" she asked incredulously. "We had an argument." Luke nearly snorted at her comment.

"Whatever you say." She could tell he was holding his tongue. While Luke was rarely serious, currently his jaw was tensed, and he was intently focused on the blank white board at the front of the room.

"What's that even supposed to mean?" she pressed, annoyed that he thought he knew something she didn't.

"I just don't get it, that's all. I don't get how a guy can treat you, or any girl, like that, and keep her. Whatever. Your business." He made a show of searching his backpack for his pen.

"You're right. It is my business," she shot back. "And I think you're blowing things a little out of proportion."

"Is it about having a date to homecoming? Because I'll take you. Just seriously, enough with the douchenozzle." He finally looked at her, and all she could read was frustration on his face. This annoyed her even more.

"Wow, how gracious of you." She paused, gathering her anger. "*No*, it's not about having a date for homecoming, but thanks for thinking I'm that shallow. Or that I'd need your pity date." She could feel her teeth grinding together, and was almost grateful when Mr. Lessner finally arrived. "Jackass," she muttered under her breath, causing Luke to shake his head. He laughed, but it lacked his usual humor.

13

The days leading up to homecoming were blissful. Brooke had finally lessened her hold on them and canceled morning practices. Zack had brought her a purple present every day, ranging from a stuffed cat to grape flavored gum. He walked her to class and texted before bed. She had a difficult time reconciling his behavior with the fact that he hadn't even brought up the word "girlfriend."

The new kid hadn't come near her since the altercation despite the fact that they had Spanish together eighth period, and she couldn't even blame him. That Friday, however, he ventured over and took the seat next to hers.

"So, *Vanessa*," he said with mock formality, "your boyfriend's a little intense. Like, should I be worried that he's going to tackle me out of this desk right now?" He attempted to be serious, but failed as soon as that smile hit his lips.

"Shut up. And he's not my boyfriend."

"Well, good for you. He's kind of a dick, honestly."

"We're still *dating*. Jesus. You are…" She couldn't put her finger on the word she needed.

"Dashing. Handsome. Drop dead-"

"Presumptuous."

He only laughed. "I've been called worse. By your non-boyfriend even. I just wanted to say I'm down to hang out some-time. Though I'm sure as hell not going out with the Hulk, but-this town is boring. Like really effing boring."

Vanessa tried to muster up the energy to be offended, but couldn't quite manage it. "Well, you're not wrong. It is boring if you don't have party invites. Unless you like to bowl. There's a big competitive bowling scene here in Gem," she teased.

"While I fully believe I could rock a bowling shirt, parties would be better."

"I'll keep that in mind," she offered as class began to come to order. He gave her a brief nod as he headed back to the other side of the room.

* * *

"Hey babe, are we good to go to the river tonight after the game?"

"Yeah, of course, I'm excited. I'm also super excited for this halftime to be over, and for regionals to be over, so I can get a freaking break from everyday practices."

"And spend more time with me," he grinned, stopping outside the locker room doors. This seemed to be their new routine, and he'd be waiting for her after practice as well.

"Except you have crazy practices for the rest of the season too, but after that, yes. More time," she agreed happily. He leaned in and she placed a brief kiss on his lips, causing him to smile and press for more. She dropped her cheer bag to the concrete and stopped caring that they were still on campus. He wove his fingers in between hers and squeezed, pulling her arms around his lower back tightly. A contented sound built in the back of her throat and he pulled back shortly after.

"Please tell me we can be alone. *Soon.* Like, I need you to come to Vader's tomorrow night. I know there's your mom, but I'm worth it, right?" he asked, only a hint of a joke coloring the question. She was out of breath and completely smitten with this broad-shouldered creature in front of her, and at that moment, she may have agreed to join the circus and live life out of a train car if he'd asked.

"I will try to figure it out. I will."

"Thank you," he breathed, pulling her in once more before disappearing behind the door.

"Well. Crap," she muttered aloud to no one.

* * *

Lying to one's parents was infinitely more dangerous in a town as small as Gem. Vanessa paced her room, dressed in her full cheer uniform while she waited for Jess to pick her up for the game. After her last grounding, and her flighty friend's direct involvement, Vanessa felt certain that asking to sleep over at Jess's house after the dance would warrant an automatic "no." She had already decided to go with Kim as her alibi, though if their mothers were to run into one another at the grocery store, or the hardware store, or the freaking *one* main street in town where everyone shopped, she would be toast. Blackened toast that was made from the heel of the loaf of bread that no one wanted to eat anyway. *One thought at a time,* she reasoned. The heat that was running through her veins when Zack kissed her hadn't dissipated, and she couldn't be sure if that was exciting or terrifying, but ninety percent of her knew she wanted to keep feeling it. *This is such a bad idea,* she knew. That bit of forethought did not deter her from going ahead and asking anyway and getting barely a second glance before the "sure, that's fine," came out of her mom's mouth. Her parents had known Kim since they were in third grade, and the girl had never so much as forgotten a thank you note after a birthday party, let alone been accused of getting in any kind of trouble. *Thank you for being a model citizen,* Vanessa praised her friend silently.

At the sound of the Jeep outside, Vanessa grabbed her overly-stuffed cheer bag and silver poms before running out the door hurriedly, lest she lose her nerve and confess. Looking at Jess, she knew her own over-the-top appearance was reflected. As mandated by Captain Crazy, their hair was in the highest form of ponytail imaginable, adorned with a comically large black sequined bow and covered in glitter hairspray.

"You look like a disco-ball," Jessi commented seriously.

"Right back at ya," V returned, wishing there was any way to get that glitter out of her hair before the party at the river later on. Unfortunately, glitter was like the plague- nearly impossible to eradicate all at once. She knew there would still be daily sparkles on her pillow in two weeks' time. They listened to some angry 90s song on the way to the field, as was everyone's ritual after the football team handed out literal mixed CDs to get everyone "pumped" before the first game. It was almost too adorable to mock.

Vanessa took a deep breath before divulging her recent activities in one exhale. "So I told my parents I'm sleeping at Kim's tomorrow so that we can go to Vader's and I think Zack wants to like, I don't know, ya know?"

"Are you channeling me tonight? Because I caught like forty percent of that," she complained, turning down the music significantly.

"Maybe? I don't know. I'm sort of freaking out, and I'm not even sure why. I can go to Vader's. If you still wanna go. Do you wanna go?"

"Truth? I was gonna go either way. But it'll be way more entertaining with you there," she grinned.

"And the other thing? Do you think I'm wrong? God, the whole issue is just annoying. I hate that I don't know what to do or say or *be*." Her nerves were almost overcome with sheer irritation.

"Well of course you're not *wrong*. He's a seventeen year old male, and he likes you. That doesn't mean you have to *do* anything about it. I've told you a million times, it's not what you say but how you say it."

"Yeah..." she responded without even knowing what she was agreeing to.

"I'm sure you'll know what you wanna do if and when the opportunity ummm, presents itself?" she stated carefully.

"Ugh, whatever. You're no help," Vanessa stated pointedly, but she felt better having just voiced what was in her head aloud. Jessi shrugged and turned the music back up. Determined to get back to that spine tingling place where her mind had been earlier, she thought about nothing but that kiss.

* * *

Vanessa found an almost immediate sense of relief after the game was over. With halftime done, Brooke seemed to return to her more human ways, and she actually complimented the whole team before they left. They also won the game, by a decent margin even, meaning Zack would not be Pouty McSad-Face for the whole night. *Thank god.* He'd played incredibly well, although she would have said that regardless, and her heart felt a small swell of pride in knowing that he was hers. *Sort of. Maybe.* No matter how forcefully she attempted to shove down the question that was bubbling up, she knew she was going to have to be *that girl* and ask him where their relationship was going before she could make any decision about the other up-in-the-air issue.

Feeling undaunted, she changed into black leggings and a long purple sweater to match the lavender heart earrings he'd given her that week before heading out into the madness that was post-game euphoria. She almost had a coronary when Zack snuck up behind her and picked her up in a crushing hug.

"Okay okay okay! I need to breathe too!" she squealed between giggles.

"Ridiculous," he smiled, finally putting her down. He smelled like a fresh shower and a hint of spearmint, which made her sigh inwardly at his general yumminess. "You ready to go, pretty girl?"

"Well you're certainly overflowing with admiration tonight," she commented happily.

"But you're so easy to admire." She knew she was blushing and willed her cheeks to stop. Vanessa Roberts did not *blush* at compliments.

"And yes, I'm ready. If we can ever get out of the parking lot," she added, watching as more than half the town hurried to their cars.

"Nah, I got a secret spot, don't you worry." Curiously, she glanced at him, but followed anyway. She saw the new kid on their way out and turned to her non-boyfriend.

"Hey, I am gonna go and tell that guy about the party tonight. And you're going to be cool about it, because you sort of threatened him on his first day of school. Got it?" Her insides were turning mildly as she wasn't sure about the reaction her little stand would provoke. He rolled his eyes but acquiesced anyway. She grabbed his hand and pulled him towards Fisher. He was surrounded by his new posse, which currently included about six females.

"Fisher," she stated clearly, waving him closer.

"Vanessa," he returned cautiously, eyeing Zack behind her as he wandered over from the group.

"I wanted to let you know there's a party at the river... you should come. I'm sure any member of your fan club over there could tell you where to go."

"Yeah, I'm not really looking for any drama tonight, so... maybe another time. Thanks though," he nodded.

"Hey man, it's cool. I'm sorry for, whatever, being an ass. There will be no drama…assuming you don't cause any," he added for effect. She could tell he was not comfortable in an apologetic role, but she was grateful anyway.

"All right, well then maybe I'll see you guys there. Have a good one."

"See ya!" She practically skipped away with Zack in tow, feeling like she had righted the wrong she'd caused. "Thank you for being nice," she murmured, nudging Zack playfully.

"What can I say? I'm in a nice mood." They finally made it to his Charger, which was parked in a nearly hidden spot next to a low hanging tree near the exit. "See? I told you I had a secret space." While climbing into the passenger seat, she was struck with the realization that she sort of had everything she wanted at that moment, like she needed to appreciate this high school memory so that someday, she could pull it out and look back on it warmly. When he slid into the driver's seat, she leaned over and kissed him intently, loving that the lips she'd once only admired in passing now felt familiar and comforting on her own. He reciprocated by guiding her slowly over the console so she was sitting on his lap, her back awkwardly leaning against the door. She could feel the butterflies people always talked about, except they were in her fingertips and her toes in addition to her belly. He slid his hand under her sweater, apparently searching for the waist of her leggings, and her breath caught. And then it stopped completely because a large human slid across the hood of the vehicle, and she was pretty sure she was in danger of having a concussion after how hard she hit her head on the window.

"Jesus Christ!" Zack was laughing hysterically though, and she almost screamed again when she looked up and Vader's face was pressed up against the glass of the passenger side window.

"Open up lovebirds!" he yelled, pounding on the window. Zack unlocked the doors and Vader slid into the backseat followed by none other than Jessi. "I knew you'd be in this stupid secret spot. Let's go. I wanna party," Vader insisted. His lopsided grin was kind of contagious, so Vanessa simply shook her head and climbed back to her own seat with absolutely zero grace.

"Did ya miss me?" Jessi asked, smoothing Vanessa's ponytail from the back seat.

"So much."

"To the river then?" Zack asked, his good mood even more pronounced.

"To the river!!" Vader shouted with what seemed to be genuine enthusiasm. She supposed it was his last homecoming before graduation and forgave him his overbearing excitement.

When they arrived, the party was in full swing with a bonfire crackling and "We Are the Champions" playing unoriginally out of someone's speakers.

"I must have food. Like immediately," Vanessa declared upon walking onto the bank.

"Agreed. Why don't you figure out the sustenance situation, and I will get us some beverages. You want something fruity and pink?"

"Nah, I'll just have water or a Coke or something."

"Babe, we're just celebrating," he said, seeming put off.

"I know, and I'll be your DD if you wanna celebrate any harder," she explained.

"You're not mad?"

"Do I look mad?"

"You sort of always look mad. In a hot way though." She gave a half-laugh through her nose and the most pleasant smile she could muster.

"Better?"

"Mhm," he murmured, kissing her cheek before heading off on his mission. Meanwhile, Jessi conned some guy into giving up a few already-charred hot dogs, so they didn't have to roast the wieners themselves. It appeared Vader had intimidated some sophomores into vacating their spots on a coveted log as well.

Having friends in high places was very beneficial. Even though sometimes she wished she lived in a bigger city, nights like this made her love that Gem was her hometown.

"So, Vanessa," Vader started.

"V."

"V, I like it that we're now on an official nickname basis. We're closer already," he grinned. "Tell me, how is my boy Zack treating you?" She had to imagine he didn't particularly care, but it was nice that he was putting forth the effort to get to know her.

"Just fine I suppose," she responded, not sure precisely how to act.

"Only fine, huh? Maybe I need to have a chat with him, you-"

"Hey dude, how've ya been?" a familiar voice spoke out from their left.

"Miller! I've been excellent, yourself?" Vader replied lightly, never losing his jovial tone.

"Just livin' the dream, you know how it is," Luke chided.

"Sit, sit, you know Jess? And Vanessa?" Luke almost snorted.

"Yeah, we're acquainted." She was somewhat glad to see him as it took some of the pressure off of her conversation with Vader, but then she remembered their last encounter and threw off a much different vibe. "I'm gonna grab something to eat, I won't impose on your private party over here. I did want to ask you if Kim was here, V. I thought I'd take your advice." He directed his full attention towards her, and she felt like he was judging her despite the benign nature of the question.

"You're going to ask her the night before the dance? Nice etiquette," she threw out sarcastically. It was the wrong thing to say, she knew; she should be happy her friend would have a good-looking date to the dance. Even in a hoodie and jeans he was something to stare at. He was just so irritating.

"I guess it's a good thing I'm not courting her then. And that it's not 1805. Is she coming?" he repeated.

"Yeah, she'll be here. Make sure she knows you're asking as a friend, ok? She has a tendency to… whatever. Just do it."

"Ok boss," he ribbed. "See ya later."

"Hey, come to my house tomorrow night if you want. It's a sleepover, so bring some jammies," Vader grinned. Luke only looked sharply at Vanessa for a moment.

"Yeah, maybe. Thanks for the invite." He walked away slowly, and Vanessa began to realize Zack had been gone for a while.

"I'll be right back, I'm gonna see if I can track down my date," she smiled. Now alone, she wandered through the sea of her classmates and pondered how arrogant Luke was just asking Kimmy to the dance last minute. *Like he's god's gift to the freaking female population.* She caught a glimpse of him in her peripheral vision talking to Ethan. Or Fisher. Whatever. *Now there's an egotistical match made in heaven,* she thought, amused. The amusement stopped abruptly, however, when she saw Zack sitting on the tailgate of a truck with a couple of guys. They were not the problem. Jenna was. She was sipping something pink and fruity while leaning flirtatiously onto the truck bed, no doubt clearing a pretty significant visual for anyone wishing to glance down her shirt. *What the hell is this girl's problem?!* The urge to rush her was strong, but instead Vanessa sauntered up slowly.

"Did you get lost?" she questioned, attempting to keep her tone neutral. Unfortunately her face almost certainly betrayed her anger.

"Nah, just catching up. Sit with me," Zack insisted, holding out a hand. "Here, I got you a Coke," he offered once she had settled next to him on the tailgate. Jenna made a hasty exit, but at least she didn't spew any more vitriol at her.

"So, should I drag you out of here and slam my fist into a locker or something? I mean, what's the protocol when I think you're flirting with someone else?" She posed the question loudly on purpose, not caring if it was passive aggressive. He cleared his throat uncomfortably.

"Guys, can you give us a minute?" he asked, or rather told, two of his teammates chatting next to them. They meandered towards the coolers without questioning his direction.

"What's wrong?"

"*Really?*"

"Yes, really. She came over here while I was talking with those guys about the game. I didn't even say anything to her; she just inserted herself into our conversation. Typical Jenna bullshit."

"Were your legs broken? Were you incapable of getting up and walking away? It really annoys me that you stayed over here this long knowing I was waiting for you, and that you were looking so cozy with her."

"I wasn't looking cozy. I don't even know what that means."

"Yeah, I need to know what we're doing. I can't just wonder if you're trying to get back with her, or if you like me, or what. Sorry to be *that girl* and ambush you with a relationship question at a party, but it is what it is." She steeled herself for an answer she didn't want, and also realized her timing could not have been worse. If this didn't go well, she was dateless for the dance.

"We're gonna do this now?"

"Looks that way."

"Can we at least go to my car, or somewhere not in the middle of a hundred drunk people?" he exaggerated.

"Sure," she agreed with a sigh. Things were not looking up. He walked quickly with his usual confidence, but she kept up adamantly.

"Can we not get through one effing event without you trying to fight with me?" he let out through clenched teeth one they were approaching his car.

"I don't have to try. It just comes naturally," she smarted off.

"Don't be a bitch. Jesus."

"That might be easier if you-"

"Stop! Just get in the car." She glared at him in response. "Fine. *Please* get in the car." The glare remained as she slid in the seat, this mood a polar opposite of earlier that night.

"So talk then," she sighed, knowing this was about to go up in flames. *And you lit the fire yourself,* she chastised. He leaned his head back against the seat and stared at the ceiling momentarily.

"Where do you want this to be going?" he asked, resignation in his voice.

"I just want to know you're with me. Or not. I can't keep guessing though."

"How can you think I'm not with you? I'm *with* you all the time. I don't know how I could be with you more."

"Stop saying the words 'with you,' they're losing their meaning."

"What words do you want me to use?" She rolled her eyes.

"Stop pretending you're stupid."

"Not pretending anything. Just tell me what you want."

"I want you to tell people I'm your girlfriend." She hated the words as soon as they left her mouth because now she was completely exposed. There was no way to play it cool, and she'd just handed him the ammunition needed to reject her.

"People already assume you're my girlfriend," he muttered in a non-committal tone. Hurt resounded in her chest as his reaction really landed. *Okay then.*

"It's fine, whatever. We can be done here. Sorry for ruining your good mood." She clicked the door handle and turned to go, praying her tears would stay trapped inside long enough for her to find a ride home. She felt his fingers around her wrist, but she wrenched her arm away. He was out of the car and standing in front of her before she made it three steps.

"Stop, ok? Just stop. I know that's what you want. And I've known that for a while. I've thought about it a lot, actually, and I just… I don't feel like it's the right thing to do. Until I feel like I can be the kind of boyfriend you deserve. A real boyfriend, who is all in. I swear to you I'm getting there; I'm just screwed up after what went down with... well, you know what I mean. I almost took that guy's head off when you were talking to him in the cafeteria. I get that that is not *normal*. I'm not trying to blow you off, seriously. I like you, I've told you that. Can you get where I'm coming from? I want to be good enough for you."

Her heart was racing as she tried to evaluate his sincerity. He looked genuinely uncomfortable, biting his lip, and she hoped it was because they hadn't had many moments like this. Desperately, she was trying to put herself in his position and not allow the sting of rejection overcome her. "I'm trying," she finally answered, meeting his eyes.

"Does it help if I say I'm having *fun*? It's been a long time since things have been like this with a girl. Are you having fun? With me?" His freaking eyes were just so damned earnest, even with just the moon to light them.

"Most of the time," she allowed herself to admit. He laughed.

"Fair enough. Can I entice you to come back over here with guaranteed enjoyment?" Her eyes narrowed. He was flirting with her. He was relentless. Vanessa didn't move. It was simply her nature to be stubborn when hurt. Despite his declarations, she still felt wounded. And pissed off that he knew he could hurt her now. His feet crunched on the gravel as he cautiously made his way towards her. "Too soon to flirt? Please don't be mad. Let me kiss you." He grinned that charming grin, and her anger faded some.

"It better be a good kiss," she muttered. With a chuckle, he leaned in, pressing his lips to hers tentatively. *Maybe it doesn't have to be so black and white,* she thought. *He's doing everything a boyfriend does anyway, so what does it matter if the word freaks him out?* While his kisses became more urgent, she was coming down from the hostile takeover of her brain and trying to understand that just because this was different, it didn't mean it wasn't good. At that moment, it was great, actually. Finally, she succumbed to his intensity and kissed him back with a little more enthusiasm.

"Thank you," he whispered in her ear, placing kisses along her jaw down to her neck, his hands becoming much bolder in their exploration of her leggings. She felt his teeth nip at her neck, but then become more insistent.

"Don't you dare give me a hickey for our homecoming picture, Zack Roads!" she yelled at him, swatting his shoulder forcefully. He only laughed again.

"You're no fun! I thought I would show everyone you were *with* me," he explained, mocking her slightly.

"Well, nice to see you're back to being yourself." She rolled her eyes at him, though the heat that had risen in her cheeks made it impossible for her to glare successfully anymore.

"Let me give you one somewhere else. It'll be hidden, I swear."

"And where would that be?"

"I need to check out my options first, so I can select the best real estate." His eyes danced with delight as he opened the back door to his car.

"You think you're so freaking smooth."

"Maybe a little bit. Will you just come here and let me touch you? Jesus, I've never had to work this hard before." His tone was light, but she sensed he wasn't lying. It made her feel better. She rocked on her toes a couple of times to keep him guessing until she thought he might explode, and then slowly made her way to him. "You're driving me crazy," he stated once she got there.

"That was my intent."

"This is why I like you." He didn't give her a chance to respond, just pulled her into the car on top of him and slammed the door shut. His hands were warm, and she had been freezing outside. He continued what he started, and apparently wasn't kidding about searching for a place to leave his mark. He bit her teasingly on her fingers, her shoulder, and even her ankle before he became much more serious.

"Zack," she breathed, trying to remember some form of the advice Jess had given her about saying things in the right way. She honestly couldn't remember, and words just sort of came out. "I'm not going to have sex in the back of your car. In case that's your-"

"V. Relax. Let me make you feel good, and you tell me if and when you want me to stop. And I'll stop. Crisis averted. Relax."

"I am relaxed."

"Good," he replied, showing off his dimples. He resumed his cross-country journey, and for the life of her she could not find anything she wanted him to stop. She also felt like she understood Jenna's refusal to disappear. This boy was deliciously attentive.

When they finally came up for air, she had nearly forgotten their spat and also felt more secure in his feelings for her than ever- regardless if he would wear the boyfriend crown or not. In an attempt to look somewhat presentable, she climbed into the front seat and pulled down the mirror.

"I think you look hot post hook-up," he said slowly in her ear. She shivered and smiled despite his obvious exaggeration. "We should probably go find Vader and Jess and head outta here. Unless your mom has suddenly decided curfews are unnecessary?"

"Really unlikely."

"It was worth asking. You wanna stay in here or come with me?"

"I'll come with. Who knows what kind of trouble you can get into on your own."

♪ *"I'm So Excited" - The Pointer Sisters*
"Pompeii" - Bastille (Glee Cast Version)
"Best Song Ever" - One Direction
"Rock Your Body" - Justin Timberlake
"What I Like About You" - 5 Seconds of Summer

14

Vanessa woke up experiencing the same mood in which she went to sleep: annoyingly excited. After just accepting where she and Zack were, there was so much more room in her brain to be excited about the newness of all of it. She grabbed her phone to text him a happy homecoming message, but checked her missed ones first.

> K: Hey! I guess I don't have to return my dress :). Going to homecoming with Luke. As friends (of course :/) but can I come over later and you do my hair?? And maybe makeup?
>
> V: Of course!!! That's awesome! Come over whenever, see you then.
>
> K: Yay! Thank you!

At least he did something right, she thought.

* * *

V: Good morning sexy :). I'm so excited for you to see my dress. I think it will meet all of your specifications.

Z: I will forgive you this early morning message, only because there are much more exciting things going through my head than there were when I was asleep. I can't wait to see it either… on you, on the floor, whatever ;). I had fun last night.

Her stomach took on a life of its own upon reading, and even though it was her intention to take their conversation down that path, she was unsure about her own boldness. *Nerves are normal,* she repeated over and over in her head.

V: Me too. I'll see you at 6?

Z: That you will.

Vanessa spent the rest of the morning dancing around her room and playing with different hairstyles until Kim got there. She practically tackled her friend outside the front door to fill her in on the "sleepover" web she'd spun earlier that week. The last thing she needed was for Kim to come in and blow her cover.

"Seriously? You *know* I'm an awful liar, why would you pick me?? Tell them you're going to Jess's," Kim pleaded, her hazel eyes showing her trepidation.

"I can't. I didn't want to risk them saying no, and they don't really trust Jessi."

"They're not the only ones," Kim muttered, following Vanessa into the house and up to her room.

"What do you mean? Did she do something?" Jess was kind of flakey, but Vanessa had never known her to be malicious. Well, at least not towards her.

"I don't know, it's probably nothing. Just me being stupid."

"Spill."

"I'm not sure... she just doesn't seem to want me to hang out with you guys. And she always has a great story or excuse, but there are only so many times I can believe it's coincidental."

"Like..." Kim had a tendency to be overly sensitive, and Jess was perhaps the opposite. She had a feeling it was probably just a misunderstanding.

"Just... the mall thing? You know how much she's on her phone. Do you really think she just forgot to text me the message and then never looked at it again? And the night of Zack's party, I had asked her to pick me up and she never responded. She said somehow the message didn't show up until way later and the party was almost over at that point. I mean, it's fine if she doesn't like me, I just wish she'd spit it out instead of pretending she does."

"I don't know if she really has it in her to devise schemes like that. She's running a million miles a minute all of the time. But I can talk to her if you want?"

"No, no. It's fine. Just..."

"What?"

Kim sighed and flopped down on the bed, which was actually made for once. "If you guys go out and she says she invited me, could you just text me? I feel like I'm missing out on everything."

"Of course! I'm sorry, I don't want you to feel like that. I will call you. Absolutely."

"Thank you," Kim let out sincerely.

"Now then, tell me about Luke, tell me about how you want you hair, makeup, where you're going to dinner, all of it," she commanded, gesturing for her friend to sit in the chair she'd dragged upstairs. "And then I'm taking you downstairs and forcing you to look at all of the decorations that arrived this week for the remodel." She could see her own eyes light up in the mirror when thinking about her project. She had just been stuffing boxes in the corners of rooms for weeks until she had time to actual sort through everything. Now that Brooke was no longer enforcing a boot camp-like schedule, she could refocus her energy on getting everything unpacked and hung up just how she wanted. The entire project was still weeks away from completion, but the common area would be done first. She couldn't wait to start drilling holes in the walls.

She flat ironed Kim's shoulder-length hair until it shone and pinned her side-swept bangs into a rhinestone accessory. Her makeup was pretty but simple to match, and Vanessa truly thought her friend looked like a knockout.

"Maybe Luke will change his 'just friends' tune when he sees you," she encouraged, even though she'd been the one to tell Luke to be clear in the first place. Vanessa wanted her friend to see how great she looked.

"Honestly? I think he likes *you*."

"What? I can assure you that he doesn't. Plus, I'm with Zack, so it's irrelevant. What would even make you say that?" Now she was just curious.

"I debated on whether to tell you or not, but he either likes you or just *really* hates Zack. When I saw him last night we sat and chatted for a bit, and he made it pretty clear he thinks you're too good for Roads."

"He does seem to have a bug up his ass about him. I've no idea why though. Maybe I'll ask Zack tonight. But that's beside the point. You look amazing. Let me do my own hair and we can take some pre-dance pictures before you leave." It took her back to getting ready for middle school dances, and they reminisced about devising ridiculous schemes to get the boys they liked to ask them to dance. "I'm so glad our awkward years are behind us," Vanessa relayed.

"Eh, I'm still in my awkward years." Vanessa just crossed her eyes disapprovingly in response. She finished her own hair with a complicated pattern of different sized braids leading back to a messy curled bun. All was secured with seashell bobby pins. Was it possible she was taking the mermaid thing too far? No.

Her makeup was smoky and alluring, or so she hoped. They took model-esque photos to the best of their abilities, and Vanessa showed off the basement before Kim headed home.

"Holy cow, V, it actually looks really different down here. Like new walls and... a hallway? Do you get to move your bedroom down here?"

"Only if my parents succumb to my persistent begging," she declared. "It's supposed to be a guest room. For now. Until I win." They discussed the beauty of the dark stained floors, and how great the Moroccan lanterns would look once they were hung.

"Thanks for letting me come over today. I've missed you."

"I've missed you too. I hope you and Luke have an awesome time tonight."

"You and Zack too."

* * *

Vanessa was still bursting at the seams with restless energy and knew she needed to call Courtney. She didn't know if she could come right out and tell her what the night might hold, but needed her friend to bring her back to earth. Courtney was *that* logical... her power could cross state lines.

"Hey friend!" Courtney answered, happy to hear from her as always.

"Hi hi hi. What are you doing?"

"For real? Or should I make some sort of attempt to sound cool?"

"Let's hear the attempt."

"Getting ready to head out with my friends to a hotel party. I'm pretty sure there will be famous people there."

"Overkill. What are you really doing?"

"Re-reading *Harry Potter* and eating cereal."

"You kill me."

"Yeah yeah, what are you doing?"

"Getting ready for homecoming."

"Ohhhh with Zack-attack?"

"You're lucky I actually get your *Saved By The Bell* references. Anyone else would think you're weird."

"That's why I love you. And I am weird."

"And yes, with Zack. I think... I don't know... but things seem to be getting more serious."

"Serious like..."

"Like we're staying together tonight." She whispered this confession, afraid it would somehow travel through the vents and directly into her mother's ears.

"Oh! Okay then. Serious. Seriously serious. Sirius Black serious."

"Is there anything that doesn't relate back to *Harry Potter* for you?"

"I sincerely doubt it. Sorry. Well, are you nervous? I would be. I also get nervous about tests, and what to wear, and the state of our political climate, and global warming... well, you know what I mean. So are you?"

"Yeah," she admitted. And would only ever admit to Courtney. "But I think it's going to be ok, you know?"

"Well, good. I'm sure it will be, it will be great. Keep me updated. I need to live vicariously through you. And also ask you a billion questions if I ever find myself needing advice in such matters."

"In such matters. Okay grandma. Glad we had this birds and bees talk," she teased.

"Well, you are a young whippersnapper; I have to set you straight."

"Dork." Courtney just laughed.

"I miss you. I wish I was going to homecoming there."

"I miss you too, and that would be awesome. I'll text you tomorrow, yeah?"

"Yeah. Good luck. Have fun. Or break a leg, but don't really."

"Bye Court," Vanessa laughed. As suspected, she felt a hundred times better. In glancing at the time, she let out a happy sigh, realizing it was now socially acceptable to begin getting dressed for the dance. She unzipped the garment bag that held her gown, and it was even more amazing than she remembered. She took the hanger out of the bag and draped the dress on the back of her bedroom door. It was a mermaid style gown, but it was also a *mermaid style* gown. The top was covered in a menagerie of blue and green sparkles, and it hugged her down to her hips. The bottom flowed out in chiffon strands of turquoise and sea foam, and Vanessa decided she wanted to wear it everyday for the rest of her life. Stepping into it carefully, she tugged the zipper up the back to get a look at the full package. Topping it off with some simple silver jewelry and heels she was determined to walk in, she felt ready. Until the doorbell rang. Then she felt like her body might somehow shrink into nothingness if her stomach continued to house a vortex of disastrous proportions. In hearing her mother chatting animatedly with Zack, and her dad managing to come out of his office, she decided it was time to get over it and head downstairs.

"Hey," she called softly as she reached the entryway. Zack turned around, looking impossibly dashing in a charcoal suit, the jacket left open to reveal a pale blue button-down that matched his eyes. His dark hair stood up perfectly, and she had a distinct urge to take a photo of him modeling male hair accessories. *Stop being weird,* she commanded her brain.

"Hey beautiful. You look amazing," he stated charmingly.

"You have outdone yourself, Vanessa," her mother commented, already taking photos.

"Here," Zack said, reaching for a box on their entryway table. He pulled out a dark purple rose corsage and slipped it over her wrist. It was perfect.

"I love it, thank you." He had insisted she not buy him a boutonniere, declaring that men didn't wear flowers, no matter the occasion. She had let that battle go. He clasped her hand and posed for pictures without so much as a covert eye roll, and Vanessa finally convinced her mother they had to leave.

"I know, I know. Just one more picture with your dad," she insisted. It may have been uncool, but Vanessa kind of liked the father-daughter photo. Her dad had a good smile- it reached his eyes when he was genuinely happy, and she liked that. "Have a good time, and call me when you get to Kim's so I know you're safe."

"I will. Love you guys."

"Love you too," they both echoed. "Bye Zack."

"Bye Mr. Roberts, Mrs. Roberts, have a great evening."

They made it out to his car, and he stopped her before she got in. His lips were against hers instantly, completely trashing her carefully applied lip-gloss, but he felt so good she let it go. "You look...so hot," he murmured between kisses. She dropped her overnight bag onto the cement so that she could participate fully.

"You think so?"

"I know so." Her skin tingled down to her sparkly toes.

"Are we going to make out in front of my house all night?" she questioned lightly when he got a bit carried away.

"I suppose not," he sighed, flashing his dimples at her. "Let's eat, shall we?"

"Sounds good to me."

* * *

Dinner felt like something out of a 90s movie montage. Zack was attentive, charming, complimentary, and she had never felt more important. She let Jess drag her off to the ladies' room to touch up their makeup before they left.

"Well, your catch of the day is certainly in it to win it tonight."

"Speak English," Vanessa commanded as she pulled out her lip gloss.

"He's like super date, that's all."

"And this is bad, why?"

"Not bad! Good! Jolly good. Cheerio and pip pip." Somehow, she'd transitioned into a British accent.

"I think British people would be offended by that impersonation."

"I will be certain never to do it in front of a British person then. Because we have so many of those in Gem," she retorted incredulously. Subsequently, she flipped her head upside-down and tousled her long red hair that had been curled to perfection. She was in a short purple dress with an off-the-shoulder neckline. Any other night, Vanessa might have been jealous of her friend's curves and overall bombshell appearance, but she was drunk on Zack's attention at the moment.

"Are you and Vader, like, a thing? You've been sort of quiet about the whole situation actually. Which is kind of the opposite of your normal... everything." She looked up from her reflection and raised her eyebrows at her friend.

"Ugh, I don't know. For now, I guess. He's not like the love of my life or anything. He's fine. Fine like wine. Valentine."

"You are truthfully the strangest friend I've ever had."

"Everyone says that," she grinned, walking back out into the restaurant.

Zack kissed her when she sat back down next to him. "You ready to head out?"

"Yes," she answered, unable to stop smiling. "Are you going to dance the night away with me?"

"Yeah no. I don't really *dance*, but I'm happy to let you dance around me," he offered as they headed back to the parking lot.

"Lame."

"Don't get pouty," he stated, amused. "I'll dance the slow songs with you, and I'd be happy to watch you dance with Jess the rest of the time."

"Ugh, don't be a perv."

"A man has to have dreams, Vanessa." She shoved him force-fully off the sidewalk, but he took it in stride and simply bounced back up, wrapping his arms around her from behind before they got to the car. "I like your sassiness this evening."

"I don't know if that's actually a compliment."

"I can assure you that it is. Now get in the car." His eyes challenged her to spout something else at him, but she refrained. It was possible she liked his gaze on her a little too much as she sank into the car, loving the way the chiffon felt against her legs. *I want to wear formalwear all of the time.*

She was forced to listen to sports talk radio all the way to school. It was difficult to understand how people did such a thing for enjoyment and not to inflict pain on others. When he shifted the Charger into park, he pulled something silver out of his jacket pocket and swished it at her. "You want any liquid fun before we head in there?" he asked, unscrewing the top and pressing the spout to his lips. He tipped his head back and let whatever was his drink of choice for the evening flow down his throat.

"I'm ok… Are you planning on having me drive us to Vader's then?" Her tone was confused.

"Not a chance in hell," he responded, laughing.

"So you're going to get wasted and then drive your car?" She could see her perfect evening dissolving in front of her.

"Do I look wasted?"

"No."

"Did I say that's what I was going to do?"

"Well, no."

"Then don't assume. I'm just making the evening slightly more entertaining. Don't get your panties in a bunch. Or if you do, at least tell me what they look like," he finished, biting his lip. She smacked his shoulder, deciding she could leave this particular argument for after the dance.

The homecoming theme was *Under the Sea,* and she didn't care how cheesy the gym looked, it was like the whole night had been designed in her own imagination. The ceiling was covered in clear balloons made to look like bubbles, and blue and green streamers echoed the look of her dress. There was already a song she had to dance to blaring from the DJ's speakers, and she pulled Zack towards the floor.

He leaned in close to her ear so she could hear him. "If you think you're somehow going to trick me into dancing to this song, you would be wrong."

She turned around and pouted. "You're going to make me dance by myself?"

"I'm not going to *make* you do anything."

"Fine, I will just find someone who does want to dance with me." Her tone was challenging, but still playful, though he did not look particularly amused.

"Do what you've gotta do, babe. Come find me when you're done." Vanessa's eyes narrowed at his refusal to take the bait. She really wasn't keen on following after him, so instead she looked around for someone to help her make good on her bluff. There was clearly a circle forming around someone, or someones, and she made her way over to see what the hubbub was about. To her utter shock, Ethan Fisher was in the middle of said circle, dropping it like it was hot. *Shut up,* she thought. *Who the hell is this kid?* The crowd started to disperse as the song came to and end, but the next beat that came up was "Walk It Out," circa 2006. Vanessa had memorized a complete routine to that song years before, and was not about to let it go to waste. She pressed through the now-smaller circle and grabbed Fisher by the wrist. He looked confused, but she motioned for him to watch her. She kicked her shoes off deftly and began to walk towards him in a very dance-battle fashion. His smirk grew bigger than normal, and he copied what she did in the next eight count. She threw in a "lean back," in addition to some more complicated arm motions which had taken her weeks to memorize, and he matched her beat for beat. The boy could move. She couldn't stop grinning as their show finally ended, and she threw him a *very* smooth fist bump with a little jellyfish action on the end of it, making him laugh.

"Thanks Fisher," she expressed during a brief silence as a slow song came on.

"My pleasure," he replied, loosening his tie. "I should probably go find my date?" he posed as a question.

"Me too. See you later." She grabbed her shoes off the floor amidst the couples now forming on the floor and looked around for Zack. He was sitting at a table towards the back with his friends, looking interested in their conversation, but she knew there was no way he didn't see that performance. Quickly, she made her way to him, not wanting to miss the first slow dance of the night.

"Come dance," she practically yelled in his ear when she arrived.

"Why don't you go ask Ethan?" he retorted. It didn't seem like he was actually mad, but it was clear she wasn't going to get away with her display quite that easily.

"Because I want to dance with you," she said more softly.

"Meh," he responded, still not quite looking at her. She whispered an answer to an earlier request about her undergarments, and he finally broke into a grin and got out of his chair. Happily, she flitted to an opening on the dance floor and turned to slide her arms around his neck. "That was mean you know," he scolded her lightly.

"What was? Dancing with Ethan?"

"No, that was just ridiculous. But I hope you enjoyed yourself anyway. I'm talking about what you just told me back at the table." She blushed at her earlier boldness.

"You asked. I answered."

"And now I want to have you all to myself, not be stuck at this dance." She could feel his words on her neck as he spoke, and she sucked in a breath. His arms tightened around her, and she might have fully appreciated for the first time how strong he was. "But maybe you don't dance with him again anyway." She smiled against his shoulder in knowing he was a little bit jealous.

She spent most of the remaining songs dancing with Jess, Kim, and other girls from her cheer squad, and Zack dutifully showed up whenever the tempo slowed down. Being held that close to him became less anxiety-inducing and more comfortable as the night went on, and she was becoming more secure in her decision to be with him. They sat out a couple of songs towards the end of the night. Her feet hurt, and she was pretty certain she was dehydrated. Zack went to get her a water, and Luke sauntered up. He looked stupidly hot as usual, but his navy suit and crisp white button down sort of made her forget how annoying he was.

"Well?" he questioned expectantly.

"Well what?"

"Are you going to join me for the traditional lab partner dance?"

"That's not a thing."

"Sure it is. Walk with me," he stated more seriously. She got up, not really intending to dance with him, but the way his eyes were cast downward made her wonder what he needed.

"What's up?" she asked once they were out of earshot of her companions.

"Right to the point then?" he questioned, putting his hands on her waist.

"Are we really dancing?"

"Trying to, V."

"Ok then. Spit it out." She placed her hands on his broad shoulders tentatively, not wanting it to look like something it wasn't.

"Are you really going to this party tonight? Like staying there?"

"How is that your business? You have a serious boundary problem, Luke." She began to drop her hands, but he caught them and placed them back around his neck.

"Can you just *listen* to me when I tell you not to go? Because if you go, then I have to go. And I feel like things are gonna get awkward."

"Literally none of that makes any sense. You go do whatever you want. You've never cared what parties I went to before. And shouldn't you be more concerned about where Kim is going after? She *is* your date, yes?"

"She's my friend. And she's going home after the dance. But I guess I'll see you at Vader's," he sighed.

"Whatever." She started to leave, but curiosity got the better of her. "How do you know him anyway? You guys seemed chummy."

"From like… forever ago, I guess. His dad and my uncle were friends back in the day, we used to play little league together. He's a cool guy. The same can't be said for all members of that group, though," he added somberly. "I'll see you later. Thanks for the dance."

"Sure," she answered, confused about the whole thing. Zack was waiting with her beverage back at the table.

"What did Miller want?"

"Honestly? I'm not sure. I don't really understand what he's talking about half the time. Something about lab partners."

"I don't really get the hype about the guy. I mean, he's kind of a baller, sure. Other than that? I don't know. Vader loves him, thinks he walks on water or some shit. Whatever. Are you ready to head out?"

"Yeah, just let me find my shoes." Her heart was attempting to jump through her throat at the moment, so shoes sounded like a good thing to focus on. *Oh my god, oh my god, oh.my.god.* Could she seriously do this? Was this like a reasonable decision? Suddenly, every thought she'd ever had and every choice she'd ever made seemed completely irrelevant to her current life situation. She had no idea what she was doing or thinking or forgetting or remembering. *Why isn't Courtney here?!* She already knew that Kim would probably just blush or fall over if she tried to talk to her about sex, and Jess would wave her hand and tell her to handle it. Courtney at least admitted it was a big freaking deal. Vanessa literally stopped in the middle of the room and leaned against the table to collect herself. *You are not this girl.* A few deep breaths later, she was at least somewhat in control of her brain. With shoes in hand, she made her way back to her date, now jacket-less and wearing his seemingly permanent amused expression.

"You all right over there?"

"Yeah. Why?"

"You just looked overwhelmed in the quest for your shoes."

"Nope, just fine," she lied. "Let's get going." He draped his jacket over her shoulders in a sweet gesture and grabbed her hand solidly. She felt better in that moment. Thoughts about the lie she'd told to even get to that party and the fact that she and Zack had never explicitly talked about sleeping together were gnawing at her nerve endings.

"Are you sure you're ok?" Zack asked, looking more confused than concerned. His tires touched the centerline, and she remembered their earlier fight. She hadn't thought to ask him if he'd had any more to drink at the dance.

"Yes. Why wouldn't I be?"

"Because we're going to spend the night in the same room?" The grin he was so fond of was still plastered on his face, and she could not fathom how he was so nonchalant all of the time. *Except when he thinks you flirt with other guys*, she reminded herself.

"Well, there's that." She felt completely exposed when he looked at her that way. Like he knew more or knew better or just knew what she was thinking. He almost missed the entrance into Vader's neighborhood and he turned the car sharply. "Jesus, Zack," she complained, grabbing the handle above her.

"Sorry, I was distracted by your stressed out expression; I forgot where I was going. Calm down. Ok? Everything is fine."

"Ok," she agreed without commitment. They pulled into the drive, and she tried to take his advice.

♪ *"I Want It That Way" - The Backstreet Boys*
"Fall to Pieces" - Avril Lavigne
"That's What You Get" - Parmore

15

To Vanessa's surprise, the sleepover was actually pretty tame. That fact almost made her feel less guilty when she texted her mom that she'd made it to Kim's. Almost. Music, poker, maybe a little bit of smoking going on out on the patio, but people mostly just sat around and chilled or played video games. She hadn't changed yet, not certain she wanted to go straight for the pajamas, though Jess seemed to have no problem prancing around in shorts and a *My Little Pony* t-shirt. Vader apparently thought she was "adorable." Even Jenna was keeping her distance and maintaining her focus on her own date.

"Come here," Zack called, motioning her over to a large oval chair like her grandma used to have in her basement. She climbed in next to him as best she could, but he stealthily maneuvered her onto his lap and brushed her sides with his fingers. "I had fun tonight, you know? I don't usually. You're kind of fun to watch dance."

"Yeah? Well, good. I had fun too." He began kissing her neck, and she let herself relax against him. Grabbing a soft gray blanket from the back of the chair, he wrapped it around them and held her tightly.

"You know I want you, right?" He traced her stomach through the sparkly fabric of her dress until she thought she might die. It was like being tickled and unable to laugh.

"I think so," she answered, unsure of what she was really supposed to say to that comment.

"Well then I guess I need to help you know so," he murmured, his hands slipping slightly lower.

"Zack," she paused, "we are in a room full of people."

"And?" he chuckled, pressing further. She sucked in air and glanced around. No one appeared to give a second thought to them sitting in the corner.

"And... just..."

"Baby, will you please relax? I told you last night, if you want me to stop, I'll stop. But you've been driving me insane in that dress all night, and I want to see how truthful you were about honoring my request," he teased, his voice deep and alluring. Her stomach flip-flopped, and it became clear that it was time to come to a decision. A reel of "first time" highlights from her favorite films began to play in her mind's eye. All she could picture was Cory in *Empire Records* trying to seduce Rex Manning. Or Cher trying to seduce Christian in *Clueless*. *Awkward awkward awkward... no movie montage,* she cautioned herself before she got carried away.

"Yeah, can we just find somewhere that's not... out here?"

"Of course. Hop up," he directed. He tugged her hand down a darkened hallway and felt along the wall for a light switch. She found herself in a clean but sparse bedroom, she assumed for guests, with a floral print on the wall and a plain white quilt over the bed. "Better?" he asked, pulling her close again. He smelled like... a man, she supposed. Like sweat and cologne and a little bit of leftover alcohol. His strong hands rested on her hips and he walked her backwards to the bed.

"Better," she breathed. He kissed her gently but with purpose, moving his mouth slowly. His lips traveled down her neck and her collarbone, and she realized this was actually going to happen. She would no longer be a virgin after this night. As scared as she was, she also told herself it was almost a relief that it would be over. The zipper on the back of her dress came apart, along with any leftover uncertainty.

"You have...protection?"

"Yeah," he answered quickly, as though this was not a new development in their relationship. "You didn't lie. This is easy to get off," he murmured, re-stating his only request for her homecoming attire. She kissed him back with a renewed energy, ready to follow his lead.

* * *

It was not particularly magical or life changing, as she'd secretly, and maybe naively, hoped, but it was done. It had hurt, which she'd expected; it was the lingering pain she hadn't anticipated. Though there were the parts that felt good too, it was all just sort of overwhelming. And the awkwardness. God, she hoped it was only on her end since she wasn't sure what to do.

These thoughts were running through her head at break-neck speed. "That was great," he breathed. "I'll admit, I had reservations about dating a sophomore, but you're...well, you're amazing. Seriously, that was worth waiting for." *Worth waiting for?* she wondered, thinking that was an odd sentiment, being that they hadn't been dating that long.

"I'm glad this was with you," she stated, trying to return some sort of compliment but not sure what to say. She pulled the covers around her, beginning to feel how she used to when sleeping over at a new friend's house for the first time. Everything was foreign. She curled into him and let his hands run over her back until things came into focus. She did feel closer to him, knowing this wasn't a memory she'd ever forget.

He kissed her forehead lightly. "Do you wanna go back out to the party? Or stay in here?"

"Oh, um, I don't know. What do you wanna do?"

"Whichever. I'm not really tired, but I can stay in here with you."

"No, no, that's ok. We can go and socialize," she assured him, trying to sound upbeat. She wasn't sure how she'd envisioned the *after* of the whole experience. Maybe that they'd stay up and talk all night? *It's not the movies, Vanessa,* she scolded herself. "Do you think you could go grab my bag from out there, though? I don't really wanna put my dress back on just to change."

"Sure, of course. I'll be right back," he answered, pecking her cheek before pulling his dress pants back on. Admiringly, she took in the sight of his bare back and shoulders before he swung the button-down over his arms.

"Hey…" she said, not quite sure what she was going to say.

"Yeah?"

"Can I… can you kiss me?" *Why did you ask that?! You sound like a moron.* She couldn't even meet his eyes, she felt ridiculous.

"You haven't had enough kissing tonight?" he laughed lightly. He stepped over as he worked on the buttons of his shirt and leaned down. He pressed his lips against her three times in quick succession. "Better?"

"Mhm."

"I'll go grab your stuff." Zack unlocked the door and disappeared into the hallway. Realizing that anyone could walk in, she tugged the blanket all the way up to her shoulders, putting a 'stay away' vibe out into the room. With difficulty, she tried not to let her mind wander. *This wasn't that big of a deal,* she told herself. *Everyone loses their virginity, and you lost yours to Zack Roads. This is a good thing.* Anger rose in her chest when she noticed her legs trembling. *How stupid.* She grabbed her knees and hugged them against her chest to show her body she was in control. *What the hell is taking him so long?*

Finally, she heard footsteps coming down the hallway, mixed with Zack's voice. The door handle turned and he popped his head in. "Here ya go, babe. I'm gonna go hop in on a game of GTA, you'll meet me out there?"

"Uh, sure, thanks." He flashed a grin at her and closed the door behind him. Fighting the urge to let hurt creep into her thoughts, she counteracted it. *At least he's acting normal. Things aren't weird… just normal.* She pulled on her favorite gray sweats and a hot pink sweatshirt, feeling the braids on her head for anything out of place that might give away what she'd been up to that evening. It felt a little frizzy but otherwise in tact. She shook out her hands, took a deep breath, and applied some lip-gloss. She hated to stuff her gown into the duffel bag, but there wasn't much choice.

The bedroom door swung open just as she bent down to grab her bag, and she almost choked on her tongue. A giggly junior named Melody almost fell on top of her, followed by some guy Vanessa didn't recognize.

"Oops! Sorry, we didn't know anyone was in here," Melody offered.

"No problem, just leaving," she replied. They promptly ignored her as she squeezed behind them and out the door. Her stomach turned slightly as she heard them shut the door and lock it.

"V!" Jess squealed once she reappeared in the common area. "Come, help me play poker. I think I'm losing. I also don't have any money." Vanessa couldn't help but laugh at the annoyed faces of the guys sitting around the table, save for Vader's, which was bathed in an "I'm-with-Jess" glow. It happened to the best of them.

"I'm coming," she answered, throwing her bag in the corner. She looked around for Zack briefly, and he was across the room amped up about something going on in his game. *Poker it is,* she decided. *It's not like you have to be with him every second.* She bumped Jessi with her butt to make her scoot over and share her chair. She wasn't losing actually. She was doing well, and almost had a straight this hand. Glancing around to check out everyone else's pile of chips, her eyes stopped on Luke, looking not quite as jolly as his normal self. "Hey," she stated awkwardly, knowing she had held his gaze for too long.

"Hey," he replied, his tone clipped.

"Hey, yeah, great, we're all acquainted. Can you just flip the next card?" an exasperated Rich complained. Vanessa essentially took over for Jess at that point, ready to orchestrate a take-down. An hour later she had amassed most of the chips on the table and incited grumbling all around. Zack had come to check on her a few times on his way to and from grabbing snacks and drinks, but she wished he'd sit and stay. She didn't want to follow after him like a puppy, but she really wanted him to be closer.

They elected to call it a night, and she held out her hand for her fifty bucks. *More throw pillows,* she thought, envisioning exactly the ones she wanted from her HGTV magazine at home. Jess had gotten distracted at some point and wandered off, so she was left with Luke giving her an off-putting stare as the rest of the guys vacated the table. She was about to get up and play video games just to escape the heaviness of the energy coming off of him, but it seemed to lift just as she made the decision. His facial expression changed and his jaw seemed to relax.

"You wanna go play basketball?" he asked randomly. His tone was almost too upbeat.

"Basketball?"

"Yeah. We can play HORSE or something. There's a hoop outside."

"You're asking me to play HORSE."

"Yeah. Did I not enunciate my words?"

"*No,*" she shot back, "it's just a weird request. It's twelve thirty in the morning, and we are at a party."

"Yeah, it's quite the rager. I think I see Jess snorting pixie sticks off the coffee table. People are gettin' all wild and crazy up in here."

"Shut up."

"I will. As soon as I beat you at HORSE."

"You're like a foot taller than me."

"Doesn't matter in HORSE."

"Stop saying HORSE."

"HORSE."

"Are you going to let this go?"

"How long have you known me?" She actually had to think about that for a moment. *Since sixth grade,* she thought. He really hadn't changed at all; he just grew into his arrogance.

"Let's do this, then." She tried to mime to Zack that she was going to play basketball, and though she didn't think he got the message, he sent her a 'thumbs-up' sign anyway. *Awesome,* she thought, stifling a sigh. She followed Luke through the now dew-covered grass to a fairly decent court. She shivered despite having on a sweatshirt.

"It's not even cold."

"The thermometer would suggest otherwise."

"What thermometer?"

"The one in my brain that tells me I'm cold."

"Ah, the princess thermometer. Gotcha." She turned on her heel to go back inside. She could be annoyed just as easily in there and be warm.

"Okay okay okay okay, I'm sorry. You're not a princess. You're a very down to earth, responsible young lady. Ok? Come back." Vanessa stopped, but held onto her glare. "You know how to play?"

"Yes," she sighed.

"You can start because you're not as good as me." His grin made her grin even though he was being an idiot. How he was out there in a t-shirt and sweats was beyond her. There was a distinct possibility he was really freezing but intent on showing his biceps. She bounced the ball without skill, using two hands, and he snorted. Standing just in front of the free-throw line, she heaved the ball towards the hoop. And missed. Embarrassingly.

"So close!" Luke yelled. She only crossed her arms. He ran to get the ball and tossed a shot granny-style into the hoop.

"You can't shoot it like that."

"Says who?"

"I don't know, the basketball rule-makers?"

"They don't preside over HORSE. It's out of their jurisdiction."

"You don't even know what that word means."

"Yes I do. I watch a lot of *Law and Order* re-runs. Just take the shot, Jesus, V." She did, and actually made it in by shooting underhand. She made the next one too, standing directly next to the basket. Luke even missed some of his shots on purpose, though she wasn't entirely sure why. He never cared about sparing her feelings before. In fact, he usually sought to it to call her out as often as possible on anything she did that was mildly stupid.

Her loss was not surprising. "So does this mean you have to be silent for the rest of the night?"

"Huh?"

"You said you'd shut up once you beat me."

"Yeah, I lied. I do that sometimes, don't take it personally." He was just shooting the ball for fun now. He didn't even have to try. Looking down, he asked, "So, are you ok?"

"Yeah, I'm fine. Cold, but fine."

"I mean… like really ok?"

"I just said I was. Why wouldn't I be?"

"V…"

"Luke…"

"I saw you come out of that room. I know it's not my business, I just-"

161

"Are you honestly trying to talk to me about my sex life right now? God you've got balls, Luke." Her face flamed at his apparent inquisition, wondering why he would drag her out there, and why he was so hell bent on inserting himself into her relationship with Zack. They'd been friends for years, but they were never *this* kind of close. Saying the words "sex life" out loud made her feel like a fraud anyway, being that she didn't have one or know what she was talking about.

"No," he replied quickly, seeming to realize he'd pushed her buttons. "I'm sorry, we'll drop it. If you say you're ok, you're ok."

"Wow, thanks for that validation." This time she kept walking when she turned around, tears springing to her eyes for no freaking reason, which just made her want to stuff Luke into the basketball hoop. And shout "HORSE" at him. And stomp off victoriously.

Instead, she sucked it up and plastered a smile on her face as she crossed the threshold back into the basement. Some people had started to go home; others were staking their claim on couch and floor space for the night. Vanessa fell into the sofa next to Zack, and she pressed her face against his shoulder, breathing him in. This was where she should have stayed all night.

"You tired, babe?" She just nodded into his arm.

"I threw some pillows and blankets over on that chair," he mentioned, tilting his head back towards the spot they were in earlier. "You can go lay down, I'll be done here in a minute."

"K. Thank you." She kissed his temple lightly and made her way to the enticing pile of blankets. Her body was starting to feel sore in all kinds of foreign places, and sleep was a welcomed thought. Jess was snoring slightly on a couch nearby, and Vanessa wondered how it was possible for her to still look cute sprawled out like that. She sighed and sank into the rounded chair.

* * *

The glow of the TV in the darkened room hurt her eyes when she opened them. It was unclear what time it was, but definitely not morning. It took a moment to orient herself with her surroundings, but concern took over when she realized Zack wasn't next to her. She assumed he fell asleep somewhere else, but waking up alone in a strange place still caused her heart to beat irregularly. With the blanket tightly wrapped around her shoulders, she scooted herself out of the chair in search of the bathroom. The sliding door from the outside opened as she was midway across the room, and Zack walked in.

"V?" he whispered.

"Yeah… what were you doing outside? What time is it anyway?"

"I'm not sure, like three, I think. Some girls were leaving and didn't wanna go to their car alone, so I walked them up there. I'm sorry."

"Oh, no, that's ok. Go lay down, I'll be right back." He nodded tiredly and traipsed over to their spot. She climbed in with him when she returned and played with the hairs on his arms until the warmth from his body calmed her nerves. His mouth found hers in the dark, and he pulled her in even closer. It was the first real breath she'd taken since they left the bedroom, and she clung to it with all that she had. *Things are ok,* she realized, letting herself relax into him.

♪ "Titanium" – David Guetta ft. Sia
(Performed by: Madilyn Bailey)
"These Words" – Natasha Bedingfield
"Really Don't Care" – Demi Lovato

16

A dull chatter began to run through the basement as the sun became more pronounced in the sky. Vader's mom, *Mrs. Vader?* came down with doughnuts, orange juice, and bagels for everyone who had stayed the night. She was now Vanessa's new favorite human being. Two doughnuts and half a bagel later, she felt awake enough to think about going home.

"Hey, I think Jess and I are gonna head out."

"Yeah, I gotta get home here in a minute too. You're sure I can't drive you?"

"I'm sure. I'm on edge enough as it is. I don't wanna have to come up with a story about how you ended up picking me up at Kim's."

"Got it. Well, I had fun last night," he relayed, those dimples coming out momentarily.

"Me too," she agreed. "I'll text you later?"

"Yeah, sounds good." He kissed her, and she let him despite the morning breath. At least the taste of doughnut overshadowed it.

Grabbing her things, she let Jess pull her up the stairs and out into the morning air after her own goodbye to Vader. She heaved herself into the Jeep, hoping the heat worked quickly, but she almost jumped out of her skin when Jess attacked her.

"Ow!" Vanessa cried as her friend clutched her arm tightly, her nails digging into her flesh.

"Tell me everything, oh my god, like don't leave out even one moment. Was it amazing? What did he say? What did *you* say? How did you do it? Was it *so* awkward? How is he-"

"You are cutting off the circulation to my hand!"

"Oh, yes, sorry. But not really. Because tell me." She loosened her grip, but only slightly.

"You're deranged. It was good, I guess. I don't have anything to compare it to."

"Well he certainly seemed to think it was good," Jess replied, finally putting the car into gear and pulling onto the street.

"Ummmm, and how would you know that?"

"He wasn't exactly discreet when he came out of that room. There may have been fist bumping involved." She told this story without emotion, as if she were reciting the school lunch menu.

"*What?*"

"I mean, he didn't like, say anything in particular. Just, I don't know, it was kind of obvious."

"Uuugggggghhhhhhhh, that is *so* humiliating." Her thoughts were swimming; she put her head between her legs and tried to breathe normally. "So everyone knows..."

"I don't *know,* I'm just telling you what I saw. It's not like he wasn't going to tell his friends anyway, though, I don't see what the huge deal is. I just wanna know if-"

"I am not talking about this anymore right now. I may throw up from mortification."

"I don't know what that means. Like you're dying? Like a mortician?"

"No. Mortification. Embarrassment. And yes, I'm dying. Just kill me and put me out of my misery." She put her pink hood on and tried to strangle herself with the strings. It wasn't going well. The look she'd gotten from some of the guys playing poker after… well, they took on a new layer of *yuck* now that she knew they *knew*.

"Don't be so dramatic," Jess mumbled, apparently coming to the realization that there would be no sordid details handed out from Vanessa.

"Just talk about something else," she muttered from beneath her hood.

"Vader wants to be my boyfriend. I told him I'd think about it. I don't know if I can seriously date someone named after a *Star Trek* character."

"Congratulations," she replied flatly. This was a very very bad start to the day. "It's *Star Wars*. And his name's Garth."

"Excuse me?"

"Garth. Like Garth Brooks. But they call him Garth Vader. That's where the name came from."

"You allowed me to go to homecoming with someone named *Garth*?!"

"Yes. I allowed it to happen. How will you ever forgive me?"

"Well that is absolutely settled. I will *not* have a boyfriend named *Garth*. Can you even imagine? Ugh. No. No. No no no. Absolutely not, no." There was a long pause, and Jess looked pensive. "No."

A giggle escaped Vanessa's mouth despite her mood. And then another. Jess's preoccupation with saying the name "Garth" over and over again had now become so amusing that she couldn't stop laughing. There were simply too many emotions at the surface for her to hold any more inside. Jess's face told her she thought a straight jacket might be needed, but she inevitably started laughing too. Her sides hurt, and tears streamed down her face, but at least she felt like she was releasing *something*.

"You're a little crazy. And coming from me? That's saying something."

"You might be right."

* * *

When Jess dropped her off, Vanessa saw the familiar sight of the contractor's vehicle in front of the house, but a truck boasting a new logo was alongside it. *The painters are here!* She practically rolled out of the car while it was still moving. Almost knocking her dad over in the front room, she threw her bag on the stairs and rushed to the basement. The newly stained floors were now covered with brown paper to protect them while they were painting and hanging wallpaper, but it looked like an actual *space.* A space she created. Most of the main room was left white so she could hang art and several mirrors she'd found at a great vintage shop, but the largest wall in the room was now covered with a turquoise and gold metallic quatrefoil pattern. She touched the textured paper with her hands, and it even *felt* perfect. Sort of worn and soft like papyrus.

"So you like it?" Mike asked, wandering into the room.

"It's perfect. They did an amazing job getting it up so quickly," she marveled. It was just incredible how fast a room could change due to something so small.

"Well, if you're impressed with that, check out the bed and bath," he bragged. She followed him happily and almost gasped when she floated into the room. She had designed it for herself even though her parents told her in no uncertain terms that she would *not* be moving into it. The walls were a French white with large pale-gold polka dots moving from one side to another. Being that it was a basement, she tried to keep the color pallet light. This room would be off-white, gold, and a washed-out gray, with hints of black for drama. She knew the pillow with the gold sequined bow was hiding in one of the boxes, and she couldn't wait to start tearing them open. A thin metal canopy bed had already been painted gold and assembled in the room. She wanted to cry. The bathroom was difficult to judge because the guys were still in there working, but the whole thing was overwhelming- in the best sense of the word. She actually hugged Mike momentarily, causing him to laugh heartily.

"I should probably be thanking you! Shots of this remodel will go a long way in client meetings. If you ever become a designer, let me know; I'm sure I know people who would hire you," he said, probably in jest, but her heart almost exploded at the compliment.

"A girl can dream," she left as her only reply. It was too frightening to admit to anyone that becoming a designer was *exactly* what she wanted to do with her life. This whole experience only solidified that for her. It was her imagination come to life.

"Looks great down here, V," her dad's voice came from the living area.

"You really think so?" she asked excitedly, hopping back into that room.

"Absolutely. Mike here says it should all be done by middle of next week. Can't wait to see it."

"Does that mean I can start unpacking boxes and hanging things up?" Vanessa was practically salivating looking at the drill on the table.

"Unpacking, yes, but just set things around the room where you'd like them hung, and Mike will do that for you. I don't want eight million holes in the walls."

"Hmpf," she huffed. "Can I at least help?"

"Sure thing," Mike promised. This appeased her. Plus, it was difficult to dampen her mood anyway. She spent the rest of the afternoon with a box cutter, ripping open boxes and staring in awe at the beautiful things that would soon occupy the space. She forgot to eat. Or shower. But she wouldn't have traded that afternoon for anything.

Dinner finally rolled around, and her parents dragged her to the table for something green and leafy. She was starving, and already envisioning a late-night trip through Wendy's drive-thru.

"So how was the dance? We haven't even seen you above ground all day," her mom asked at dinner. The dance seemed like it took place eight years ago.

"It was good! I danced, we took a photo, I had a dance battle with this new kid named Ethan. All in all, a good time."

"A dance *battle?*" her father questioned, confused.

"Just look it up on YouTube. I can't explain it otherwise," she laughed.

"Sure. I'll get right on that." Her good mood continued throughout dinner, and then fatigue set in. Her late-night Frosty run would have to be postponed. She grabbed her bag from the night before and ventured up to her room for the first time all day. Her phone screen was full of messages, and she realized how odd it was that she hadn't checked it all day. She had texts from Jess, from Kim, even one from Luke that was a picture of a horse, but there was nothing from Zack. Her heart slowed some, but she realized she told him she would text him before she left Vader's that morning. Hoping he wasn't mad, she shot off a message.

> V: Hey, sorry I didn't text you before now. I've been unpacking everything in the basement- it's almost done! You have to come see it next week. I had so much fun last night. Thanks for a memorable home-coming ;).

She threw her phone on the bed and showered quickly, wanting the warmth and comfort of her own bed. Zack hadn't responded by the time she was about to pass out, so she set her alarm and figured she'd see him in the morning. That rational thought, however, didn't stop a pit from making itself known in the center of her stomach.

"Vanessa Roberts, get up before you're late for school," her mother's voice stated sternly as she shook her daughter awake.

"Huh?"

"School? That place you go every weekday?"

"What time is it?" she asked, rubbing her eyes. Why hadn't her alarm gone off?

"Almost seven thirty"

"What?! Okay okay, I'm up. Why'd you let me sleep this late?" she questioned, throwing clothing from her closet onto her bed.

"I assumed you were up. You're sixteen, not six. I'll drive you, and you can eat in the car. Just get dressed."

"Ugghhhh," she groaned. She hated being rushed. A messy bun, some mascara, and a hoodie with jeans later, Vanessa was being ushered into the car with a piece of toast in her hand. In sprinting through the parking lot, she made it to her first period class seconds before the tardy bell rang. Kim shot her a look that resembled confusion, but she brushed it off. She had no time to really care that she looked like crap as her math teacher decided that the Monday morning after homecoming would be a perfect time for a pop quiz. Vanessa closed her eyes and willed the whole morning to be a dream, and she'd wake up with plenty of time to look presentable and ideally look over the homework she should have done while decorating.

It was possible she got two of the eight questions right. Visions of a math tutor being forced upon her by her parents danced around her head.

"Are you ok?" Kim asked on their way out of class.

"Other than looking like a homeless person and failing that quiz? Yeah, I'm good."

"Really? I thought... I don't know, that after Saturday you might be..."

"What do you mean 'after Saturday'? What happened on Saturday?" *Besides the obvious.* But Kim didn't know that. Fear shone in her friend's brown eyes. "Spill, friend."

"I don't know. I guess nothing? I must have heard incorrectly."

"Well, tell me what you heard incorrectly, because I'm really not having the kind of morning that inspires patience."

"Just that Zack and Jenna had... I don't know, reunited?"

"Stop saying you don't know and just spit it out"

"I'm sorry! I just heard they hooked up after homecoming, but I must have been misinformed. Obviously. You know how things get-"

Anger surged from somewhere deep. It was just *enough* already. "Could you just stop being so freaking interested in what everyone else has going on? I seriously don't know where you 'hear' this shit anyways. Are you lurking around people with actual lives? Just let it go, ok? Zack was with me all night on Saturday. I can't even believe you're throwing this at me right now. I've gotta go." She could feel the blood rushing through her body, and she knew she left Kim in the hall with her eyes full of tears, but she felt no guilt at the moment. She just couldn't take any more idiocy from anyone.

Second period passed without incident, and the reality of what she'd said to one of her closest friends started to settle over her like a thick layer of dust. It was suffocating. Replaying the scene back in her head, she knew she crossed a line. An apology was forthcoming, but she didn't have the words yet. Instead, she slinked into bio without making eye contact. Luke wasn't in class, which was odd in and of itself, but she would have welcomed a comedic reprieve, even if it was at her own expense. Mr. Lessner began his lecture on the respiratory system or something, and she just couldn't follow. *You'll have to watch The Magic School Bus later,* she thought, knowing Ms. Frizzle had to have something in the way of the respiratory system. The classroom door swung open, and as if mesmerized by this occurrence, the whole class refocused their eyes at the back of the room. Luke sauntered in, his usual grin gracing his face, but it didn't reach his eyes. This was mostly because one of his eyes was covered by the wrapping of an ice pack pressed against his cheek.

"I trust you've all seen a human walk through a door before. If we could please continue on..." Mr. Lessner scolded. Luke sat down next to her and got out his notes. Vanessa grabbed his notebook and wrote *Are you ok?* on the corner of the page. *Peachy,* he wrote back, and she just grimaced and attempted to focus on the lecture.

While everyone was packing up, she asked again. "Hey, what happened to you?"

"Nothin'" he answered with a cold smile.

"Ok? What's the deal here... I thought we were cool?"

He sighed. "We're fine, V. Nothing happened. I got elbowed in the face in P.E. That's it. Just embarrassing."

"Oh. I'm sorry. It's not that noticeable," she lied, looking at the darkening bruise along his cheekbone.

"Sure," he laughed as the bell rang. She hung back and allowed Kim to leave before her. That conversation was going to be a level of uncomfortable she just wasn't ready to get into in the hallway. *Lunch,* she resolved.

17

The cafeteria seemed stifling when she arrived, knowing what she had to do. Her stomach was in knots already, so food was out of the question until this part was over.

"Hey, um, can I talk to you?" she asked Kim softly.

"I don't really want to talk to you."

"Maybe you guys just need to cool off?" Jess offered, attempting to break the tension.

"I just need to apologize. Please let me." Kim said nothing, which Vanessa took as an invitation. "I had no right to say the things I said to you earlier. You know I don't really think... You know I love you. I was stressed from being late, and I just didn't want to hear gossip about Zack right then. I'm so sorry I hurt your feelings."

"It's fine."

"It's not fine. I know it's not. I can eat somewhere else today if you want. Just... I'm sorry."

"Yes," she answered with a frosty tone.

"Yes what?"

"Yes, please eat somewhere else today."

"Seriously?"

"You offered. Why did you say it if you didn't mean-"

"Ok, ok. I'm going. I'll see you later. Bye Jess." Jess simply offered a stiff wave. *Apparently the tides have turned,* she contemplated in regards to Kim's thoughts about Jess from literally three days before.

While in the lunch line, Vanessa looked around for Zack, finally realizing she hadn't heard from him. He was nowhere to be seen. She could sit at the heavily populated cheer table, but that didn't sound appetizing either. Luke was sitting at his usual spot with a couple of guys from the basketball team, and she thought she'd brave that rather than listen to anyone else talk at her.

Vanessa slid into an empty chair without asking permission, and opened the burrito that looked as if it'd seen better days.

"V…" Luke started.

"Luke…" she finished in a mocking tone.

"Are you lost? Do you need me to show you the way back?"

"Nope."

One of the other guys at the table was looking at her curiously. "I don't get it," he stated cryptically.

"The English language? Basic math? Dental hygiene?" she retorted, not caring that she was being a complete bitch.

"You seriously took that hit for this bit-"

"Watch yourself, Aimes," Luke warned his friend, his muscles suddenly tense.

"Whatever man." He just shot daggers at her again and walked away.

"Was it something I said?" Vanessa asked with feigned sheepishness. She wasn't a big fan of Troy Aimes.

"Nah, why would telling a guy he's stupid with bad breath offend him?" She just shrugged her shoulders. "What are you doing over here anyway?"

"I said some mean things. I'm waiting for the ice to thaw."

"Wow, you're just alienating people right and left."

"Yeah well, sometimes my mouth gets me in trouble. What did he mean about taking a hit? I thought it was a P.E. accident."

"We can chat about anything you like. Except that. Pick a new topic." Vanessa was quiet for a moment, thoroughly confused by his response.

"Ummmm, my basement's almost done."

"Sweet. When's the party?"

"Yeah, there is very little chance of me inviting hoards of messy, dirty people over to screw up my creation, so never."

"You're just going to sit alone and stare at the walls?"

"They're very nice walls." He just shook his and leaned back in his chair.

"I remember you being more fun than that."

"I'm fun," she relayed, beginning to feel annoyed. Though to be fair, this was bound to happen sooner or later when sitting at the same table as Luke.

"Fun people don't have to say that." He grinned, shoving a french fry into his mouth.

"You're dumb." *That was the worst come back in history.* She was embarrassed she had even let it come out of her mouth. His grin turned into a laugh.

"And you're losing your touch. You came to sit by me, so you're free to leave at any time. You already chased away my friends. Are you trying to get me to leave too?" She bit the inside of her lip, wishing she could tell him where to go and be okay sitting by herself.

"Whatever," was all she could muster.

"So tell me, what'd you say to get exiled from your own table?"

She breathed, recalling exactly what she'd spouted off, and the look on Kim's face afterward. "Stupid, mean, unkind things. I don't even know why I said them. I've just had a crappy morning, and she is always saying 'I heard this, I heard that,' and I just didn't want to listen to it. But I was in the wrong, so here I am. In exile until Kim forgives me."

"*Kimmy* kicked you out? I thought for sure you'd been cat fighting with Jess. You must have screwed up; Kim thinks you're like the Beyoncé of Gem City High."

"Shut up, she does not."

"Does so. I went to homecoming with her. We chatted. A lot. The girl likes to talk."

"That she does. It was nice that you guys went together though. I know she-"

"Hey, do you wanna get outta here?" he interrupted, suddenly sitting up rather straight in his chair.

"What? We still have four periods left."

"Yeah, and? We could go to the mall, or the zoo, I don't really care, let's just go."

"I can't cut school, my mom would ground me until senior year. What's going on with you? You were fine, and now you're weird." His green eyes were hard as she tried to read them. The chair next to her was pulled out suddenly, causing her to whip her head around.

"Hey guys," Zack offered without sincerity. He placed his fingers at the back of her neck and pressed slightly. She was sure it was supposed to be a comforting gesture, but his mood was off.

"Hey, where were you?" she asked.

"Went to pick up food. I brought you a cheeseburger, though seeing how you've been spending your time this period, I'm not sure you've earned it." Luke unceremoniously stood up and stormed away from the table without a word. *What the hell is going on?*

"Shut up. Give me my cheeseburger." She looked after Luke, but he was gone. "What was that about?" she asked as Zack dropped a Wendy's bag in front of her. Her mouth watered as soon as the scent of grease hit her nose.

"What, Miller? Eh, just a misunderstanding." He waved her off, and she had more pressing questions to ask.

"I didn't hear back from you yesterday."

"What do you mean 'hear back from me' "?

"I texted you, and nothing."

"I didn't know your text required a response, babe."

"All of my texts require a response." He held her gaze, but never let his dimples disappear.

"Aren't you feisty today?"

"I tend to get that way when one of my best friends tells me you hooked up with Jenna Saturday night." He laughed, almost choking on his soda.

"I what?"

"That's what I hear. So you must've been pretty busy."

"V, I was with you all of Saturday night."

"I know. I didn't say I believed her. I actually said some really... well, I didn't react in a ladylike manner. So now I'm sitting over here."

"Aw, you were jealous."

"Why would I be jealous of something I know didn't occur?"

"Calm down, babe. I'm just messing with you. Thanks for defending my honor to Jess. Weird though, I thought she liked me."

"Not Jess. Kim. Why does everyone assume Jess?"

"Wow, Kim's talking smack, huh?" He looked over at her former table and waved obnoxiously at Kim, who refused to make eye contact.

"Oh my god, stop it. I'm trying to get her to forgive me."

"Sorry. Couldn't resist. And speaking of things I can't resist," he continued, pulling her chair next to him, "come out with me tonight?"

"When?" she giggled.

"I'll pick you up at eight," he whispered in her ear. "Please wear the purple dress." She shivered, wondering where he was going to take her.

"I can manage that." The lunch bell rang and she scarfed down the remainder of her cheeseburger and let Zack hold her around the waist on the way to class. She hated people who walked that way, often judging them loudly in the hall, but she wanted to ensure that anyone else who'd heard the Jenna rumor would know it was balderdash.

* * *

A feeling of déjà vu settled over Vanessa that evening as she sat at the window in her dress, waiting for Zack. Waiting. Waiting some more. Then waiting some more. She was bad at waiting. Her heartbeat pounded behind her eyes. The last time, she had only been pissed. This time was different. The last road she wanted to walk was the one of "Did I Make a Mistake Boulevard." *Dammit.*

Her phone vibrated in her purse, and her hands were beginning to shake as she pulled it out.

> Z: Hey, something came up last minute. Can I make it up to you later this week?

Every part of her being wanted to tell him to go to hell. She typed out the words even. Four times. Each time she deleted them, looking for any way to justify his actions. She could *not* be the girl who lost her virginity to a guy who couldn't be bothered to call to cancel their date. Her stomach was twisted, and her breaths came faster. She shoved the phone under her pillow before she could text back without thinking it through. *You will not cry. Not one.single.tear. Nothing has even happened. You're just overreacting.*

She forced herself to calmly change into her favorite white sweats from PINK, and go downstairs to admire the almost-completed basement. The TV was now mounted, and the cable would be connected the following day. *But you don't need cable to watch a movie,* she told herself. *Can't Hardly Wait* was at the top of the pile of DVDs she needed to organize. *Yes. 90s goodness.* Unfortunately, she made it about twenty minutes in before remembering what a douche canoe Jennifer Love Hewitt's ex-boyfriend was in the movie. It did not improve her outlook on the male gender.

Deciding to give up on the day, she trudged back to her bedroom and, even though she thoroughly hated herself for it, took her phone out from under the pillow and let her heart sink when there were no further messages from Zack.

> V: Hey, you around?
>
> C: Yeah, studying for midterms. Everything ok?
>
> V: I don't know.

All of four and a half seconds later, her phone rang.

"Hi," Vanessa answered, trying to sound cheery.

"What's going on?" Courtney demanded, clearly not buying it.

"I think I may have been really stupid," she admitted for the first time out loud.

"I doubt it, but why?"

"I... well, I did what I said I was going to do. The night of homecoming. But now..."

"Please tell me this is not an 'I think I might be pregnant' talk."

"Oh god, no! No, we were safe. Sorry, I didn't mean to make it sound like that."

Courtney let out a deep breath. "Ok. Now we can continue."

"I just don't think he likes me anymore," she blurted out before she could talk herself out of it. It sounded so *weak*, but that's exactly how she felt.

"Why?" Courtney pressed, sounding sympathetic. Vanessa told her about him standing her up for their date and lack of texts since homecoming, and she of course said all of the right things. Courtney didn't push her for any details about that night like Jess would have. She just let her say what she needed to say, and re-living that night was absolutely *not* part of that plan.

"It's possible something really did come up, you know? And if it didn't? If he's honestly *that guy*, then you don't want him. That's a seriously screwed up game to play, V."

"I know. You're right. I just… god I'm so stupid. Why couldn't I have figured this out *before*?"

"I'm so sorry. Maybe things are honestly fine, ok? Just talk to him tomorrow and then at least you can move forward one way or another. And you're not stupid. Please call me if you need me."

"Ok I will. I'll let you study, I'm fine, honestly."

"Are you sure? I can study later."

"I'm sure. I need to sleep anyway. I'll call you soon."

"Yes, let me know what happens. Love you, V."

"Love you girl, thanks."

Her brain had slowed down enough to process a thought after her conversation with Courtney. *Just talk to him tomorrow.* To feel more prepared, she pulled out a killer outfit from her closet, determined to look better than she felt the following day.

♪ "Out of the Woods" - Taylor Swift
(performed by Anthem Lights)
"Rather Be" - Clean Bandit
"Counting Stars" - One Republic
(Performed by: Alex Goot and Chrissy Costanza)

18

Sleep had not come easily, but Vanessa awoke feeling stronger than the evening before. She was going to figure out what the deal was once and for all. Decked out in skin tight black jeans and knee high boots, she pulled on a tight blue t-shirt and a fitted gray jacket before feeling satisfactorily presentable. She left her hair down and curled the ends, determined to look ready to kick-ass on the exterior.

"Mom, can you take me to school early? I need to talk to my math teacher about extra credit." That wasn't strictly the case, but it was a good idea, so she could do that too.

Extra math project in hand, she set off for the library where she knew Kim should be. It was not in her nature to eat any type of humble pie, but she had to make things right with her. She was running over what to say in her head, and that focus allowed her to walk right past Zack without noticing.

"Hey," he called, leaving whatever conversation he was in with Rich. Her pace did not slow at first. She hadn't had time to play out that confrontation in her mind yet. "V… seriously?"

he asked, obviously frustrated. "We're not twelve, you can't just give me the silent treatment." He had caught up to her easily and grabbed her elbow.

"Don't touch me," she warned him in a low tone.

"I like touching you," he asserted, his eyes dancing. The hurt and anger she'd been suppressing was just below the surface, and it would not be pretty if it found its way out. His grip only tightened. "Ow, you're hurting me."

"Then stop being dramatic. Seriously," he growled at her once he realized she wasn't backing down.

"I'm not being dramatic; I'm telling you I don't want to talk to you right now." Her voice shook slightly as he pulled her over to the doorway of an empty classroom before releasing her arm.

"What is your problem? I don't really find it amusing to have to chase you down the hallway."

"I'm not really here for your amusement." He chuckled at her quip, and her anger surged again. "What could you possibly be laughing at right now?"

"I'm just thinking that I should have anticipated this. I'm sorry. I should have been more... sensitive to your ah, situation."

"What the hell are you talking about? I don't have a 'situation.'"

"V... the other night, that was your first time, right?" Her face flamed, and she felt more exposed with his eyes on her then than she had during the actual act.

"I...what does it matter?" She looked around, really needing their exchange to be over. Immediately. He stepped in closer to her and set his hands on her waist. It was too close, and she placed her hand on his stomach to stop him.

"Baby, I'm sorry I canceled our date last night. I was beat, and I fell asleep after practice. I've been sleeping like crap lately. When I woke up, I was already late picking you up, and I hadn't showered- I just figured I'd see you tonight or tomorrow night.

It wasn't a big deal, but I didn't know you were feeling this insecure."

"I'm not insecure," she shot back immediately. He grinned again and pressed forward, overcoming her weak attempt to keep his body at bay.

"Of course not. You're just feeling like this because we were together. And it was really good, by the way," he flashed his dimples at her, now within kissing territory. Tears threatened to spill over for five different reasons. She needed to believe he wasn't avoiding her, that she hadn't let him take advantage of her, that she wasn't that stupid. "Come on, V. Please don't be mad about last night. Let me make it up to you." He kissed her lightly, his tongue still tasting like spearmint toothpaste, and she crumbled. He pressed himself into her, and she felt wanted again. The halls were becoming more and more populated as the first bell drew nearer, and she broke their embrace.

"I need to go to class."

"Tell me I can pick you up tonight."

"You can pick me up tonight. Whether you actually will or not remains to be seen," she continued.

"There's the girl I know," he laughed deeply. "I'll be there. I like these pants by the way." He smacked her butt lightly and kissed her again before walking towards his first period class. Vanessa cursed under her breath for feeling so much better after kissing him. She also realized she'd lost her moment to speak to Kim with any type of sincerity. Sighing, she pushed off of the wall and made her way to class.

The day passed slowly. That seemed to be a by-product of everyone being mad at her, or acting like she didn't exist in Luke's case. She spent lunch in the library working on the math assignment, and finished the day passing notes with Jess in Spanish class.

So what's the deal? -J

With what? Kim? I'm sure she's told you. –V

Not anything specific. And I texted you fifty bajillion times yesterday.

I know I'm sorry. I was in a mood. Kim and I will be fine, I'll talk to her.

Wanna get dinner tonight after practice?

Can't. Going out with Zack. Tomorrow?

Yeah, tomorrow.

Jess dropped her at home after one of the best practices Vanessa'd had all year- her tumbling even earning her a compliment from Brooke. She was cautiously optimistic about her date with Zack and wanted to get in the shower as soon as humanly possible. When she waltzed in the door, her mom practically pounced on her.

"Oh my god, I've been waiting forever for you to get home," she exclaimed.

"Jesus mom, you almost gave me a heart attack. And why? What's wrong?" Her immediate thought was that she was in trouble. Her mom was never this happy to see her.

"Nothing! It's done! The basement, it's finished. Mike finished this afternoon, and I've been waiting for you before I went down there." Her heart started thumping in her chest. Her project was complete? In six weeks? Weren't contractors supposed to drag these things out and make the homeowners' lives miserable? It also struck her that her mom had waited before going to look at it. The expression on her face conveyed that she actually *got* what a big deal it was.

"Are you sure? Finished? What about the outlet covers, are they back on?"

"I don't know, Vanessa, I just told you I've been waiting for you! Mike said he'll come by tomorrow and check on everything again, so you can leave him a list if there's something missing. Now can we go downstairs or not?"

"Yes!" Vanessa nearly shouted as it hit her that everything she'd been working for was *done*. Dropping her cheer bag where she stood, she flew down the stairs and into the main living space.

There was nothing like the feeling of walking in to a completely finished design. She had seen all of the pieces, separately, but together? It was magical. He had hung the Moroccan style lanterns in turquoise, yellow, red, pink, and midnight blue exactly where they'd discussed, and low light glowed out of them and filled the space. She ran her fingers along the back of the clean lined white sectional and took in the sight of the *pillows*. There were so many pillows. Beaded ones, some with lace, some embroidered, in every color imaginable. It looked like a bazaar from somewhere in the Middle East. It was beautiful.

Turning, she watched her mom take in the sight as well. "Vanessa... this is incredible."

"I know, right?!" she joked. She knew her mother hated that phrase. This time though, she just shook her head and continued to inspect the art on the walls-some wrought iron work, some prints in heavy metallic frames.

"I can't believe this is my house," she murmured.

"Come! Let's see the bedroom and bathroom!" She urged, unable to wait any longer. If the main room was a Middle Eastern bazaar, then the bedroom was a Parisian loft. It was elegant and sophisticated and Aubrey Hepburn-esque, just as she'd imagined. The bathroom was small, but felt airy with the arabesque tiles and the gold and white shower curtain surrounding the tub. The whole thing was surreal. It was impossible that all of this had only been in her semi-organized binder two months ago. "Please can I live in here?" she asked, unable to force her feet to leave the room.

"Vanessa, please don't start. Let's just enjoy your accomplishment right now. Please."

Vanessa realized this was as good as a "no," but agreed to drop it and enjoy the moment. "Can I shower down here to get ready for my date?" she questioned, needing to experience the space.

"Yes," her mom breathed, seemingly happy to be able to agree to something. Vanessa knew she needed to hurry to be ready on time, but she still appreciated the detail work in the mirrors on the wall and the curve of the tall faucet in the sink. While applying the finishing touches of her makeup and perfecting the tight plaid button down she'd chosen to wear, she heard the doorbell ring. A pair of camel boots and a denim mini skirt completed her ensemble, and she waited for Zack to join her downstairs.

"Hey babe," he greeted her as he jogged down the steps, planting a kiss on her mouth.

"Hey! So… what do you think??" she asked, gesturing to the rest of the room.

"I think you look incredible."

"Not about me, Mr. Charming, the *room*."

"Oh! Well, I still think you look hot. And the room is cool. I like these things," he stated, tapping one of the lanterns.

"You are not excited enough," she complained.

"I'm sorry! I don't like, look at people's decorations. I am *very* excited by other things in this room though. Namely this skirt," he explained, being certain to speak softly as he let his fingers travel under the hem of her shirt.

"You're lucky you're so smooth," she answered. "Where are we going anyway?"

"Well let's get going and find out." She followed him out and appreciated his biceps in his Gem City t-shirt, sighing inwardly when he put his jacket on prior to leaving the house. He swung his arm around her shoulder and pulled her close on their way out to the Charger.

"Did you miss me?" she flirted, feeling back to her old self.

"Miss you from when, this morning? Tons," he answered snarkily.

"At least pretend like you mean it," she chastised him.

"I'm sorry. I do mean it. I missed you." He kissed her quickly before opening her car door. They drove towards the outside of town with some form of his horrible music on the stereo. The car pulled off of a gravel road towards the river, and some of her confidence rushed out of her system.

"This is our date?" she asked incredulously.

"What? You were thinking champagne and caviar?"

"No, I was thinking it would be a date."

"Are we together?" She rolled her eyes. "Are we having fun?" She sighed. "Are we about to have more fun?" he asked, his stupid blue eyes sparkling at her.

"Fun for you or for me?" she paused. "That's rhetorical," she added quietly.

"*Dammit* Vanessa," Zack yelled, slamming his fist into his steering wheel and sounding the horn. She jumped at the sudden noise. "I like being with you because it's *fun*. I have a good time when we're together. The rest of life is stressful, and when I'm with you, I can ignore it. But now you're turning this into one more effing thing I have to deal with." He got out of the car unexpectedly.

There was a convergence of fear and anger taking place in her mind as she watched him throw a pretty legitimate tantrum. She could tell there was deep breathing involved. *Do you want this to work or not?* she questioned herself. It was apparent that it was either time to walk away or accept that what he said was true: He liked her, he enjoyed being with her, and he wanted to keep seeing her. Sitting with both options, the idea of *not* being with him made her stomach drop to her knees. She would see him at school every day, knowing that they had been *together*. That he knew what she looked like naked. That made her ill. The other option settled her nerves some. She could try to relax about their relationship status- for a while. She could give him time to work through his issues about Jenna. She tugged on the door handle and steeled herself for more honesty than she might be comfortable handing out.

He turned around and looked at her, his face still giving off irritation. "Look-" he began, but she stopped him.

"Let me say what I want to say, all right?" He said nothing in return, so she proceeded. "You might have been a little bit right this morning. I'm feeling... like..." this was harder than she thought.

"Insecure."

"*Yes,*" she stated as a warning. She wanted to get this out on her own. "But we do have fun together, and I like hanging out with you. I just need for you to be a little bit more...forthcoming, I guess, with your communication. You can't just text me and say 'something came up,' and then *nothing*. Ok?" She felt like that was concise enough to get her point across.

"Ok. I get that," he agreed, walking closer to her. His demeanor was relaxed again, the tantrum seeming to be over.

"Yeah?"

"Yeah. I should've, I don't know. I should've realized... sooner. Come here." He tugged on her shirt to pull her into him, and he wrapped his arms around her tightly. "You're such a small fry."

"I'm not even that short with these boots on."

"I know. I'm just huge," he joked, flexing his arms as he held her."

"And humble," she kidded back.

"Can we make out now?"

"Well, since we're here and all," she acquiesced playfully. His mouth found hers, and there was an all around better energy between them. The entire family of butterflies that typically lived in her stomach when she was around him returned, and she felt light headed as he pressed her back against his car and his focus became much more intense.

"Did I already say I liked this skirt?" he murmured in her ear while his hands found their way under it.

"It's possible you mentioned it."

* * *

It really hadn't been her intention to have sex with him. Especially not in the back of his car. *Cliché, trashy, and awkward,* she thought. *The trifecta of stupid girl moves.* She really hadn't even been certain that's what was happening, until it was. And something about the way her name passed through his lips when he wanted her made her an idiot. It was more uncomfortable than painful this time, but she just felt unsure once it was over and her brain began working again. They were in such a precarious place in their... relationship, if she could even call it that.

"I'm glad we're ok," he told her as he drove her home. "I needed you tonight."

"Me too. Everything okay with you?"

"Yeah, just a lot of pressure. Football, and the SATs, and I don't know, just shit."

"Ok. Well, if you want to talk about it..."

"I know," he smiled, and left it at that.

"I'll see you tomorrow."

"Give me a kiss," he commanded before she got out. She obliged, and without thinking, she asked the question she'd really wanted to ask all night. Perhaps she'd wanted to ask it since Vader's bonfire.

"You're not seeing other people, are you?" she inquired with a confidence she didn't feel.

"What? Where did that come from?" He shifted in his seat uncomfortably.

"Just answer the question."

"Ok? No, I'm not seeing anyone else."

"Ok then. Just wanted to make sure we were on the same page."

"Goodnight, V."

"Goodnight."

She held her head slightly higher than normal, putting one foot in front of the other with certainty. She greeted her parents, she took the stairs calmly one at a time, and she closed the door to her room. Then she came apart at the seams.

♪ *"Congratulations" –Rachel Platton*
"Love Yourself" – Justin Bieber
"Face Down" –The Red Jumpsuit Apparatus
"All You Wanted" – Michelle Branch
"I Knew You Were Trouble" – Taylor Swift
(Performed by: Madilyn Bailey)

19

Liar liar liar liar liar. The word just kept running through her head like an unending freight train as she sat against her bed, staring at the ceiling. He had lied through his mother-effing teeth. She'd seen him lie before... when he played poker. He ran his tongue along the backs of his teeth and looked at his nails. It didn't register until he did it again while answering her question. The feeling of his hands and his lips on her, the things he said to her- all of them now lingered incessantly, and she couldn't shake them off. Her skin crawled, and her stomach tried to expel contents that didn't exist...because she never ate dinner. *Because that stupid selfish asshole didn't take you to dinner... he picked you up for a booty call. Oh god.* How could she have been so *weak* as to believe everything that came out of his mouth? The insides of her chest literally felt as if they were on fire, and she could not take a breath deep enough to calm her brain. She had become a cautionary after-school special. *Don't sleep with the smooth-talking pretty boy. It's like the first lesson girls learn from watching Lifetime movies, you incredible idiot. You are going to be the laughing stock of the entirety of GCH.*

The longer she sat, the number of nausea-inducing thoughts entering her brain increased. She had to assume that everything Kim "heard" was true. That he was still hooking up with Jenna. The image of him slipping through the sliding glass door the night of homecoming played on repeat. He'd been outside doing god knows what after they had just... And she let him snuggle right in next to her afterward. The possibility of actually vomiting was becoming more real by the moment. Shaking, she pulled her phone out of her purse. Her thumb hovered over Courtney's name for a while, until she decided against making that call. While it was true that her best friend would talk her down, she also knew she'd be distraught and disappointed in hearing her like this. Their whole friendship was sort of built on Vanessa being the outgoing, fearless one, and Courtney being the more levelheaded and timid one. Not that she wouldn't support her, but Vanessa couldn't envision how ashamed she'd feel in telling the whole sordid tale. Jess was out. The sympathetic type she was not. Kim would get it, but of course they weren't speaking. She was completely and utterly alone.

* * *

Tears came quietly off and on for the rest of the night and into the early morning. She looked like hell, but there was no way she was missing school. At some point during her nervous breakdown, she decided she would show up and laugh and flip her hair and flirt with whomever she wanted and make that bastard look like an idiot if it was the last thing she did. The tears would stay hidden until she was safely in her room that evening. It may have taken a rather thick layer of green concealer to cover up the redness around her eyes, but she looked worthy of a cover of *Seventeen* when she was through. Her hair was artfully fishtailed to the side, and her outfit could not have been more cheerful if she tried- a red tank top with red chiffon ribbon threaded throughout the neckline, her favorite blue jeans, and the highest wedges she owned. She chose some oversized sunglasses to keep her eyes hidden whenever possible and a fitted black jacket to keep her from freezing that morning.

Her mom even commented on her over the top put-togetherness as she dropped her off in front of school. She still didn't feel well, but she had a mocha in her hand, which was certain to remedy that, plus two extras for her friends. Well, she hoped they were still her friends.

"I come bearing gifts and an apology," she started off, sliding into the space next to Kim on a silver bench in the front courtyard. Kim's warm eyes already showed their forgiveness, but she took the coffee and listened intently. Vanessa had plenty of time to practice these words during her newly acquired insomnia. "You were saying some things that I didn't want to hear because they hurt, and I tried to hurt you back. And that's not what friends do. I'm sorry, and I hope you can-"

"I'm sorry too!" she blurted out. "I didn't mean to hurt you. It was a stupid thing to bring up; I don't know what I was thinking," she confessed, her eyes now welling with tears. It really wasn't in Kim's nature to hold a grudge, and Vanessa imagined it had been eating her up for them not to speak for this long.

"You were thinking I'd wanna know. Which I should have. But that's a conversation for another day," she explained, throwing her arm around her friend's shoulders and hugging her like they were twelve. She knew she wouldn't make it if she started talking about Zack. Not yet. She had to get through the whole day in character first, and it was time for step two. A head of blond curly hair passed in front of where they were sitting, and she plastered a flirtatious smile on her cherry-glossed lips. "Jared! Come here," she commanded. He looked thoroughly confused, as did Kim, but Vanessa continued on as if it were perfectly natural for her to be chatting up the toe-headed musician before school.

"Hey? What's up?"

"Just come sit with us."

"Did I do something to piss you off?" She narrowed her eyes at him. He was sort of pissing her off currently. She had been counting on his flirtatious nature to make this easy.

"No silly. I just haven't talked to you. How are things with…"

"Valerie?"

"Sure, Valerie."

"Uh, I don't know."

"Hmmm, that's too bad. You're too cute to be single," she giggled.

"Are you high, V?"

"Yeah, are you?" Kim echoed.

"Ugh, no. You two are no fun."

"Yeah, I'll never complain about you having your hand on my thigh, but I also sort of don't want to be run over with your boyfriend's Charger. Or his fist. Really, any part of him."

"Not my boyfriend, so not a worry," she explained, still smiling, still full of cheer.

"Well, if you're looking for a rebound, you've got my number," Jared grinned. "Lovely chatting with you ladies," he stated before he left."

"What the hell was that about?" Kim questioned.

"Just… nothing." Her façade threatened to crumble even saying that much. So instead, she insisted they find Jess before the coffee got cold.

* * *

Zack hadn't been at lunch that day which helped immensely. Vanessa hadn't quite devised a plan for that event, and she had been carrying all of her books around with her in order to avoid her locker. She also managed to avoid running into him after school by having her mom pick her up in the other parking lot after practice. All in all, it was a successful day of evasion. She made it home, did her homework, and ate dinner- all without cracking. Once she was alone in her room, however, she began to feel trapped again by the sheer magnitude of his game and how good he was at playing it. Her phone lit up next to her, and she was afraid to even look. Curiosity got the better of her, though, and she viewed her messages.

Z: Hey, I'm on my way over.

V: I'm at dinner with my parents.

Z: Ah, bummer. Rain check?

V: Sure.

She wasn't really sure why she wasn't cussing him out or slashing his tires. *Something*. Really, though, she needed to be able to do whatever it was without crying. He would not see her come unglued and know he had that power. After she got ahold of herself, she could deal with it.

The next couple of days passed in much the same manner. She showed up looking fierce and chatted with anyone and everyone to solidify the impression that she was doing just dandy. She convinced Kim and Jess to eat in the library to study for their Spanish test on the day Zack stayed on campus. They both looked at her like she'd grown an arm out of her head, but they obliged. He'd texted both nights, and she'd legitimately been at Jess's on the first and feigned illness on the second. She almost felt ready to confront him, and by the frustration coming through in his messages, she could assume that would be sooner rather than later.

* * *

Things got real fairly quickly the next afternoon when Zack showed up at her locker before her final class. "Why does it feel like you're avoiding me? I thought we were good the other night." He started in without so much as a 'hello,' and his arrogant grin was now making her ill instead of making her swoon.

"I have no idea," she answered calmly, searching in her locker for her Spanish book. His jaw ticked at that response, and she felt a deep sense of satisfaction in knowing she was getting to him.

"Don't be a bitch, V."

"Again I say, I have no idea what you're talking about." She finally looked him in the eye, wondering how it would feel to lie straight to his face like he'd done to her. She was taken aback by the gleam of anger emanating from him. He grabbed her wrist roughly and pulled her closer to him.

"Be very sure you know what you're doing before you screw with me," he warned her, sending a shiver down her spine that she prayed he didn't notice.

"There will be no screwing with you. That's a promise." Her knees were practically knocking together, but she knew her meaning was crystal clear when he dropped her hand and laughed coldly.

"I find that hard to believe, slut," he spat, loud enough for people around them to hear. He slammed her locked shut so hard the sound sent a clang all the way down the corridor, causing people to look up from their conversations. She breathed out slowly, ignoring the stares. It was done, and it was done without her shedding a single tear in front of him.

* * *

She practically broke into a jog headed out to the parking lot, feeling eternally grateful that her mom let her borrow the Durango. It was imperative to get out of there without running into Zack again. She'd hung back while the lot cleared out, hoping he'd be gone well before she ventured into the courtyard. Their earlier confrontation had been working its way into her mind, and the word "slut" kept bouncing around, causing pain wherever it landed. She'd kept it together during her last class, but as soon as she'd hit the parking lot, the tears had started to form. *You are such an incredible idiot,* she thought as they stung her eyes. Her vision blurred as she searched through the too-large bag for the keys. *Dammit!* Her hands were furiously fishing in all corners of the bag when she heard his voice.

"You look like you could use some help, babe." *Do NOT let him see you cry.* She did everything in her power to continue looking through her bag and avoid glancing upward until she absolutely had to.

"Did we not establish that this," she gestured between the two of them, "was over? I thought that was pretty clear when you called me a slut in front of the entire junior bay not one hour ago."

"Eh, you pissed me off," he shrugged. "Plus, you have to admit, you jumped in bed pretty-"

"You're a sociopath. Get the hell away from me." She glared at him, hoping the expression on her face was defiant. Tears gone, she stood up and squared her shoulders, determined to appear more sure of herself than she was.

"Aw, why? I was hoping I could get a re-play of the other night. I know how much you like the backseat of my car."

"I'm sure you can call Jenna. Or any other number of girls who fawn over your very existence."

"Is that what this is? You're jealous because I hang out with other girls? God you are such a sophomore. Just come over and let me show you they don't matter." He flashed her an arrogant grin and she cringed involuntarily- at both the insult and the thought of being alone with him.

"I do not know how to be more clear that I'm done coming over, hanging out, whatever it is you wanna call it. And right now I'm going home." She swore internally at her shaking hands.

"Yeah, I'm thinking that's not really your call."

"Who else's call would it be?"

He took a slow step towards her, and regretfully, she flinched, making him grin even more. Alarm bells were ringing in her head, and she quickly looked around the parking lot. *Where the hell is everyone?* "Don't worry babe, we're alone." He pressed her against the SUV and brought his lips to her neck.

"Zack, seriously, get off me."

"I hear a proposition in there somewhere," he whispered in her ear. Her heart thudded in her chest. *Get out of here.* She took a step to her right but he grabbed her wrist harshly.

"Let go of me. Now. We are done here." Thankfully, her voice sounded strong. "We are done, period, you son of a bitch." She didn't even see him move, but felt her head jerk sideways and a searing pain radiate through her cheek. More tears formed immediately.

"Again, that's not really your call." His voice had lost all amusement. She pressed her hand against her cheek and kept her eyes cast towards the ground, willing herself to think of a way to get out of this. The air around her was not cooperating with her lungs. *Just tell him you'll meet him later. Lie, lie, lie, lie.* She began to straighten up, and as her frightened eyes found his glaring ones, he was suddenly and forcefully pulled backward and onto the asphalt.

"You are so going to regret the last five minutes of your life." Vanessa took in the sight of Luke placing his body between her and Zack, never having been so happy to see him in her life.

She heard a laugh, but there was no humor behind it. "Seriously Miller? Walk away before you cause yourself more trouble than she's worth."

"Yeah, ok, so new rule. From this moment, you don't speak to or about her. Ever." Zack had gotten to his feet and was shooting daggers at them both. She could practically feel the fury radiating off of Luke's shoulders, his fists clenched and his muscles rigid.

"Get bent, man. What do you actually think is going to happen right now?"

"I think if you take one step towards Vanessa, I'm going to deck you in the face. That's what I think is going to happen. So maybe you just walk back to your douche-mobile." Luke was bigger than Zack by probably twenty-five pounds, but Vanessa was flipping out. *He's not seriously going to-*

The rest of that thought was lost in the sound of Luke's fist connecting with Zack's jaw, sending him effectively back to the pavement. "Or maybe I don't actually care if you take a step. Don't.Hit.Women. You 'roided out piece of shit." Luke's voice was low and calm, but no less angry. Zack spat blood onto the gritty parking lot surface. "Not so tough without your lackeys to hold me back, huh?" Luke asked, referencing his almost-healed cheekbone.

"You *will* regret this." Zack was up and walking away, probably more quickly than he'd admit later.

"Not even for a second," Luke shot back, shaking out his hand. "V, get in the car." She didn't move for a moment, still in shock at what had transpired in the past ten minutes. "V," he said more gently, touching her arm and causing her to jump slightly. "It's ok. Let me drive." He took the keys firmly from her and guided her around to the passenger side.

"But. Your truck?" She knew somewhere in her brain it wasn't important, but it was the only thought that showed up.

"It's fine, let's just get you home." She allowed him to help her into the car. All of the adrenaline had left her body and was replaced by uncontrollable shaking. From her pinky toes to her teeth, she couldn't get a grip. He placed himself in the driver's seat and pulled out of the lot slowly. She could only assume he was checking to make sure Zack was not still on the premises.

"I, um, you were. Just..." And then the tears came. Not just for what had occurred right then, but for all of it. For losing a piece of herself to someone who could treat her that way, for allowing it, for making excuses, for being so weak that such a prick would think he could... She just cried. Not a girly cry. A big, ugly, hiccupping cry. She sucked in breaths quickly, not able to get enough air.

"V. You have to take slower breaths. You're going to hyperventilate. You're ok. You're safe. Just breathe." He spoke in an even tone, like any sort of fluctuation in his voice might hurt her. Purposefully, she slowed her breathing.

"I can't. I can't... I don't..."

"You don't owe me an explanation. You don't owe anybody anything. You're ok." She leaned out of the shoulder strap of her seatbelt and onto his shoulder, not caring that it was awkward. She needed to feel something stable, and he immediately put his arm around her and pulled her in tighter. His arms were warm, and she was freezing. Her eyes remained closed tightly on the drive, as if she could keep out reality if she simply refused to acknowledge it. The tears wouldn't stop though. No matter how hard she tried to stay present and recognize that she was physically OK, her mind never stopped imagining what would have happened if Luke hadn't shown up. The look that was in Zack's eyes was almost *happy*- he enjoyed the power he had over her. Vaguely, she realized Luke had shut off the ignition and was now holding her with both arms.

"V," he almost whispered. "Let's go inside." She only nodded, but made no move to get out. Luke hurried around to the passenger door and tugged her arms slightly. "I'll carry you if you want," he expressed sincerely, seeming unsure of how far to push her.

"I can walk," she breathed, sliding off of the seat and onto the ground.

"Is your mom home?"

"Um, I'm not sure? The other car's not here, so I guess not." Her voice sounded off in her own head. Far away. She was mildly concerned she had a concussion, but she didn't think he hit her that hard. He had *hit* her. She had never been hit by anything other than a misplaced arm in a cheer formation. Her feet followed Luke up the walkway to her front door, and her fingers made their way over the painful redness still present along her cheekbone.

"Do you want some ice?" Luke asked, setting her bag on the floor. He hadn't been to her house since her birthday party in seventh grade, but he didn't look the least bit uncomfortable taking care of her.

"Um, yeah, probably. I don't... will it leave a bruise?"

His fingers gently brushed her jawline, tilting her injury towards him. "The ice should help. It's not turning purple yet, so maybe not. You'll know in the morning." He moved into the kitchen and found a bag of frozen peas and a dishtowel, handing them to her. His expression was kind when he looked at her, but his body was still tense. Her gaze dropped to his hand to see that it was swollen.

"Your hand. You need ice more than me," she offered.

"Nah, I'm fine. He just had a hard face." She almost smiled, but that made her cheek hurt more. He positioned himself on the ottoman in front of her.

"Luke..." The only response he offered was a pleading look. She didn't know how to say thank you for this. "Your timing was good. Today." It was the lamest expression of gratitude known to man, but it's what came out. He chuckled slightly.

"I think it could have been a little better," he admitted, pointing at her current state.

"Maybe just a little," she agreed.

"V, I think maybe we should call the police or something. I can call them, and I'll stay with you, but you need to report this."

"No. Luke, no one can know that this happened. Please." Tears started to form again, and their heat pricked at her eyes.

"If he tries to… Vanessa, I can't think about what would have happened if I had left school on time today. I was helping with open gym for new freshman, and that's the only reason I was there. No one else was there, V. He needs to pay for whatever he was going to do. What he *did* do. He put his hands on you." His sea-green eyes searched hers for some form of understanding, but she couldn't do it. She shook her head forcefully.

"You know how small this town is. You know who his parents are. There is very little in this situation that would go well for me." She gripped her knees tightly into her chest. "Please," she begged.

"Do you want me to kill him?" he asked, his tone giving away no hint of a joke.

Her eyes softened slightly at his earnestness. "No, but thank you for offering."

"I'll totally kill him. Seriously. Dead. People would thank me." She laughed through her nose.

"You don't have to stay and babysit me. If you need to go, you can."

"Well, no, I can't. My truck's at school. And if it's all the same to you? I'd rather not leave you alone anyway."

"I'm a big girl, Luke," she pressed, hating that she really didn't want him to leave either.

"Yeah, it's not really for you." She looked at him, confused. "If I leave, I'm going straight to his house. And you told me not to kill him. So it's probably better if I hang here with you for a while."

"Well, as long as it's for your benefit," she agreed, knowing exactly what he was doing.

"Oh yeah, absolutely. Nothing to do with your safety. I mean, who cares, right?"

"Right," she grinned, the ice finally taking the sting away. "Do you want to watch *The Breakfast Club* with me?"

"I don't know what that is, but ok. Is it on the Food Network?" Her mouth opened slightly in disbelief.

"Are you being for real right now?"

"Yeah, why?" She just shook her head and pulled him to his feet with his uninjured hand, leading him down the stairs to her new sanctuary.

"Whoa... this is your project? It's done?" he asked, glancing around the room in awe.

"Yes!" she practically shouted at him. "*That* is the appropriate reaction to this room. Jesus. Thank you," she finished. *Stupid ass,* she cursed to herself, thinking of Zack's blasé response to her design.

"Well, you clearly feel strongly about that," Luke laughed. "It looks cool in here. I mean, there are sort of a lot of pillows, but I like it."

"I do like pillows," she admitted, scouring the built-ins for her DVD. "Here we go," she announced, popping the movie into the player and turning back towards him. "Come, sit," she requested, sinking into the low-backed sofa. The squishiness of the pillows calmed her, and she tugged a pink and gold one to her chest. He fell into the space next to her and stretched his long arms along the back of the couch.

"I like it. It's comfy," he declared. "Are you going to be a decorator or something?" She slowed at the question, not sure if he was joking or not.

"Like... in life?" she asked cautiously.

"Yeah, in life I guess. Do you go to school for it, or do you just do it? Or intern or something. I don't know."

"There are design schools."

"Ok, are you being vague for a reason? Do you wanna go to one?"

"Who knows? Probably not. It's hard to get a job as a designer."

"Well, I would hire you," he mused. She didn't continue on, afraid to sound naïve about being on HGTV or something, but her heartbeat did make itself known at the compliment. "So... I take it this is a movie. Is it about breakfast? Because that sounds lame."

"Just shhh. It's not lame. Don't say that." It was becoming easier to pretend they were just hanging out, and forget that the whole reason he was here was because she was literally assaulted in a parking lot an hour before. *No. Don't go back there,* she scolded her brain. She felt safe with Luke there, and *The Breakfast Club* could only bring happiness, so she let the hurricane of reality fade to the outskirts of her focus. Silently, she forked over the frozen peas for his hand, and this time he didn't argue. "Do you need water or anything? I have snacks..." she trailed off, suddenly aware that she was being a terrible hostess, which was not like her. *Not that this situation is particularly normal in any way.*

"I'm good. No worries," he assured her, nudging her shoulder slightly with his outstretched arm. She leaned back against the cushions and draped her stocking clad feet across his lap. The non-awkwardness of the situation was beginning to weird her out. The opening scene was finally up on the screen, and she let herself be transported to Shermer High School.

* * *

"Vanessa," her mom's voice sounded softly. She was too comfortable to possibly wake up. *What time is it?* she wondered. She lifted one eyelid.

"Hmpf."

"Nessa, I need you to wake up." Her mom never called her Nessa... since she was about seven anyway.

"What's wrong?" she asked, now concerned.

"That's what I was going to ask you." Her mom's brown eyes were glimmering with worry, her mouth drawn in a tight line. The events of the day started to make themselves known in her head.

"Oh."

"Yes. Oh. I just took Luke back to his car."

"Luke? Oh god, I fell asleep? What did he say?" She would kill him if he spilled his guts to her mom.

"I'm really more interested in what you have to say. What happened today? I promise I'll just listen. Please tell me the truth."

Vanessa swallowed hard, her throat sticky from crying. "I don't... I don't think I can."

Her mother's eyes teared up at her admission. "I know that... things between us aren't easy most of the time, but I need you to believe me when I say I'm on your side."

She began to play with her braid instead of answering, contemplating just letting all of it out. The whole truth. How stupid she'd been, how gullible and naïve. There was no way her mom could let her get through all of it without an "I told you so." She sighed, expecting a lecture, but her mom just sat with her, quieter than she'd ever been.

"Can you tell me if you're ok?"

"Yeah. I think I am."

"Vanessa. Are you *really* ok?" For some reason the addition of the extra word and emphasis made her breath shake. No, she was absolutely not ok. She shook her head, unable to get words out properly. She breathed as evenly as she could.

"What did Luke tell you?" She needed to know how angry she was with him before continuing.

"Not much. There was a fight, and he's worried about you." Unsure if she believed that was all he said, she proceeded with caution.

"Zack, ah, he wasn't super pleased when I told him we were done." Speaking was painful as her throat tightened to try to keep her sobs in. "He... he grabbed me, and he was just *so* angry." Even as the truth tried to force its way out, she knew if she confessed it all- that he'd hit her- her mother would call the police. It took physical strength to keep it in. "Luke saw us and laid him out. I don't know where Zack went after that."

Her mom only nodded, several tears making their way through her lashes. Something about their current connection made Vanessa turn into a child again. She just wanted to be told that everything would be OK.

"Has he done anything else...or made you...?" It took her a minute to catch up to what her mother was asking.

"No. He didn't... no." The relief she let off was palpable.

"What do you need?" The question threw her. She had no idea what she needed. A time machine, maybe. Then she could prevent all of it. He wouldn't have a piece of her that she'd never get back, and she could be fighting with her mom about her midriff showing, or how much she spent on magazines.

"I... I don't know. I just don't want to feel like this." That realization, that she had no way of *fixing* it, the pain in her chest, it was heavy, and the dam finally burst. Her mom hugged her in a way she hadn't since Vanessa was small, tightly and protectively.

"I know..." her mother repeated to her until her breath evened out. "Vanessa... I have to ask you something, and it is important that you're honest, even if you don't want to be." Vanessa just looked at her with trepidation, wondering if she knew more about that afternoon than she'd let on. "Were you *safe*, with Zack?"

Vanessa stared at her blankly, unsure of how to take that question.

"I'm not asking to get you in trouble. This is more important than that. I need to know if you should see a doctor."

"Oh," she breathed, the reality sinking in that she and her mother were having a safe-sex talk. "Yes, we were safe." She was fairly certain that her body temperature was at a dangerous level from her discomfort trying to convince her to crawl out of her own skin to get away from this conversation.

"Ok. Good." The suspended moment in time they'd been sharing was over, and a new feeling settled over them. It was as if, in the time they'd been sitting there, her mom went from seeing her as a kid in need of reprimand to a young adult in need of a confidante. It was unfamiliar but not unwelcomed. "Do you want pancakes for dinner?"

"I'm not really hungry, to be honest. But for breakfast tomorrow?"

"I can do that," her mom promised, moving to get off of the couch. "And Vanessa?"

"Yeah?"

"You show up to school tomorrow looking like a Miss America contestant, ok? He's not worth the heartache, and he needs to know that," she advised. Vanessa almost snorted through her nose at the image of her walking the halls with a sash and a crown. School was a million miles from her thoughts, but she nodded to acknowledge her mother's comment. Her body relaxed for a few minutes, and she foolishly began to believe she was OK. It was all fine until her mind found its way back to the vomit-inducing thoughts of their last "date." It pissed her off even more that the first time she was really able to sit in her beautiful new basement was forever going to be marred by this disgusting day.

With difficulty, she hauled her butt up the stairs to take the hottest shower she could stand. There had to be some sort of layer of Zack scum on her that needed to come *off*. She stayed in until the water ran cold. Once in her room, she promptly took her purple dress and buried it in the garbage can. *Never again.* Not wanting to stand in front of a blow dryer, she braided her hair tightly and found the largest pajamas she owned. Only after she was wrapped in a sweatshirt and blanket did she stop the slight tremor in her hands. She even dared to pick up her phone, wanting to ignore it, but knowing she would never sleep wondering what people were saying. She only had two messages, both from Luke.

> L: Hey, I just wanted to make sure you were OK. I wanted to wake you up when your mom got home, but I thought maybe you should sleep?
>
> L: Just let me know you're ok.

Well, it might have been a miracle, but it appeared that the Gem City rumor mill hadn't gotten ahold of this one yet, which meant she could sleep for now and deal with whatever she was going to face at school later.

> V: I'm ok. Thank you- for a lot of things, but also for not giving my mom a play-by-play.
>
> L: I'm not gonna say I didn't want to. But I guess you're welcome. Do you want me to pick you up in the morning?

As tempting as it was to take Luke up on his apparent desire to be her personal bodyguard, she did not love the added layer of feeling helpless on top of everything else.

> V: Thank you, but I think I've gotta be all right on my own. I'll see you at school though.
>
> L: Ok. If you change your mind… text me. See you tomorrow.
>
> V: See ya.

Her brain was beyond the point of exhaustion, and she was asleep before her eyelids had time to flutter.

♪ *"Bad Blood" – Taylor Swift*
(Performed by: Tanner Patrick)
"Don't Turn Around" – Ace of Base
"Fire to the Rain" –Adele

20

Vanessa found herself sitting on the edge of her bed the following morning, fully dressed but unable to leave. *What the hell is going to happen when you see him?* The idea of him being at her locker or waiting for her after school was too much. Her muscles already wanted to go into fight or flight mode, and she wasn't even actually looking into his soulless blue eyes yet.

V: Pick me up please.

L: I was already on my way.

She let out a long breath, knowing she'd typically be annoyed at him for treating her like she couldn't take care of herself, but in this instance, his arrogance was a welcomed trait. While her mother had told her to go all out with her wardrobe, she went understated instead and paired a black sweater with jeans and boots. Her mermaid necklace remained her only jewelry while her blond hair hung in waves from the braids. Her cheek hadn't bruised. It was one less thing that she had to explain, and for that she was grateful.

Once downstairs, she scarfed down four chocolate chip pancakes under the watchful eye of her mother, though she seemed satisfied with her renewed appetite. When Luke's truck pulled up outside, she grabbed her bag and hurried towards the door, not particularly wanting her mom to have a second chance to speak with him.

"Vanessa- take these to Luke, will you?" Her mom held out a foil wrapped paper plate full of pancakes. Vanessa's gaze softened as she realized they were gratitude pancakes.

"Sure, thanks." She squeezed her mom into a hug. It was probable that when her dad returned from his trip that evening, there would be further uncomfortable conversations about what happened with Zack, but she felt closer to her mom than she had in many moons. Plate in hand, she walked carefully down the front porch steps and out to the truck. Luke hopped out to open her door like he was a southern gentleman or something.

"Good morning," he greeted cheerfully, almost like his usual self- minus the manners.

"Morning," she murmured. "These are for you," she explained, placing the plate in his hand.

"You made me food?" he asked incredulously.

"No, I carried you food. My mom made it."

"Sweet, I might actually eat it then," he shared, his eyes shining before closing her door. She only had time to glare at him. Once he started his truck, she shut off his stereo as soon as the beat dropped. "Did you literally just touch my stereo? And cut off the new Lil Wayne album?" His tone was harsh, but his eyes were playful.

"Yes and yes. It's too early for Lil Wayne," she declared, finding a station more to her liking on his radio.

"You are a brave woman, Vanessa Roberts. I could have taken your hand off for that."

"Yeah, yeah. You're so big and bad. I'm shaking in my actual boots," she teased. He raised an eyebrow at her and reached his hand over the center console. She thought for a brief moment he might try to hold her hand, but at the last moment, his fingers dug lightly into her side just below her ribs. "Oh my god!" she squealed. "Do *not* tickle me." She grabbed his wrist to fend him off.

"Sorry. You can't just get off without any consequences," he explained calmly, pinching her side one last time before turning his music back on.

"*Rude*," she chided him. "And you should be watching the road anyway." He almost snorted. A snort didn't quite suit his features. A semi-awkward silence filled the cab of the truck as they both struggled to find something to fill it that didn't involve the previous afternoon. His hand was cleaned up, though it still looked a little gnarly. She cleared her throat nervously. "Any idea what we're going to walk into today?" she asked quietly. He glanced at her out of the corner of his eye.

"Honestly? Probably nothing. No way he's going to admit to people that I get the better of him, or that he… well, you were there. I was surprised when he didn't make a thing out of giving me that black eye the other day. I'm still not sure why he didn't run his mouth."

"*Zack* gave you that black eye?"

"Oh. Yeah. I thought you knew that after yesterday, sorry. We, ah, kind of got into it in the locker room. His douchnozzle of a friend practically tackled me first, though."

"Jesus, Luke. Why didn't you say anything? An accident in PE, really?"

"Would you have listened? Honestly?"

She gave a silent response, knowing she wouldn't have. "Wait. Yesterday… you called him… is he on *steroids*?" She had blocked out a lot of the details from their altercation, but now there were some things that started to click in her mind.

Luke sighed. "I'm like ninety-nine percent sure. He's not doing them very *well*, mind you, but yeah."

"How do you do steroids *well?* Stop. You don't…"

"God, no. V, seriously? Come on. I don't even get flu shots. They freak me out. And I just mean… most guys who, like, enhance themselves, or whatever, are actively trying to get ripped. In the gym every day, eating only lean proteins, etcetera. Your boy was eating like crap and is one of the laziest sons of bitches I've ever met. Sorry for my language," he added as an afterthought.

"He's not my boy," she replied solemnly.

"I'm sorry. I know. That was a stupid thing to say."

"I'm really kind of an idiot, huh?" She thought back to picking up random bags at Rich's, and Zack's angry outbursts. She never even questioned any of it.

"V… you're not an idiot. Your taste in men could use some work, because that guy was a dick long before he ever took anything, but don't like, beat yourself up about it."

"Yeah… I just left that part to him." GCH was coming into view, but she suddenly felt much less prepared. He was quiet as they pulled into the parking lot, and he seemed to purposely maneuver the truck to the furthest possible point from the "incident." She took a few deep breaths, trying to think about putting on a normal face.

"Do you have practice today?" Luke asked, lightening the mood.

"No. We have a break before our insane regionals schedule. Well, as much as three days is a break."

"I have an open gym thing, but I can take you home first after school if that's cool."

"Oh, I'm sure Jess can give me a ride, or I can call my mom. I don't want you to miss practice."

"I'd feel better if I took you home. I won't be able to concentrate wondering if you got there ok. Coach will be fine with me being late. It's just an open gym."

"If you're sure, ok. I'll meet you after school." Luke slid out of the driver's side and came around to let her out. The whole dynamic between them was weird now. He wasn't giving her nearly as much crap as usual. Admittedly though, she wasn't either. She sort of owed him…and when he wasn't being annoying, his jawline was distracting. It was like walking around with a Ken doll. Almost involuntarily, she looked around the lot for the familiar black Charger, and finally breathed when she didn't see it. Still, she scooted in closer to Luke as they walked into the courtyard. It was a natural motion for him to rest his long arm around her protectively.

"Hey guys…" Jess greeted as they walked up. Luke abruptly stepped away from her and put some space between them.

"Hiya," Vanessa responded, trying desperately to remember what she would say on any other day when she wasn't waiting for her sociopathic ex-boyfriend to jump out from behind a trash can. Or ex-non-boyfriend. *Ridiculous.*

"Buenos dias," Luke replied, ruffling Jess's hair obnoxiously before continuing down the hall. "See you later, V," he added as an afterthought.

"What the… why did he just touch my hair?" Jess asked, concerned. She frantically flipped her head over to fluff it back to its unnatural state.

"I cannot claim to know why Luke Miller does anything he does." She meant that truthfully.

"Um, why was his arm around you? Don't you two like hate each other? And where is Zack? And what the hell is going on? You know I'm just going to keep asking you questions until you start talking because I'm so confused right now. Why did he say he'd see you-"

"Jess! No more questions! I don't even know the answers to any of them. Zack and I are no more. That's all I've got for you." The two of them made their way into the building and towards their lockers, Vanessa trying to act natural, and Jess trying not to run into anyone else as she conducted the second coming of the Spanish Inquisition.

"Wait, what? Why? I'm sorry for the alliteration. I just feel like Alice in the rabbit hole or something. You know how I feel about that creepy movie. Giant caterpillar smoking a hooka. Gross."

"Yes, Jessica, I'm aware."

"Don't call me *Jes-si-ca!* I'm not a three-syllable name person."

"I want to understand you, honestly I do, but what does that even mean? *My* name has three syllables."

"It's completely different."

"You're insane."

"And you're deflecting!! What happened?!" She was now digging her nails into Vanessa's arm to slow her pace.

"He just… he's an ass. There was a scene. That's it."

"A *scene,* like Steven Spielberg? Were there dinosaurs? What do you mean a *scene*, I need to knooooooow."

"Just let it go for right now, ok?" Vanessa dropped the playful banter and shot her a serious look. Her façade would not hold with the artillery Jess was shooting off.

Jess pursed her lips, but she backed off. "Do we loathe him?"

"Yes. We *loathe* him," she agreed, mimicking her friend's emphasis. They gathered their things in near silence and started towards first period, though every few minutes, Jess would breathe in purposefully like she had another question to ask before thinking better of it.

Other than that, there was no indication that anyone knew anything of what had transpired in the parking lot. There were no whispers or averted eyes; she didn't have to yell at anyone for staring. She still turned every corner that day with bated breath, not sure if she was about to meet his eyes across the hall. It did not appear that Zack had shown up to school at all.

* * *

"You ready to head out?" Luke's voice came from behind her. She had been watching the parking lot anxiously for any sign of that stupid Charger, but turned to face Luke instead. He had on a pair of mirrored aviators, and while she wanted to scoff at his trendiness, he looked *hot*. Even so, she couldn't let it slide.

"Yeah. Nice shades, Top Gun," she teased. He chuckled and shot her an arrogant grin.

"You know I look good."

"Do I, now?" she retorted, following him towards his truck. He just tugged on her braid playfully.

"Interesting that you didn't disagree." She almost couldn't glare at him for the smile that was creeping out. He had been uncharacteristically quiet during bio, but seemed to be more himself now. "So... how was your day?" he asked, his meaning clear, once they were in the cab.

"Other than Jess? Not a word. You were right, I guess."

"I'm sorry, could you repeat that?"

"Shut up."

"Hmmm, that wasn't quite what I was looking for."

"You were right," she repeated slowly, widening her eyes, making Luke's smile reach his. His expression was satisfied as he turned on something raptastic. She even found herself moving to the beat of whatever it was, and she appreciated that Luke didn't call her on it.

"Thanks for the ride," she relayed as he pulled into her driveway. "Do you think it's too much to hope that all of this just blows over, and I never have to see him again?" she asked, turning serious.

"I'm not sure if you want me to be nice or honest."

"Neither," she sighed. "I guess it was kind of rhetorical. Thanks again though." She turned to get out of the truck and head inside. To her surprise, Luke got out as well and was waiting for her next to the hood of the car. She raised a perfectly plucked brow at him. "You know I can make it to the front door. I'm not an invalid."

"Ah, Vanessa, people wonder why chivalry is dead." She chuckled at the idea of him as a knight, but the laugh died in her throat as she realized how close he'd come to being exactly that. Her face grew warm as she walked up the steps to the porch, remembering him standing in front of her in the parking lot and shielding her from god-knows-what. She silently called out to all of the woman-friendly goddesses in the universe not to let her cry. "Hey, are you ok?" Luke asked, his eyes trying to catch hers. She just nodded briefly and rifled through her backpack for her keys. *Freaking keys. Causing more problems than they're worth.* "V," he stated again. She nodded again, more forcefully this time, but by the time he finally locked her gaze with his, the tears had started to escape. The whole "normal" day had taken all she had. "I'm sorry. I should have said the nice thing. I'm sure it will all be fine. I will make sure it's fine. Even if I have to stand in front of you everywhere you go for the rest of the year to block the sight of him. Just, please don't cry."

"I'm not crying," she managed through a closed throat. "I'm ok. Really, I don't want you to be any later for practice. I'll be fine."

"I'm not going to open-gym. It's for guys who need pointers. Guys who are not me." His hubris made her smile despite the turn in her mood. She finally managed the task of unlocking the door and allowed him in without much more of a fight. "Hold up, I know what will make you feel better," he announced before abruptly turning around and jogging back to his car. *What is his game?* she wondered, narrowing her brows and having a hard time believing he was just in good Samaritan mode.

Throwing her bag and jacket on the couch, she went on a hunt for something even remotely unhealthy to eat in their pantry. *Bingo,* she thought when she came across a bag of chocolate chips. She was unabashedly pouring a handful and funneling them into her mouth when he returned.

"*Really*? Not even bothering to bake anything huh? Just straight from the bag. Respect," he joked, holding out a poorly wrapped rectangular package.

"Whaisis"

"Huh?"

"Whad is dis?" she repeated more slowly, her mouth full of melting chocolate.

"What does it look like? Jesus, it's a present, will you just open it?" She shrugged and tugged off the purple paper. Her breath caught, and she almost very seriously drooled chocolate saliva down the side of her mouth when she read the title of the DVD. It was an anniversary edition of *The Little Mermaid,* including the crappy sequels made too many years later to be classics. There were so many raw emotions already floating at the surface of her brain from holding them all in throughout the course of the day. The only new feeling to join the party was something fluttery that made her even more confused.

"I love this," she managed. "Why... why did you have this in your car?"

"Ah... it was for my sister?"

"You don't have a sister."

"Yeah, I know. But can we pretend that I do? And that I bought this for her, but gave it to you instead so you'd stop crying?" He looked almost as uncertain as she did, all traces of his usual arrogant expression worn away and replaced with flecks of... nervousness?

"Yeah. We can do that," she agreed softly. When he started to turn towards the basement, she reached out without thinking. Her hand caught his and pulled gently. The look in his eyes was almost pleading as he turned back around, their bodies much closer now.

"Vanessa, I . . . " He stumbled over his words, very unlike him, and she found herself pulling on his fingers again. He leaned down, almost apologetic in his stance, and she held her breath when he finally kissed her. She had known it was happening. She had, in fact, been the one to make it happen, but still her brain was shocked when it finally occurred. His kiss was tentative, like he half expected her to push him away, but when she kissed him back and secured their fingers by weaving them together, he found his footing and pulled her hips firmly against his. It felt good to feel wanted. And safe. It dawned on her that subconsciously, she was waiting for him to try to press for more, but he seemed perfectly content to stand there and kiss her like it meant something. It was almost sad that such a scenario was surprising to her rather than what was expected. Reality slowly crept back into the space in her brain being occupied by the way Luke's biceps felt under her nails. The fact that she was full-on making out with him in her kitchen gave her pause. She stepped back, shock taking over her face without her consent.

"What . . . Do you? Do we . . . We've always hated each other." The words came out despite the fact that she knew they were a lie. She had hardly hated him when she was plotting his ex-girlfriend's death.

"That didn't really feel like hate. And I've never hated you, V." Luke looked ready to crawl out of his skin as they stood in Vanessa's rooster-adorned kitchen. Yet another movie montage began in her head, and all of his actions over the past months seemed to take on new meaning. Unfortunately, most of those moments running through her mind included Zack, and she began to feel ill at the fact that if she'd listened to Luke in the beginning, she would still be *whole. Stupid proud stubborn girl*, she berated herself. Her heightened breathing brought her back to the present.

"How did you know? To tell me to stay away from him, before anything even happened?"

He looked at his shoes. "I really don't see how that can possibly be useful *now*."

"Tell me." The mild nausea her memories had induced began to increase. "It's making it worse with you just standing there like you're hiding something."

"He just… he's not shy about… things. When he's around his friends. And I doubt any of it's even true, he just… *dammit*. He likes to run his mouth."

"What kinds of things?" Luke leaned his head back and groaned to the ceiling.

"I can't talk about this."

"I asked *what kinds of things*, Luke."

"About… stuff you guys did, or what he wanted to… at homecoming. Jesus, Vanessa, please don't make me do this. I already got punched in the face for telling him to lick an electrical outlet." Luke's breathing had picked up, and he refused to make eye contact with her. *He thinks you're a slut too*, she realized, listening to him dance around what he knew. Her stomach heaved as she envisioned Zack's friends and god knew who else sitting around thinking about… *Oh god*.

"You couldn't have mentioned any of this *before?* Your timing really blows, Luke. How could you let me stay with him knowing…I don't even want to know what you know. I want to throw up."

"I *tried*, Vanessa. You don't effing *listen,* ever! Would you have even heard me if I tried to tell you all of it? Or would you have told me to go to hell? If you think that I don't regret doing more, you're dead wrong. As soon as I saw his hands on you, I knew I didn't do enough. I can't get that image out of my freaking head." Somewhere in her mind, she knew he meant the parking lot, but that wasn't the image she was concerned about people getting out of their heads. The settling wave of humiliation had knocked her off her feet, and she was in no state to admit that he was right.

"Well I guess all of this explains the kiss. And why you've been so... nice. At least I figured that out before I made myself look any worse."

"What the hell is that supposed to mean?"

"If you're hoping that I'm just easy, you can kiss my ass. Figuratively," she added angrily.

"You're *joking*. You're pissed at me because Zack was talking shit... and I stood up for you, and I beat the crap out of the guy, and I freaking brought you a mermaid. You seriously think I'm just looking to get some? I could go troll the freshman hallway if that's what I wanted, and you *know* it."

"You're so full of yourself."

"Un-believable," he growled.

"You can go."

"Yeah, I gathered that. Enjoy your stupid movie." She let the front door slam before she dissolved to the floor, unable to shake off the knowledge that when any of those guys looked at her now, all they would see was a whore-ish sophomore who tried to sleep her way to popularity. *You are the walking embodiment of a cliché.*

21

A mass of red hair nearly assaulted Vanessa when she stepped onto the sidewalk the next morning. "True or False- Zack got into a fight with some guy from Central over *Jenna*, and that is why he's sporting a messed up face?"

"Run that by me one more time. I'm tired." This was true. Another night of nearly zero sleep had resulted in lovely bags under her eyes.

"This is what I hear. Zack, Jenna, guy from Central, punch punch pow."

"He's very good," she admitted, more to herself than to Jess.

"Soooooo, false?"

"False. But I don't wanna expand on why right now. Ok? I gotta keep it together knowing he's on campus today."

"Fine. Ummmm, why are you wearing sweats?"

"Oh my god, are you in charge of coming up with new ways to make me depressed? I feel like crap, I wore sweats. They're still *Pink*. You'd think I'd shown up in gold lame stirrup pants or something."

"Actually, I hear those are making a comeback," Jess retorted, now completely interested in that discussion. With herself. Truthfully, Vanessa had tried on fourteen different outfits, all of which made her feel like she was trying to draw attention to some area of her body, and it became too much. The way Luke had looked at her, like he was embarrassed *for* her, was enough to make her want to transfer schools. Or apply for a foreign exchange program. By third period, no less than seven people had asked her if she was sick, and she was starting to feel like she was ill indeed. *Only in this town are sweatpants cause for a national state of emergency.*

After taking in her surroundings when she trudged into bio, Vanessa nearly pivoted and walked right back out. There was a lab set up on all of the tables, and Luke's arms were already crossed in front of him in a hostile gesture. *Shit shit shit. Could this day get worse?* With shoulders back, she marched to her seat without a clue as to how they were going to act. There was so much anger lying in wait just under her skin, but she was having a difficult time remembering why exactly she had unleashed all of it on Luke. *Because he thinks he has to save you. And he kissed you, thinking you were going to hook up in the middle of your kitchen.* She was searching her brain frantically for any way to make those reasons sound less asinine. *Shiiiiiiiiit.*

She was suddenly struck with the knowledge that she had no idea how to sit properly on the stool. It was either she was having tea with the queen or she was an invertebrate. *What the hell is wrong with you?*

"What is wrong with you?" Luke questioned, looking at her like she was an idiot.

"*Nothing,*" she snapped back. "This chair is just uncomfortable."

"Uh-huh. As it has been since the beginning of the year. Perhaps you're feeling uncomfortable for some other reason." He now looked more intrigued than angry, his head cocked to one side, but she was starting to feel much better about being mean to him.

"I can't imagine what you're referring to."

"I can. It involves you flipping your freaking lid over *nothing.*"

"It wasn't nothing." Whatever had happened, been discussed, thought about... it wasn't nothing. She still felt the aftermath of it.

"How is it even possible that you take literally *everything* I say the wrong way?" He had been attempting to be discreet, but his volume was slowly creeping up to attention-gathering levels.

"Can you just... we can talk about this later."

"Or not. Whatever." His arms resumed their former position across his chest, and she knew he was flexing his stupid muscles at her. Her fingernails were digging into her palms at the memory of running her hands over them. Mr. Lessner finally called the class to order and explained the directions for their cell-cycle lab. The whole scene tickled a memory in the back of her mind, and she actually giggled out loud when it registered. She was about to complete a cell-cycle lab with a very hot, very angry male who had saved her in a parking lot. She was in the *Twilight* zone...pun intended. *At least he doesn't sparkle*, she told herself, making a mental note to relay this story to Courtney at some point. She was the only one who would appreciate the literary parallel. "I'm not even going to ask what you're laughing about," Luke declared once they were set free to work on the first slides. "I think you're off your rocker."

"Blah blah blah. You wouldn't get why I was laughing even if I told you." She let out a sigh and put the first slide under the microscope. He was still glaring at her when she looked back at him. "You can go ahead and glare at me all day. If you've ever met my mother, you know I can handle it." Luke just rolled his green eyes at her and looked through the eyepiece. They continued for the rest of the period with as little communication as possible. Thankfully, they managed to complete the part of the report needed for the day, and Luke was out of the room before the bell had finished its first "ding."

Her ears began to tune out whatever Jess was going on about in the hallway on the way to her locker; she was simply too overcome with regret about the sweatpants. Forcefully, she was jolted back to reality when several manicured nails dug their way into her forearm.

"Ow!"

"Shhh! Just act like we are really involved in our conversation," she advised mysteriously as they arrived at Vanessa's locker.

"Ok? Pretend away."

"Ummmm, it's really hard to think of something to say when I'm really just trying to pretend not to see Zack standing across the way. Like really hard. Raspberries? Can you think of anything to say about raspberries?" Jess's eyes held concern, but Vanessa knew her own held dread. Not that it was a surprise; she'd known he was at school, and that she'd run into him eventually. Risking a glance towards where Jess refused to look, she saw him leaned up against the wall, face still bruised from his run-in with Luke, and Jenna perched at his side, though preoccupied with her phone. Involuntarily, Vanessa sucked in a breath, but unfortunately swallowed at the same time and found herself in a coughing fit. Before she could correct her eye-line, Zack met her gaze and *winked* at her. Legitimately winked like he was some sort of a freaking *winker*. Well, she was almost certain he winked. Her eyes were watering from coughing, but it was a pretty distinct one-eyelid-closure.

A tsunami of nausea threatened to overcome her once she was able to breathe again just thinking about all of it. Him and her and Jenna and homecoming and his car, and that everyone standing over there knew all of it. The *flowers* even. She could never smell tulips again without wanting to projectile vomit. She pulled her jacket tighter around her body, willing all of them to look elsewhere. Rich had the audacity to blow her a kiss and wiggle his eyebrows suggestively, causing her ears to burn. Jess was trying to save her by patting her back, as though that would stop her coughing, but she could finally breathe. And focus on regretting her entire existence.

A much louder voice carried down the hallway. "Hey Roads... That sucks about your face, dude. It looks like shit," Luke conveyed with feigned concern.

"Miller, I swear to god-" Zack spat through clenched teeth.

"Yeah... I don't really buy it, sorry. You can swear to anyone you want though, if that makes you feel better," Luke chuckled as he continued on his way. A smile tugged at Vanessa's lips as he passed her, and then *he* winked at her. She was certain about that one.

♪ *"Bad Day" – Daniel Powter*
"This" – Ed Sheeran
"Why Don't We Go There" - One Direction
"So Yesterday" – Hilary Duff

22

The brick covering the building behind her kept catching on her t-shirt as she leaned on it, increasing her annoyance. Jess had agreed to give her a ride home but was taking her sweet time getting there. Vanessa really just didn't want to be wearing frumpy clothing any longer, and her sneaker began to tap rapidly on the cement.

"What has you looking all pissed off now? Did someone say 'please,' or 'thank you,' or perhaps open a door for you? Want me to take 'em out?" Luke walked up wearing those stupid aviators that she wished she didn't love, his hands shoved in his pockets. He looked like a Hollister ad, and she hated him even more for it when she *again* remembered her ensemble.

"Shut up. I'm waiting for Jess."

"Really?" he asked, sounding oddly surprised.

"Um, yeah."

"Ok, whatever. I could just give you a ride you know. It's Friday, do you really wanna hang around school any longer?"

"I'll walk if necessary." This response made him chuckle. "What? You don't think I could walk to my house?"

"You're now trying to fight with me about your hypothetical walking prowess? Give it up, V. I know you don't dislike me as much as you're pretending to. Get in the truck. I'm driving you home."

"No," she replied coldly, though her face was flushing red at the probable truth in his words.

"What do you want to do then, like what will make you less *this*?" Luke questioned, gesturing rather wildly. His tone was sincere and pleading, and she had to admit that he just seemed to be trying to make her feel better. It made her pause.

"I want to get dressed up and go out dancing," she requested even though that thought hadn't existed prior to this moment. She knew full well he wouldn't do it.

"Then get in the car."

"Wait, really? You don't dance, do you?" She didn't even attempt to hide the shock in her response.

"Of course I don't dance, V. Look at me. I can't be this awesome *and* know how to dance, it wouldn't be fair to the rest of the world."

"Fisher can dance," she said tauntingly, knowing it would make him give her his most annoyed expression.

"Fisher is a freak of nature. He's lucky I find him entertaining, or I would really effing hate him." This made Vanessa laugh genuinely; she already felt better. "I may not impress anyone on the dance floor, but I can sure as shit keep guys from hitting on you. Maybe you can get out whatever girly angst you have going on. Get in."

"We don't have to go dancing, but thank you for offering. I doubt anyplace even has a sixteen and over night on a Friday. They're all on random weeknights. No big deal." His kindness was starting to rub off on her, and she was feeling guilty about being bitchy.

"Yeah, no. We're going somewhere, even if it's not dancing. Though I've honestly never been happier to be under twenty-one than I am right now," he admitted with a perfectly symmetrical grin. It didn't sound like it was really open for discussion. She looked at him for a long moment, not sure how she felt, but the sincerity of the look on his face made her melt a little inside. Stepping towards him, she surprised herself by standing on her tiptoes to kiss him on the cheek. Making her way around towards his truck, she didn't look back at him, but she could feel him smiling anyway. The weight sitting on her chest had dissipated for the time being, and she remembered how much she liked the taste of oxygen.

"Can I go home and change before we go anywhere?" she blurted out, really ready to feel more like herself.

"You don't need to, but yes, we can."

"And then we can go to a movie?"

"Which movie? A girly one?" he questioned, a pained look on his face.

"Absolutely not. I think there's a Die Hard marathon playing at the Columbus."

"That movie theater is lame. And it smells. We can go to Fairfield."

"But... Die Hard." He looked over at her with an admonishing glance.

"All right. Die Hard," he agreed.

"And we can smuggle in candy?"

"Again, not necessary."

"That's not the point. It's about rebelling against the establishment."

"Who *are* you?" His tone was flat, but his face gave away that this was exactly what he'd wanted when he insisted on taking her out- her regular sassy self.

"I'm Vanessa, and I like to break stupid rules for kicks. So can we?"

"Yes, we can smuggle in candy." Vanessa just gave a satisfied smile as he turned onto her street.

"I'll be right back. Do you wanna come in or stay out here?"

"Are you asking for my assistance in changing your clothes? Because then I am one-hundred percent coming in," he confirmed with the return of his arrogant grin.

"*No*, Lucas," she scolded him. "I was being polite."

"Manners are overrated. I'll be here," he responded, still beaming at his own joke. She flitted up the front steps and found herself smiling too. Him flirting openly with her should have been weird. They'd only ever sparred before, or annoyed the crap out of each other. This was different. Her feet carried her happily up the stairs, and she began the ritual sacrifice of clothing in her closet. None of her normal going-out outfits were right, ergo they landed on the floor. Every garment she laid her hands on, she knew Luke would make fun of in some way or another. About fifteen minutes in, he honked the horn at her. *Shit,* she thought, still standing in her bra and a plaid mini-skirt she'd just decided was the ugliest thing ever to grace her presence. It was too cold for it anyway. She spied a pair of nearly shredded jeans peeking out from under her bed, and sighed relief when they appeared to be mostly unwrinkled. After a white tank top and a black leather jacket and boots, she felt a little bit like Sandy from *Grease*, but it was going to have to be OK. There were worse female leads to resemble on a date, she supposed. If this was even a date. *Is this a date? Oh my god.* The front door opened, and she jumped.

"I am coming up there, so you better be decent. Or not. Really depends on-"

"I am ready, geez. Don't get your panties in a bunch," she voiced nonchalantly, appearing breezily at the top of the stairs and going down to meet him.

"Really? You had to use that word? You know I can't let that go. I-"

"Do not finish that statement. We are going to see Die Hard. Vamanos."

"As you wish," he agreed, allowing her to pass him at the bottom of the staircase. Vanessa locked up the house and was surprised when Luke reached back for her hand.

"Are we-" she began before thinking better of it. Instead, she laced her fingers with his and marveled at how nervous she wasn't.

"Are we what?" he asked, pulling her along.

"Nothing," she chirped. She was going to make a snarky remark along the lines of *are we really going to hold hands in my driveway,* but she was thankful her brain hadn't let her get away with it. As it turned out, she quite liked holding hands in her driveway.

* * *

"All right. What kind of candy do you like?"

"I don't really like candy. I'm more of a chip guy."

"I'm sorry, what?"

"I like *chiiiiiips,*" he repeated slowly, and she swatted him on the arm fairly hard, making him laugh.

"I *heard* you, I just don't think we can be friends if you're actually telling me you don't eat one of the main food groups."

His eyes danced a bit at her frustration. "Fine. Pick out some candy for me, and I will eat it. But I'm getting chips too."

"Suit yourself. Chips are hard to smuggle. They make too much noise." He just rolled his eyes and grabbed some Doritos noisily. As a literal kid in a candy store, she weighed her options before choosing several candy bars to cover her chocolate craving, then onto the movie staples- Red Vines, Milk Duds, and Sno-Caps. She didn't even like Sno-Caps; they just looked like they belonged in glass case at a multi-plex. "K, done."

"You're joking."

"I don't joke about candy. Or movies."

"Fine, fine," he acquiesced and paid for their snacks. Standing by and watching him pay for their food made awkward feelings take up residence in her stomach. Money had been spent. Now it was like a date. *A date with Luke Miller,* she thought, having flashbacks to eighth grade when she was determined to catch his attention.

"Earth to Vanessa. Are you ready?"

"Huh? Yeah, of course."

"What were you thinking about there?" he asked, clearly amused with her zoning out as they headed toward the Columbus theater.

"Just, you know, stuff. Things, and such."

"Things and such. You are an *awesome* bullshitter," he declared facetiously. He had really good eyebrows, she noticed. They moved up and down very dramatically when he was animated. They weren't wishy-washy eyebrows with stray hairs popping out willy-nilly- just good solid, manly eyebrows.

"You have good eyebrows." He paused and looked at her, and she felt good about catching him off-guard. It was not often that he had nothing to say.

"So you were thinking about my eyebrows?"

"No. I was thinking about the crush I had on you in eighth grade. Then I was thinking about your eyebrows." For no particular reason, she felt bolder sitting there in his truck. His brows had hypnotized her. *You might be losing it,* she thought seriously. She did feel a certain sense of comfort in hanging out with him, though. Like nothing she said was going to shock him... he'd already put up with her worst.

"Yes, my eyebrows are awesome, thanks for noticing. Now about this crush? How big was it? Like, writing *Vanessa Miller* on your notebooks big?"

"Oh look, we're here! That's a shame; this bonding time was super fun," she responded cheerfully. When she went to open the door, however, it was locked. When she unlocked it, it went right back. "Unlock the door."

"Hmmm, that's not the magic word."

"Before I punch you."

"Manners, Vanessa."

"I believe a wise man once said, 'Manners are overrated.' "

"So he did; I remember that fable. I wanna know how hard you were crushing on me. Come on. Scale of one to ten."

"Right now? Zero."

"*Zero,* huh? Let's test that theory." The center console was up and his hands were firmly around her waist before she even had a chance to utter a reply. Her butt slid across the bench seat easily, despite any amount of giggling and squirming, and she ended up sitting on Luke's lap, her lips tauntingly close to his.

"That's cheating. You're bigger than me."

"I am. I have to use my advantage in the name of science. I'm testing a hypothesis. We're lab partners, and you're obligated to help me." Her eyes rolled back hard in her head at his lame metaphor, but she wasn't totally hating the situation, so she kept her mouth closed.

"What's the hypothesis?" she muttered.

"That you're totally still in like with me. And you only fight with me because one, you're stubborn, but two, you like it that I can keep up. Stop me if I'm wrong. In the name of science, of course."

"Who says you can keep up?" she questioned, torn between hating and loving that he *got* her. Something between a growl and a laugh rumbled from Luke's throat, and he leaned forward only slightly to drop a kiss on her lips. She kissed him back slowly, having been more ready for it this time. Carefully, she pressed herself into him, noting the fact that her heart thudded excitedly rather than thundering like a freight train. While she traced his hairline along the back of his neck, his fingers danced along the rips in her jeans and she shivered, shrugging her shoulders into her body.

"I'm sorry," he stopped, "should I not…"

"No, no, no, you're fine. Just, goose bumps," she explained.

"Oh, good. Ok," he breathed. "Do you wanna go in or…"

"Right, the movie," she remembered, struggling with thoughts after drinking him in. He smirked at her flustered reply.

"Told you I could keep up," he stated under his breath, opening the driver's side door and letting her off of his lap. "You, ah, you look pretty, by the way. I didn't say that earlier."

"Aw, thanks. Now put this licorice in your pants."

"I'm sorry, what?" Vanessa burst out laughing.

"Put these Red Vines under your waistband. And the candy bars too. Then cover them with your shirt.

"Don't you have a purse for this contraband?"

"I would, if you hadn't insisted on chips. They take up all the room I've got," she described, showing him the inside of her adorable black suede bag. "Now stop being a weenie and put these in your pants." She shot him a look much too serious for the situation.

"The things I do for you, woman." Minutes later, and after a lot of complaining, Luke was holstered with boxes of candy. "You know this is insane," he stated, walking awkwardly into the old theater. There was a sticky quality to the carpet that was completely unnatural, and the air wasn't exactly fresh either, but it was also where she saw her first movie when she was little.

"Pretty bold words coming from the guy with candy in his underwear. Just sayin,'" she teased him.

"Says the girl who's still going to eat it," he shot back, not missing a beat. She pinched his stomach rather forcefully, making him twist away from her. Abruptly, Luke stopped moving and stood stoically in the middle of the hall while Vanessa appraised the look on his face.

"You all right over there?"

"There are currently Milk Duds in my pants," he managed with a straight face.

"Yes… and?"

"No, like *loose* in my pants. And if I move, I am going to leave an inappropriate looking trail behind me." At that, his composure broke, and he busted up laughing.

"Oh my god," she exclaimed, realizing what it would look like. The laughter bubbled up from somewhere deep and she couldn't contain it.

"This is your fault!" he yelled, but was unconvincing as there were tears in the corners of his eyes.

"Okay okay okay. Here," she giggled, walking over to him, "just shake out your pant leg and I will pick them up." He rolled his eyes and did as she asked. Sure enough, ten or twelve chocolate covered caramels fell to the floor, and she laughed even harder as she gathered them. "Is that all of them?"

"I sure as hell hope so. I really don't look forward to sitting on one of these through a whole movie. These jeans make my ass look good; ruining them would be a shame."

"Well, at least this experience has humbled you," she laughed again, throwing the candy in a nearby trashcan. "Let's go find seats."

"Noticing you're not disagreeing about the jeans though," he reiterated, his arrogance back in full force as he grabbed her hand while they walked.

"I'm ignoring you now."

"Mhm." The theater was almost completely empty, as was typical for their "vintage" film series, so Vanessa chose the middle of a middle row and threw her feet on the chair in front of her.

"See? You totally couldn't do this in Fairfield."

"I wouldn't have to do this in Fairfield because I wouldn't be afraid of what substances lie on the floor there." He wasn't wrong. The older she got, the less charm the place held.

"Shush," she scolded him, trying to wrench her hand away out of spite, but he held on without even trying. "Whatever. Can I have my candy now?"

"I'm sorry, what was that? You want to get in my pants? I feel like that's a little bold of you, V. This is only our first date." She was about to hit him again for his relentless innuendos, but the word "date" threw her.

"So this is a date?"

"We already made out, I put candy in my pants for you, and you complimented my ass. I would venture to say that yes, this is a date."

"We did not *make out.* And you complimented your own ass." He was tickling the underside of her palm with the tips of his fingers, and she was trying desperately not to react. It was driving her insane. "Fine. It's a date."

"Yeah, I know." The lights went down and the previews began. Vanessa unceremoniously reached over and yanked the licorice box from Luke's waistband and opened the package victoriously.

"You're so hot," Luke laughed.

"Shut up."

The movie was as good as she remembered, in all of its late eighties glory. Her heart was appreciative of the fact that Luke actually watched the film. His arm was around her shoulders at times, and his lips found a space below her ear to kiss that she didn't know she liked, but he actually was sort of chivalrous when all was said and done.

"Do you need to get home right away? Or do you wanna go down to the river or something?" he asked, seeming unsure of his question. The chivalry sort of ended there. Her stomach dropped thinking about the last time she'd been at the river. She just shook her head, not sure what would come out of her mouth if she set any words free.

"No, you don't have to be home, or no you don't wanna go anywhere else?"

"Can we just pretend the river doesn't exist for a while?"

"Ok? Am I allowed to take you canoeing on it? Or should I pretend we're going bobsledding? I don't know, that's kind of an odd request."

"You're going to take me canoeing?"

"Yeah. I mean, not tonight, though we could go night canoeing sometime if you're feeling adventurous. I now know how much you enjoy rule-breaking," he explained, raising an eyebrow. "I have the keys to the storage gate, but I figured we could just go during normal business hours. Tonight I thought we could hang out. It doesn't have to be at the river if Mother Nature has done something to offend you."

"We can hang out," she affirmed, "just not there. Maybe at the park? I like the merry-go-round."

"Are you six?"

"Teen, yes."

"Merry-go-round it is." He was incredibly agreeable that day, and she hoped it wasn't all some part of a master plan to get her to sleep with him. *If it is, it's not a very good master plan,* she thought, having decided she may not have sex with anyone ever again. A convent was sounding more reasonable. If she could decorate it.

Once they were back in his truck, Luke plugged in his phone to his stereo and tapped the screen until music filled the car. Vanessa had braced herself for something about "making it rain," but the tune that surrounded her was by One Direction instead. Almost immediately, some form of chiding began to fly out of her mouth, but thankfully, just as quickly, she realized the playlist was for her. So she shut up. At the first stoplight, she leaned over and kissed his cheek. He then proceeded to sing along to every pop song that he'd compiled until they reached the park, and Vanessa felt very strongly that her eardrums could be ruptured. It didn't matter how many times she covered her ears or even his mouth, the boy was passionate about belting it out... really off key.

"Ohhhhhhhh I wanna dance-"

"Oh my god, please stop singing. I will…"

"You will what? Please, continue on," he teased her.

"I will nothing. I will let you live."

"You're so tough, V," he laughed, parking the truck in the darkened lot without killing the engine. At least the park itself was illuminated with lampposts.

"C'mon… put those muscles to good use and spin me on the merry-go-round," she commanded, pulling her jacket a bit more tightly around her chest to block the cooler night air. The rips in her jeans were suddenly very apparent as the breeze nipped her bare skin.

"Yeah, you know I'm not actually going on that thing right? I'm fairly certain it was built in 1923, and it is probably a death trap," Luke explained, meeting her around the side of the vehicle.

"Then why agree to come?" she asked, suddenly a bit more nervous about why there were in a dark parking lot.

"Because I was planning on making an ass out of myself at the river, but that is now forsaken ground, so I agreed to come here."

"Why would you be making an ass out of yourself?"

"Because I'm going to ask you to dance to some ridiculous song, sung by a bunch of no-talent, sell-out mother-"

"You're going to ask me to dance?"

"That was the plan, yeah." It was so odd to see him look at all vulnerable, though he honestly appeared more annoyed with the whole idea than anything. His green eyes remained in a half-rolled position, and he leaned against the tailgate with his arms crossed.

"Why- no, forget that. Just ask."

"Can we dance to a really lame song?"

"What a lovely invitation, of course," she replied with a straight face. His body finally relaxed with the emergence of his more recognizable grin, and he popped open the passenger door to choose the soundtrack he wanted. An old Ludacris song came on first, and Vanessa scowled at his back.

"Sorry, sorry, not the right song, don't lose your temper," he called over his shoulder. The song "Story of My Life" began to boom through his speakers, and he turned around smiling, very proud of his selection. *God he's cute.* He held out his hand like freaking prince charming, and she couldn't help the eye roll that found its way to her expression, though it was more contented than annoyed. She curtseyed back and placed her hand in his. Slowly, he pulled her towards him and wrapped her arms around his neck. Rather than looking into his chest, she tilted her chin up to meet his eyes. Taking advantage of their proximity, Luke gave her a picture-perfect nose graze before kissing her. It felt like, after this, there was no going back. They couldn't blame this kiss on the heat of the moment, or an error in judgment, because the whole night was a fire they'd meant to light. And lit it was. His hands grasped her ribcage under her jacket, and the kiss couldn't have been more romantic if he'd take notes from Romeo himself. The only piece missing to her movie montage was rain, but she suspected that took quite a bit of cinematography to actually look good. "This should have been how homecoming went, by the way," he murmured.

And with that? The lovely moment they were having evaporated into a cloud of *you shouldn't have said that.* Her hands dropped from his neck to her sides, and the spell was broken.

"Ah, what did I say?"

"Nothing," she stated coldly and rather passive-aggressively.

"V, I didn't mean to bring up... I'm sorry." He looked genuinely apologetic, making her hostility die down a little. It was just the stupid *memory* of her own stupid stupidity from that whole night. She'd just *let* Zack treat her like she... *Stop thinking about it.*

"Just... I can't think about that right now. Your timing sucks."

"Not the first time someone has told me that. I didn't think..."

"Clearly. Whatever, it's fine. It's cold anyway, we should probably get going."

"I totally lost all of my smoothie points for the dancing in the park, huh?"

A small smile returned to her face at that remark. "Not all of them."

"Good to know." He opened her door and lingered for a moment while she got in. "So, if you're already mad at me, does that mean I get to listen to my own music on the way back to your place?"

"Not even the tiniest of possibilities." He chuckled and started the car, beginning the whole four-minute journey to her house. Despite his faux pas of mentioning homecoming, she didn't mind when he reached for her hand.

"Can I walk you to the door?" he asked, seeming unsure of where her head was. She wasn't entirely sure either.

"Of course. That's part of the new chivalry thing you have going on, right?"

"Right." They sauntered up the front steps and stopped in front of the door, playing out a scene from every chick flick ever produced. "How mad at me are you? Should I be afraid to kiss you goodnight?"

"Moderately mad. And no." The corner of his lips twitched upward before he kissed her squarely on the mouth.

"I am sorry. I wanted tonight to be… well, when you're happy, I'm, I don't know. It's good when you're happy." A sigh escaped her, taking with it most of her moderate anger. Hastily, she stood as tall on her toes as possible and kissed him back in earnest this time. He still tasted vaguely of licorice, and that almost made her laugh. He was playing with the ends of her hair while she traced a path down his ridiculously solid arms. *Is he seriously flexing right now?* she wondered. *Probably.* That kiss turned into five minutes, and then ten, and Vanessa was starting to think they might have to relocate. Then the door opened with a creak and interrupted their goodnight.

"Good evening Luke," her mom greeted them dryly.

"Mrs. Roberts, lovely to see you. I was just on my way out. V, I'll call you."

"Mhm," she agreed minimally, humiliated by her mother's spying. There was no lecture that would help her jumbled mind at that moment. She still giggled a little at the cartoon-ish speed with which Luke vacated the premises.

"Drive carefully," her mom called after him, leaving the door open for Vanessa to enter. Much to her surprise, she went back to her book on the couch, and nary another word escaped her lips. Vanessa wasn't one to look a gift-horse in the mouth, so she scurried upstairs and tried to keep all of her relationship baggage at bay. Instead, she focused on that freaking kiss- the kind she could still feel tingling in her toes as she fell into her unmade bed and pulled the covers tightly around her.

V: You might have gained some smoothie points back. Thanks for tonight.

L: Thank god. I thought I was going to have to come back with a boom box tomorrow and serenade you from under your window. You've heard me sing, so I'm sure your neighbors thank you for this text :P. I had fun tonight. Thanks for making me put candy in my pants. It was a new and liberating experience.

V: NO SINGING. You're welcome. Goodnight.

♪ *"Nobody's Fool" – Avril Lavigne*
"Bye Bye Bye" – N'Sync
"1000 Ships" – Rachel Platton

23

It was a bad sign when she awoke to the sound of the vacuum and it was still dark outside. When her mom got a bug up her ass about *anything*- a diet, cleaning, organizing, the latest fitness craze, *anything*, they all suffered. *Maybe if I just keep sleeping, she will get bored and go away.* This line of thinking was futile, of course, the same as hoping a hungry bear would simply walk away from that tasty picnic basket. Mere seconds passed before-

"Up up up girly!"

"Mommmmmmm, it's Saturday." Vanessa desperately clung to her soft purple pillowcase.

"Yes. A day full of possibility. You've been moping around here for too long, but if you're energized enough to tangle tongues with Luke Miller, you're energized enough to go with me to yoga. Up."

"Please, for the love of all that is holy, do not *ever* use the phrase 'tangled tongues' again. I'm going to vomit."

"No, you're going to yoga. Namaste. Get up." Her mother unceremoniously pulled all of her covers off the bed and marched out of the room. She heard them being shoved into the washing machine in the distance. Petulantly, she kicked her feet in the air like a four year old before accepting her fate. She put on a pair of oversized sweats and a t-shirt, knowing it would piss off her torturer. Her hair was in a messy bun by the time she made it down the stairs.

"Vanessa," an annoyed tone called out.

"Mother."

"You have nice workout clothes. That you insisted you had to have. That cost a pretty penny. Find them."

"You want me to yoga before the sun? I wear this." It was painfully obvious that her mom was trying to decide if this was a battle she wanted to fight. Apparently, it wasn't.

It was proving difficult to find her Zen, or align her chakras or whatever while she was continually swearing at the instructor under her breath every time she said "just breathe into the stretch and relax." Vanessa was plenty flexible, but she was *not* a spotted zebra, or whatever the stupid pose was called. All of the quiet in the room was overwhelming. The quiet led to thinking, and thinking led to feeling, and despite the high note on which she ended the previous night, worries of what was to come with Zack and his friends consumed her. It was an awful feeling to have people with whom she wouldn't even share a flax-muffin knowing the most intimate parts of her life. *Ugh.* Just thinking about it left an acidic taste in her mouth.

"See? Don't you feel better now?" her mother gloated as they came out of savasana.

"I feel entirely the same," she lied. In fact, she felt worse. Being busy was better.

"Whatever you say." The ride home was quiet, but at least her mom let her choose the music. It was a rare day when they weren't jamming out to the local "easy-listening" station. The whole concept of "easy-listening" was ridiculous anyway. *When the music is painful, it's not easy to listen to.* Her phone buzzed, and she was somewhat surprised to see a text from Kim. While they had made up from their fight, it felt like things had changed between them. They somehow reverted back to just "at school friends," after being much closer for several years.

K: Hey. Do you think I could swing by today?

V: Sure. I'm on my way home from the gym now.

K: Ok. Like an hour?

V: Ya, see you then.

Odd, Vanessa thought. Until recently, she wouldn't really have asked. She'd have just shown up. Maybe eventually things would start to go back to normal.

* * *

The doorbell rang while she was finishing up her hair. It was still poufy and un-flat-ironed, but that could wait.

"Hey," Vanessa stated once she made it to the door.

"Hey," Kim replied with a small smile. Even her outfit appeared timid- a cream colored sweater and wide-legged jeans.

"What's up? Is something wrong?"

"I don't know. Maybe. Can we just go downstairs?" She chewed on her lip as she asked.

"Yeah, come in." She led them down the steps and heard a gasp from behind her. "What?!"

"Oh my *god*, V, it's completely finished! I mean, I know you said at school it was finished, but it's like... incredible." She breezed past Vanessa and began to wander around the room. The fact that she hadn't even shown her friend the completion of the space began to make her chest tight.

"I'm sorry Kimmy."

"For what?" she asked, still inspecting the hanging lanterns.

"Just, that things are weird. I can't believe we haven't really hung out since... well, for a while."

"I know. Me too. It was just easier to lay low, I guess. You and Jess had your thing going, but it's fine. Things are fine," she repeated, turning around to give Vanessa a reassuring look. It was unclear where to go from there, and an awkward silence began to stretch out between them.

"So you like it? The room? I'll have to show you the rest."

"Yes, I love it. Like, it's perfect. I, well… can I tell you what I need to tell you first? Because I'm not sure I'll keep up the nerve if I wait."

"Yeah, sit. You're making me nervous."

"I'm making me nervous too," she uttered quietly, her hazel eyes cast downward. "Given our last fight, and whatever's going on with you and Zack or Luke or I don't know, I wasn't sure what to do, but I'm not good at keeping secrets. This isn't gossip. I need to say that before I tell you. I saw… I saw Jess sort of making out with Zack after school yesterday? She, or they, didn't see me; I was leaving late after getting some notes I missed from Mrs. Fletcher, but they were in the hallway, and I turned to go in the other direction when I realized-"

Vanessa hadn't really registered anything after the part about the making out. She struggled to find her normal breathing pattern, the sting of betrayal knocking it out of alignment. It hit later that she'd been waiting for her friend in the parking lot about the same time. Her flashbacks were taking on a new mutation, and she was envisioning Zack with Jess instead, in the back of his stupid car at the river. Or of Jess's feigned solidarity to hate him. "*Loathe* him." Those were the exact words as she recalled. The wave of anger was too strong to meet head on, so she decided to dive under it for a while.

"Are you ok?" Kim asked, her expression almost afraid, and Vanessa snapped back to reality.

"Yep."

"V."

"I'm fine, honestly. They're both single, I guess. Whatever." The more upbeat she attempted to sound, the tighter her vocal chords became. "Hey, do you wanna go shopping?"

"You wanna shop?"

"I always wanna shop, of course. I wore sweats to school on Friday, I have to wear something to redeem myself on Monday."

"Are you sure?"

"Nope, but we're gonna go anyway," she admitted, attempting to address the obvious denial from which she was suffering. Kim relaxed a bit at that, and Vanessa showed her the rest of the basement before they headed to the mall.

* * *

Her arms hurt from carrying far too many garments around for too many hours, but she succeeded in finding an outfit for Monday. And another outfit that was perhaps for the next time Luke asked her out, though she wouldn't have admitted that to Kim despite her numerous attempts to get her to talk about him. It was much too soon to be running her mouth about things with Luke. She had been an idiot with Zack, and she was not going to be that girl again. There would be no getting hurt, no public humiliation, and *no* sweatpants. Ever. Again. She didn't even know if she was mad at him at the moment... she had to investigate further to figure out if he had kept the Jess-kissing-Zack scandal from her.

"Thanks for going with me," she expressed sincerely when Kim pulled up to her house.

"Of course. I really am sorry to be the bearer of bad news. What are you going to do? About Jess I mean?"

"Honestly? I'm not entirely sure. I guess normally I would be devising a plan to dissolve her reputation and make them both look like the slime that they are; I just don't know if I have the energy for it. Does that mean I'm getting old?"

"Can I admit that I'm relieved to hear that? While your schemes are always entertaining, they're kind of terrifying too. Maybe 'growing up' is a better term than 'getting old.' I don't think you can be classified as old before you can legally vote or drink or like, rent a car."

"Maybe," she contemplated. "I'll see you Monday regardless. In this freaking awesome ensemble," she added, lightening the mood and grabbing her bags.

"Sounds good, talk to you later."

After hanging up her purchases, she decided she was capable of getting to the bottom of the Luke matter, even if she couldn't yet deal with the root cause of it.

> V: Are you alone? Call me.
>
> L: That sounds *very* enticing. Are you going to tell me what you're wearing?
>
> V: Omg, just call me.
>
> L: Haha, just a sec

About a minute later, her phone rang in her hand, and she forced herself to wait an appropriate five seconds before answering.

"Are you prepared to be totally honest with me?"

"Hello to you too."

"Yeah, I don't really know if I can be nice to you until you answer my question." He sighed.

"Yes, I'm prepared."

"Did you or did you not see Jessi making out with Zack at school on Friday before you saw me in the parking lot?" She felt pretty secure in the formation of her question, like she was an investigator.

"*What?*"

"You heard the question."

"No, V, I didn't see them making out. I would have told you."

"Would you though?"

"Yes. Stop. I would have. I did see her talking to him, which is why I looked at you weird when you said you were waiting for her. But for all I knew she was ripping him a new one for being a dick to you. I couldn't hear their conversation, and I sure as *hell* didn't see them *making out*. Jesus. Please tell me she doesn't know about-"

"No. She doesn't. No one does but you." She hated that her voice sounded small when she answered. She was just so relieved that she didn't have to be angry with him too that she couldn't control it.

"Shit V, you didn't tell anyone? I should have been better about checking on you."

"Stop, you're not my keeper. And you did check on me. And drive me to and from school, and take me out, and dance with me in the park. I think your conscience is clear."

"And I totally got you all hot and bothered on your front porch, don't leave that-"

"Please stop talking immediately before I hang up on you." He just laughed.

"I'm coming over."

"I didn't invite you."

"Yeah, but you want me to."

"Now you're just annoying me."

"I'll even wear a tank top."

"One, it's fifty-five degrees outside, and two, why do I care if you wear a tank top?"

"Please don't pretend like you're not totally into my guns."

"Are you even a real person right now?" she asked, shaking her head even though he couldn't see her. A reluctant smile crept across her face, however, because he wasn't wrong. *Dammit*, she thought, not really wanting him to know that he affected her. He was still laughing on the other end of the line.

"So that's a yes on the coming over and the tank top then."

"Goodbye Lucas," she teased.

"See you in ten," he replied in the same sing-song tone. Intently, she stared at he closet for a good eight minutes, convincing herself she wasn't going to change clothes because she didn't care if he liked her outfit or not. It was just that the gray-wash jeans and the off-the-shoulder black and white sweater were so much *newer* than what she had on. There was a thing about new clothes. They just hung there having never been wrinkled or folded the wrong way or left in the dryer for three days. They were so crisp and clean. Even while giving herself a disapproving look in the mirror, she knew it was silly to resist. Forty-five seconds later her clothes were changed, her boots were zipped, and Luke's truck was in the driveway. Smiling, she let him wait at the door for a bit before answering.

"Aw, you bought a new outfit just for me," he announced, stepping inside.

"I did not," she argued, her face flushing. He reached towards her and pulled the tag from her sleeve.

"K." His grin almost overtook his face at that point.

"Whatever. Shut up." He had shown up in a gray canvas jacket and jeans, and it made her even madder that she was feeling actual disappointment that he wasn't in a tank top. *Stupid.* He grabbed her hand to start towards the basement, but she wrenched it away and walked ahead of him down the stairs.

"Don't be all butt-hurt that I called out your outfit. You look amazing. I should have led with that, ok? Now let me hold your hand," he insisted as he walked up behind her.

"Fine."

"And let me kiss you hello."

"Fine," she repeated, feeling his hand slip into hers. He smelled like he'd just gotten out of the shower, though his face had a bit of stubble that tickled her face when he pressed his lips to hers. This struck her as funny. She'd never kissed anyone with actual facial hair before. It made him seem more man-ish, which was ludicrous because she'd known him since he was twelve. His large hands held her hips tightly and he kissed her like he'd been missing her. Maybe she'd been missing him too.

"Do you guys need snacks??" her mother called down to them, causing them to break apart. Rather than backing away, however, he wove his fingers back through hers and kept her close.

"No, I think we're good, Mom!" she yelled back, trying to sound like she wasn't out of breath.

"That's a lie," Luke added, "I would love a snack!"

"Coming right up!"

"Your funeral," Vanessa murmured. "I hope you like roasted chickpeas."

"Wait, what?" he asked, now concerned. His worry made Vanessa laugh, hoping her mom really did bring down something disgusting.

"So are we watching *The Little Mermaid,* or what?" She plopped down on the couch and arranged the pillows accordingly.

"Do it up. I don't think I've ever actually seen it."

"Excuse me?"

"What? I'm a guy. It's not a guy movie. I don't have any sisters."

"I don't know what kind of childhood you must have had."

"Not seeing *The Little Mermaid* was the least of my problems. But let's do it, come on. I'm on the edge of my seat."

"What does that-" she began, but was interrupted by a tray of Oreos and milk. "What are these?" she demanded accusatorily at the woman who claimed to be her mother.

"A snack?"

"No no no. Where are the rice crackers or the hummus or the flax seed muffins? How were these even in the house and I didn't know about it?"

"Honestly, Vanessa, you're too dramatic. Just eat your cookies."

"I am not going to forget about this!" she called as her mom sauntered back upstairs.

"And to think you didn't even want a snack. I guess these are mine then."

"Touch my cookie and you will lose a hand," she warned seriously, moving her Oreos safely to a napkin on the end table while she readied the DVD.

"If I get scared will you protect me?" he asked. The intentionally vulnerable look on his handsome face made her let out something between a resigned sigh and a laugh.

"Yes. If you and your big guns get scared, let me know."

"I knew you liked them," he grinned, unzipping his jacket slowly, and, she assumed, trying to look sexy. Sure enough, he had on a green and white striped tank top underneath, and he casually flexed as he laid the jacket across the back of the couch. "You can touch them, I don't mind."

"You are a special breed of conceited."

"Would you like me any other way?"

"Who says I like you this way?" she asked, brow raised, and then squealed because he grabbed her around the waist and pulled her onto his lap so quickly her feet were airborne. He easily held her wrists and tickled her with his other hand. "Ohmygoddonottickleme," she got out between bouts of laughter.

"You are a mean girl, Vanessa Roberts," he declared, "and now you have to tell me that you are totally in lust with my biceps. Or I will continue to tickle you. And I have a *lot* of energy, so don't think you can just wait it out." To prove his point, his fingers snaked lightly across her ribcage and she squirmed, no matter how she tried to fight it. She thought about just kicking him in the head, but that seemed extreme.

"Fine. I like your arms," she gasped.

"No no no. You're in lust with them," he repeated, pressing his fingers into her sides harder. She could hear the opening music to the movie playing just under her incessant involuntary giggles.

"Okayokayokayokay, I'm in lust with them just stop it!" He released her hands and sat her up on his lap, wrapping his arms around her.

"I can't believe you said that, V, you're so forward. It's making me blush," he teased her, prompting her to elbow him in the abdomen. He finally released her completely and laughed, rubbing his side. "I'm just trying to watch this Disney classic, geez. Can you try to keep your hands to yourself for the next hour?"

"Oh, I'll have no problem with that," she assured him, stuffing an Oreo in her face. She got comfy two full cushions away from him and continued to enjoy her snack and sing along to the first songs of the movie. Luke took that opportunity to lay all six feet two inches of himself across the couch, ending up with his head almost on her lap.

"Hi," he whispered.

"Hi," she said back.

"Can I take back what I said about you keeping your hands to yourself? That was dumb. Will you rub my head?"

"Will I what your what?"

"Get your mind out of the gutter, woman, just like run your nails through my hair."

"That is a weird request."

"No it's not, it feels good. C'mon, I danced with you to One Direction. In public."

"There was no one else there."

"There's no one else here."

"Ugh, fine, come here," she agreed, patting her lap, mostly because he looked so earnest when he asked. He scooted himself down another foot so that his head was resting on her thighs. She began to comb her nails through his hair, and it was surprisingly soft and thick between her fingers. "Ok, well you can't just stare at me while I do it. You have to watch the movie." He just smiled and shifted his body so he was facing the TV. She continued to eventually let her nails run down his neck, and she scratched his shoulders and his back lightly. Despite the fact that they weren't even kissing, this felt more intimate than anything she'd done with Zack.

"That feels good," Luke sighed. She risked tracing a trail down his bare arm, confirming that she liked that particular part of his anatomy. She didn't have that kind of intel on him- though being a guy, she could guess where his favorite female body parts were. "Do I have to watch this whole movie before I can kiss you?"

"Yes. It's mandatory."

"It's kind of hot when you hand out demands." She laughed and swatted his arm. The way he could so easily jump between sweet, vulnerable Luke and conceited, inappropriate Luke was sort of starting to grow on her. She liked them both for very different reasons. With one fluid movement, he pushed himself up to a standing position in front of her and scooped her off of the sofa like a bride being carried over the threshold. She let out a squeak but was otherwise amused. Turning, he sat down and situated her on his lap, effectively reversing their previous positions. His eyes gave her a "now what?" look, and she kissed his cheeks, the stubble along his jaw, his ears, and his forehead. He leaned in to find her mouth, but she evaded him.

"I'm pretty sure I said you had to watch the whole movie first." The new look said something like "challenge accepted," and he changed tactics. Instead, he pressed light kisses along her neck and down her collarbone before heading back up the other side. This was ticklish in a completely different way. When he found the spot beneath her ear that only he had discovered, she was done playing. It appeared that he was as well, and he let her break her own rule without another word. When they finally shut up long enough to connect, it was all kinds of *right*.

"Vanessa, is Luke staying for dinner?" her mom called out, causing her to jump and remember where she was.

"Is it tofu related?" he whispered softly.

"He says he would love to, and he hopes you're making tofu!" she yelled back, giggling at the expression of irritation he now wore.

"You know I'm going to tickle you again now, right?"

"Worth it to see you eat tofu."

24

There was no sleep to be found. Every time she closed her eyes, the only things she saw were Jess' French manicured hands pressed into Zack's neck. And she had no effing idea what to do about it. Were it anyone else, messing around with *anyone* else, she'd tell her off, talk shit behind her back, and it would just be another Monday. Jess was a wildcard though. She was the only sophomore at GCH who might be crazier than Vanessa, and it could get very... messy. Not to mention her ego couldn't take anymore. Or her heart, if she was being truthful. As of late, Jess was her closest friend. Courtney would always be her best friend, but it wasn't the same as seeing each other every day and sharing in the moments like she did with Jess. It just freaking hurt to know that she could do this to her. Various scenes played out in her mind's eye- some that ended in blood and others in tears, but she had yet to find a solution that made her feel any better. The worst part was that no matter how pissed off or hurt she was, she still didn't want her friend, or ex-friend, or whatever she was, to get hurt by that creep. The pillow went from under her head to over her head to on the floor maybe sixteen times before she gave up on sleep.

V: I can't sleep.

L: Well I can. It's freaking three am.

V: Yes. You can see the problem.

L: I can. You woke me up.

V: What do I say to Jess tomorrow?

L: Oh. I don't know. This is really girl territory.

V: Bah. Goodnight.

L: Night V.

Despite the hour, she made the call she should have made many times before.

"Hey, are you ok?" a sleepy voice answered.

"Yeah. And no. I'm so sorry to wake you up, I just didn't know who to call."

"You always call me. That's the answer to that quandary."

"You can't possibly use a word that fancy in the middle of the night."

"It's not that fancy. If I were really awake, I would have gone with conundrum first."

"I sort of made a mess of my life."

"Well, start talking then." She took a deep breath and tried to pour as much of her Zack saga as she could stomach without giving away the actual physical nature of the pain he inflicted. It was also possible she tried to downplay her own stupidity in rushing into sleeping with him. Three breaths later, she had somehow spit out a jumbled up mess of words that she sincerely hoped her brainy friend could decipher, so she didn't have to repeat any of it.

"I really am not fond of this *Zack*," she finally replied after too many moments of silence.

"Yeah. I get that."

"Why didn't you tell me any of this was going on, V?" Her tone was soft, but it still induced guilt.

"I don't know."

"Liar."

"I didn't want you to think I was weak."

"I could never think that. You're a force of nature. Fire, most likely. I'm more like water. It's why we work." She smiled at that, for it was the truth. Courtney was levelheaded and deep, though there was a quiet possibility that she could turn into a hurricane if someone pushed her far enough. Vanessa was simply always blazing forward with no thought to what lay before her or the destruction she'd cause... most of the time to herself.

"Please tell me what to do."

"Well... I don't know Jess, but I think even if you can't be friends with her, you owe her the story you just told me. If you walk away at that, at least you tried to spare her from living the sequel. What she did was incredibly injurious, but I think it says a lot more about her than it does about you. If you're happier now, with this other Luke person, then don't let them drag you back to unhappy."

"You make it sound so easy to be calm."

"Eh, I just take lessons from fictional people and apply them to real life. I'm a nerd."

"Stop it, you're not a nerd."

"Oh I am. I'm kind of an oddball, but it's ok."

"So you're telling me to take the high road."

"I suppose I am."

"I've never been there before," she joked.

"The view is nice."

"I'll talk to you later."

"You sure as hell will. I gotta know how this one ends."

* * *

Once she finally got up, Sunday passed quietly in a boring mess of homework, laundry, and a little bit of stewing over the whole debacle that was her weird ex-non-boyfriend/ex-non-best-friend love equation. It may have been a lot of stewing, but at least talking to Courtney had given her some perspective. She would try to keep her temper in check and wash her hands of the whole situation. If she'd had any doubts about Jessica's guilt, they certainly disappeared by Sunday night when she hadn't heard from her friend all weekend. The vindictive side of her wanted to call and trap her in a lie, but she resisted.

Walking into school on Monday, that same resistance was crumbling like the delicious piece of coffee cake she'd convinced her mom to pick up that morning. Just crossing the parking lot was enough to rile her anger in looking at the place where Zack had hit her. She tried to focus on the image of him lying on the pavement instead. *Deep breath in, deep breath out. Now you sound like Courtney,* she realized with her constant mantra chanting. At least the new outfit was working for her. Purposefully, she'd purchased a replacement purple dress. This one was much more modern with a sheath silhouette and long sleeves, which she'd paired with gray boots and a long silver chain. Hopefully, the memory of her Friday ensemble would be forgotten.

The rest of the hallway chatter faded when she caught a glimpse of long red hair in the distance. Her footsteps matched her heartbeat, but when she came up behind her friend, it was like breaking the surface of the water after being submerged. Her brain began working again. "Walk with me," she murmured, linking her elbow with Jess's and pulling, perhaps with more energy than was necessary.

"Ohmygod you scared me. What? Where are we going? My locker is still wide open, and why are you holding onto my arm? Is this a new dress?" Vanessa continued calmly until they reached the library. It wouldn't be her typical venue for such an event because there was usually yelling, but she had committed to trying something new. Once inside, she released the other girl's arm and flipped around dramatically.

"I'm going to pretend for the next five minutes that we're still friends. Then I'll walk out of here and you can do whatever you want."

"What does that even mean '*pretend we're still friends'?*" Jess's eyes narrowed considerably.

"It means that I know you were making out with Zack on Friday. Super classy since I was actually waiting for you to give me a ride home."

"What are you *talking* about?" This was posed more as a statement than a question, but Vanessa figured she'd respond anyway.

"Well, usually *making out* refers to when two people have their tongues shoved down each other's throats. Perhaps there should be a different word for it in this case, being that it was such a shitty thing to do to your *friend.*" The location choice was starting to become an issue as her volume level was teetering on the edge of the inside versus outside voice boundary.

"This is ridiculous, I'm not going to stand here and let you call me a slut," Jess spouted off, turning on her heel to leave.

"I'm noticing you didn't deny it. And if I were you, I'd wanna hear what comes next." Jess took a breath and turned back around, her eyes refusing to meet Vanessa's, and her arms crossed defensively across her chest. She let out a shortened version of her story in a hushed tone, ensuring no tempted ears could hear them. "I'm telling you as someone who's been your friend for the past year, do not get serious with this guy. I don't want him to do to you what he could have done to me." The tears forming behind her eyes were kept in check, and she felt assured she'd done her due diligence in trying to warn the girl. There was nothing left for her to do.

"I don't really think that he *hit* you, Vanessa," Jess hissed as she began to walk away.

"And I don't really think that Friday was the first time you hooked up with Zack, *Jessica*. Happily, I don't give a shit what you think. I was trying to do you a favor, and now I'm done. Enjoy my leftovers." She allowed her lips to turn into a small smirk as she clicked the heels of her boots extra loudly on the tiled floors of the hallway. So there'd been a small detour off the high road with her last comment, but *really*?! *She is such an idiot.* Even as the thought formed, she knew others had probably contemplated the same when she was following Roads around like he walked on water. Now she wished she could hold him under it for a while.

As she strode down the hallway back towards her locker, her breaths were easier, her posture straighter, and her steps lighter. She hurried around the corner towards first period, adjusting the silver bangles on her wrist, and ran smack into the last thing she could handle seeing- which was Luke with his arms around a mousy-haired freshman. Any sense of pride she had about taking the high road with Jess tumbled straight down the rocky cliff with her to the low road. Her brain shut off, and she picked up her pace. He didn't see her coming, and though he was no longer touching the anonymous female, there were too many thoughts of murder or serious injury running through her head to form a coherent sentence, let alone something witty and biting. Instead, she breezed past them both, and in doing so reached up to find the corner of his open locker. She slammed it closed with the force of the tsunami that threatened to be unleashed if she opened her mouth.

Most people around them ceased in their chatter as she walked on, tilting her chin up to combat the anchor in her stomach. *How could he do this too?*

"Whoa whoa whoa," she heard his voice coming up from behind her. She just stomped on into her math class, acting as though it were normal for her to be there ten full minutes before the first bell. He reached for her elbow, and she put all of her weight into wrenching it away.

"Do.not.touch.me," she hissed through clenched teeth.

"Can you explain to me what is going on, like, at all? Because I am totally lost."

"You are worse than both of them, because you pretended to be something else. Go be a hypocrite somewhere else." She took in a gulp of air and whipped her hair around to stalk to her seat before he could see the tear leave her eye.

"I guess I will attempt to talk to you when you've returned to reality," he muttered after her, leaving the room. Vanessa squeezed her eyes shut and took long, deep breaths to steady herself before having to suffer through this god forsaken day.

* * *

Fortunately, there was no lab scheduled in bio, and she was able to convince Mr. Lessner that she'd ripped a contact that morning and was completely blind. He allowed her to switch seats with a boy in the front of the class, meaning she could feel Luke glaring at her the entire period.

"Vanessa," he began as he caught her on the way out the door.

"I was crystal clear earlier. Go away. I'm not going to look like an idiot, *again*," she added more quietly.

"I am so unbelievably confused, V. Tell me what I did."

"It's worse when you pretend," she got out with a straight face, but she swallowed back the lump in her throat thinking about him laying on her lap and watching *The Little Mermaid*. There had to be something wrong with her for guys to keep running to other girls.

"I'm not pretending anything, will you please talk to me?" His green eyes showed legitimate concern, and if she wasn't mistaken, a little bit of hurt. *Good,* she thought. She needed to hurt someone back.

"No, I'm sort of all talked out for the day. Maybe go find your new freshman friend to converse with, she seemed very interested."

"What freshman friend?! Are you talking about-"

With the last of her will power, she clicked her heels to the girls' bathroom and let her backpack fall to the floor. She leaned over the sink, unsure if she was going to cry or throw up or break the mirror with her fist. *What a waste of a great outfit*, she told herself miserably into the mirror. Trying to push away the onslaught of emotions confronting her, she shook out her hands and rubbed her lips together, hoping that her control returned. *Zack with Jenna, Zack with Jess, Luke with Girl X*, she repeated. No amount of breathing could stop the slow trickle of tears down her cheek. It wasn't even clear over whom she was crying. It might not have been any of them, but more the loss of her former self. Where had the girl gone who didn't take crap from anyone, who couldn't help but laugh at girls in the bathroom crying at lunch, and who definitely wasn't *alone* when she had a problem? The reflection staring back at her was someone foreign, and she wasn't fond of her at all. She let people hold her back and walk all over her. "Suck it up," she spoke aloud to herself. She managed to fix her eyeliner and swipe some lip-gloss onto the plastered smile she forced to her face.

25

The rest of the day was jumbled. She couldn't eat and decided to spend lunch in the library. While she knew she could have sat with Kim, and she assumed Jess wouldn't be arrogant enough to attempt to sit anywhere near her lunch table, it was just enough already. Coupled with the fact that regionals were in two weeks, making the idea of skipping practice an impossibility, her head was ready to explode.

"The library is for reading, not sulking," the old bat of a librarian clucked at her. Vanessa made a show of grabbing the nearest book off of the shelf and opening it upside down in front of her. *Back to the sulking,* she thought. How she had fallen from such high hopes for this year just months before, and now she was hiding in the media center, desperate to stay away from any attention. She gritted her teeth to let those persistent tears know who was in charge. Vanessa Roberts didn't really *do* pitiful. There had to be some spark of the fiery girl who once either drew people to her flame or cautioned them to stay back. Currently, she was simply a forgotten ember waiting to go out.

"Well screw that," she voiced aloud, albeit quietly, drawing a warning brow raise from the woman behind the desk. Her eyes rolled somewhat apologetically. She would make it through this day, and this week, and this year.

That resolve was easier to hold onto in the quiet of the library than with sidelong glances coming from several junior football players. She forced herself to meet their eyes with a glare instead of casting her glance elsewhere. Rich only smirked at her, and she had a burning desire to smack the look off of his face. "Hey V," he called happily, falling in step next to her.

"Go to hell, Rich," she replied just as happily.

"Aw, I was just going to ask you to take a look at my car. I've heard you're really into back seats, so-"

"Let one more word come out of your mouth, and I swear you will look back on this as the day you used to have balls." *Angry is better than sad,* she calmed herself. Rich licked his lips like he might be readying himself for round two, but instead shook off her unwavering stare and headed towards class. He may have muttered a few unsavory names under his breath while he did so, but she'd been called worse by a lot better. Luke caught her eye from across the way and shot a questioning look. If she were to give him any indication of her current level of discomfort, she had no doubt he would be by her side. She shook her head slightly to dismiss him, and he turned his back in response. There was a minute possibility that she had misjudged the situation with him that morning, but there was an even smaller chance of her ever admitting that. She was sort of committed to her irrational anger at that point.

"So it would seem you've gotten a little bit of your scary back," a mildly familiar voice stated beside her before Spanish began.

"Hello Ethan." His presence drew jealous glares from a few other females in class. Those were her favorite glares.

"I believe it would be 'hola,' but I'm new here, so what do I know?" he grinned with those now-infamous dimples. His hair fell just past the tops of his ears, and he donned a hoodie with a band she'd never heard of on it.

"And what are you talking about?"

"Your scary? I dunno, it's like a force field. I noticed people avoided you when I first met you. I didn't know if it was because you were a bitch or just, you know, intimidating. It's the latter, if it makes you feel any better," he explained, stuffing his face with what was left of his Cheetos, she assumed from lunch. Were it anyone else, the *senora* would have taken the bag and trashed it, but no one treated Ethan Fisher quite the same.

"Gee, thanks. I thought you were supposed to be charming."

"Is that what you've heard?" he asked, looking pleased with himself. "Well, I tend to be more flattering when there's an actual chance to hook up. You and me though, we're cool. We're friends."

"Yeah, no. We're acquaintances. Although my friends do seem to be running in short supply lately."

"I mean, if you want me to flirt with you, I can turn it on. I just figured you and Luke… well, whatever." She couldn't tell if he really didn't care, or if he was trying not to pry. Either way, it didn't matter; he was a pretty distraction.

"Yeah, let's hear what you've got."

"Wait, seriously? You want me to flirt with you?"

"Yep. You've got about a minute and a half until the bell, so go."

"All right, first time for everything I guess," he grinned. "I, uh, I hear you just remodeled your basement?"

"*Really,* that's what you're leading with? Fine. Yes, I did."

He just kept on smirking like he knew something she didn't. It was annoying. "So you're into decorating and design?"

"Yes, it's a hobby. And?"

"I could kind of tell that about you when we met."

"What?" she questioned, her irritation coming through loud and clear. This was not impressive.

"Well, when you walk in, the whole room becomes more beautiful." The cheesy line finally sank in, and she felt a laugh begin in her belly.

"Oh my god."

"I know; it's a gift."

"So lame, but I will give credit where credit is due," she agreed, still chuckling. "We can be friends."

"Wow, a bump up from acquaintances with one line. I'd say I'm living up to my rep," he boasted, flashing his irritatingly captivating smile at her.

"Adios, Fisher," she replied, waving him back to his seat. Jess scurried in at the last moment and let her eyes brush over Vanessa's head, never meeting her harsh gaze. *This should be fun.* She spent the next hour of her life being oh-so-interested in Spanish. Something about Fisher's description of her *scary* prompted her to be as over the top as possible. He was damn right. She *was* scary. Her participation was quite out of character; even her teacher looked at her like she thought it was sarcasm, but she kept the same sweet smile all through class, grinning even wider when she heard Jess sigh in annoyance from the back of the room. She only paused in her horribly accented question to flip her hair. *Bite me,* she silently added.

* * *

Practice was monotonous, but she sort of rocked it. All of her newfound aggression was easily transformed into power in her tumbling passes, and the compliments from Brooke in front of Jess, who was sucking that day, only brightened her spirits. It didn't even remotely bother her when she left practice still covered in sweat. She didn't want to hang around the locker room and listen to whatever rumor was running through the mill. It was probably about her anyway. In a scene quite reminiscent of their first meeting, she ran her shoulder into none other than Zack Roads coming around the corner of the building. The token arrogant grin she'd once liked lit up his face, but she refused to shrink in front of him.

"Vanessa," he let out slowly.

"Asshole," she greeted in the same relaxed tone.

"Tsk tsk," he replied, his jovial expression clouded momentarily. "Such language."

"Would you prefer I call you a slimy woman-hitting bastard?" Her voice rang with a feigned genuine tone. His jaw set harshly, and a grim line took the place of his smile.

"You stupid little slut," he spat, his eyes glowing with a barely confined rage. The word 'slut' still stung, but she didn't show it.

"Takes one to know one," she winked at him. It was an awkward motion, but she was starting to understand why people did it. It was like putting an exclamation point on a statement with her face. *Who knew?* she thought. She was reveling in getting under his skin, as he had done to her for months, and it tempered the voice in the back of her head telling her to be afraid. Obviously too stupid to come up with anything wittier to say, Zack glared in silence. She mimicked the same stare back at him and moved to walk around him, utterly unimpressed that she had been so smitten with such an idiot. Her stomach still turned thinking about certain aspects of their *relationship.*

A large hand reached out for her shoulder to prevent her from passing, but before he could get out the words "Where exactly do you think-" she had planted her left foot firmly on the ground and was bringing her knee forward with all the force of the hurt and shame he had caused. A soft give between his legs let her know she'd hit pay dirt, and the groaning on the ground portion of the performance confirmed her precision.

"If you *ever* so much as breathe near me again, your grandchildren will feel the repercussions of it." As her adversary was unable to speak, she took his silence as a sign of understanding. With difficulty, she strode with her chin up to the parking lot, only glancing back once, or twelve times, to make sure he hadn't followed her. Once the adrenaline left her system, she was trembling slightly, but this did nothing to suppress her victory. *Finally,* she breathed. She spied her mom's Durango pulling in the parking lot and sank into the passenger seat, relieved.

"Everything ok?" her mom asked, assessing her still-sweaty appearance.

"Yes. Everything is ok," she declared, feeling like it might actually come true.

* * *

It was very odd to lose most of her close friends in a relatively short period of time. She was never without company if she wanted it, as she had acquaintances aplenty, but it wasn't the same. Kimmy came around more often, but it felt like they were trying to remember their past friendship rather than move forward with their current one. It dawned on her a week or so later while picking up the basement, that who she missed the most wasn't Kim, or Jess, or even Courtney, but Luke. That realization just wasn't ok. Vanessa had done little to repair the rift between them, finding it easier just to ignore him rather than allow him back in. The thought of him being with someone else bothered her more than she wanted to reveal, even to herself. Absently, she stared at her entertainment center, chewing her lip at the DVD cover boasting Ariel's red hair and the fancy Anniversary Edition script across the top.

"Mom!" she yelled, her voice harshly interrupting the silence. "Yes?"

"Can I borrow the car to run to the store?"

"Sure! Keys are on the table!"

While Vanessa always liked to be the recipient of grand gestures, the idea of being the giver of such a favor both excited her and went against her very clear rule about opening herself up to rejection. Once again, however, her very nature of doing first and thinking later won out, and she was in the car singing along to a playlist of old school divas on her way to the supermarket. Their confidence overshadowed her uncertainty. After suffering through the odd looks from the grocery store clerk, she was armed with a seemingly random peace offering and on her way to Luke's. She'd never been to his house before, but she knew roundabout where he lived and figured she'd see his truck outside. She did, and while there wasn't really a "bad part" of Gem City, some comments he made about his life were beginning to make sense. Pulling open the chain link gate, she traversed the cracked paved walkway to the old screen door at the front of the house, passing some overgrown weeds on her way. In the absence of a doorbell, she knocked loudly, the metal of the door clanging loudly against its frame. She could hear Luke's 180-pound self lumbering down the stairs before the inner door swung open.

"Vanessa," he stated like it was a question.

"Lucas."

"Whaaat are you doin' here?"

"Aren't you going to ask me in?"

"Wasn't planning on it, no."

"Were you planning on at least opening the screen door?"

"Hadn't thought about it."

"Fine, will you just come out here then? I have something for you."

"Is it a big fat apology?" She was really starting to regret her impulsive visit.

"There is a possibility that it includes a small skinny apology." He snorted, but pushed open the remaining barrier between them and stepped onto the porch. He wasn't exactly dressed for the weather in an undershirt and gym shorts. "Were you working out?" she asked, now nervous about the speech she'd hastily thrown together in her head while driving there. Looking at him was also proving distracting.

"Does it matter?" he asked, more annoyed than she thought he'd be.

"What's your problem?" she asked, ready to take the gifts and get back in her car.

"My problem is that you're jerking me around, V. You can only push me away so many times before I'll stop coming back. You can't just kiss me one day and decide I'm your punching bag the next." Her face flamed at his rather accurate accusation, but she didn't let it show in her eyes.

"I don't do that," she claimed with pursed lips.

"Uh-huh. What's in the bag?" *So he is curious,* she realized, some of her confidence returning.

"Before I launch into that... who was the girl?"

"Again I ask, does it matter?"

"I don't know. It might." She had come with the intention of offering him friendship, but it was eating her alive wondering why he was hugging female x in the hall.

"That was Aimes' sister," he stated, giving her no further information. He was going to make her work for this one.

"Ok... why were you hugging Troy's sister?" she asked through clenched teeth, trying desperately to remain civil.

"I wasn't. She was hugging me."

"Because..." He simply raised his eyebrows at her suggestively. "God, never mind. This was a stupid idea. I'll be going." Luke only chuckled at her discomfort.

"I had been helping her get ready for basketball tryouts. Troy's parents paid me to like, I don't know, coach her. She found out she made JV instead of the freshman team, and she came to say thank you. It was not quite the clandestine rendezvous you imagine. And I would have explained that to you had you not burst my eardrum with your locker slamming."

"Why didn't Troy help her?"

"Because Troy's an ass. I don't know, but I could use the money, so whatever. I don't need to explain myself in this case. You, however, do. So what's in the bag?"

Vanessa sat on a worn out cushioned chair on his porch, still wondering how he wasn't noticeably shivering, and began to take items out of the bag. "I... I do sort of owe you an apology. And I kind of miss hanging out with you... as a friend," she added quickly, not ready for this to be a declaration of feelings. First, she pulled out a package of Red Vines and Milk Duds and held them out for him. "I know how much you enjoyed having candy in your, well, whatever, it sounded funnier in my head and not so inappropriate, but here," she said quickly, shoving the candy towards him. He grinned and sat down next to her, taking the boxes.

"Are you blushing thinking about things in my pants?"

"Shut up or I'm not giving you the rest of the present." He held up his hands in surrender, and she continued. Next, she handed him the DVD of *Die Hard* and a One Direction CD with the song he'd played for her in the park on it.

"Aw, how nice of you to buy me an expensive coaster," he joked, referencing the CD.

"Yeah yeah, you know you're gonna listen to it and think of me," she shot back, feeling more like herself now that he'd dropped the cold and stony façade. Next up, she held out a sheet of cliché temporary tattoos. Some barbed wire, a heart, and a lightning bolt included. He took them skeptically.

"To show off your guns," she elaborated. He grinned at that and flexed, winning him an eye roll. With hesitation, she held out a tiny plastic horse.

"What is this one for?"

"Homecoming."

"Ah, HORSE. Got it."

"And not just that. You... well, you're the only one who cared about... or asked me if I was ok. I never said thank you. Because this is awkward." She couldn't meet his eyes at that point, just willing him to know that he had taken care of her without her even realizing that she needed it.

"You don't have to thank me for that," he mentioned softly, resting his arm around her shoulder. Being that close to him made her breaths more shallow; he still felt warm despite the temperature. He leaned in closer to her cheek. She knew she'd kiss him back if his lips found hers, so she tore her attention back to the last item in the bag. Grinning, she pulled out a plastic version of a gold chain with a giant dollar sign hanging at the bottom.

"In case you ever wanna take your love of rap to the next level."

"Hell yes!" he nearly shouted, taking the trinket from her palm and putting it over his head. He looked completely ludicrous, or *Ludacris*, she supposed, but his smile was genuine, or *Ginuwine*. She couldn't stop making stupid rapper references in her head.

"You totally want me right now, looking like this." She bit her lip, unsure of where to go from there.

"Listen, Luke, I don't know what we're doing here, but you and I... we'll kill each other if we try to date, or be together, if that's even what you want. My head's all over the place, but I do like hanging out with you, if you wanna be friends?"

"Nah," he replied lightly.

"Nah?" she questioned. "What the hell does that even mean?"

"It means you're being dumb."

"I am not being dumb, I'm being *reasonable*. I'm trying to keep us from tearing each other's heads off."

"Yeah, I just don't buy it. Sorry," he shrugged, taking his arm off of her shoulders so he could face her properly.

"Care to elaborate?"

"You like me. I know you do, so don't try to play whatever game you're playing. You like me, and you like making out with

271

me, and you like my arms. You just do. And I like you. You're completely impossible and annoying, but I like you anyway. I'm not proposing marriage to you, but I don't think you really just wanna be my friend. So if we kill each other, then we do. At least we'll have fun doing it."

"That sounds psychotic."

"You're the one who loves to fight with me, I don't know what to tell you. If you can honestly tell me you have no interest in me beyond friendship then fine, but you can't." She took a deep breath, and knew she'd be lying.

"Fine."

"Fine..."

"We can try not to kill each other."

"Aw, honey."

"Don't call me honey."

"Baby, babe, sweetie, sugar lips, Milk Duds?"

"Milk Duds? No. And NOT babe. Just V. Just call me V."

"K, V. Thank you for my presents. And my big fat apology." He leaned in much closer and she didn't try to dissuade him this time, allowing his lips to touch hers and his arms to make her feel protected. It was a dangerous game, but it felt right. This was how butterflies were supposed to feel in her stomach- light and fluttery. His kisses became more intense and he pulled her onto his lap, his fingertips playing with her waistband. "Do you wanna come inside now?" Her heart leapt, not sure what the implication was behind the question, and she felt her shoulders tense.

"Oh, um, sure," she assured him, determined not to let Zack ruin every romantic encounter she had in the future.

"No, I'm sorry, I didn't mean it like... I just meant it's cold out. Not that we needed to like go to my room, Jesus. Ok, that was not smooth. Do you wanna go out?"

"It's fine, let's go to your room," she pushed, overcompensating for her nerves because she refused to be afraid, or timid, or any other stupid adjective that did not define her. Her palms were sweating, and she cursed inwardly.

"V, stop. I can feel how tense you are right now. Let's go get coffee, or whatever sugar-filled beverage you call coffee. I really didn't mean it like that. Ok?"

"You don't have to treat me like I'm a damsel you know. You don't always have to save me… I don't need saving. At least not all the time."

"I'm not saving you, I'm saving me. I have no interest in doing anything with you unless the real you is there with me. Not the you who thinks she has something to prove. Let me take you to get coffee."

She was quiet for a moment, contemplating his honesty. "Aren't you supposed to be a dumb jock with only one thing on his mind."

"Dammit, I knew I was doing something wrong. Thank you for pointing out the error of my ways," he joked, pulling her into a crushing hug and kissing her neck sweetly.

"Carry me to the car," she requested, feeling more relaxed and bossy again.

"You carry *me* to the car. You're driving. Only damsels get carried, sorry." Vanessa put on a pout, but began to stomp towards the SUV. Luke sighed, threw her over his shoulder, and stalked his way to the fence with her giggling the whole way there.

26

The smell of ground coffee beans was nearly euphoric. She had been burning the candle at both ends trying to keep herself together, and she was tired. She even let Luke wrap his arms around her so she could lean against him while they waited in line at The Bean. This was one place in town where she sincerely admired the décor. Old books and whitewashed floors and lots of windows- plus the caffeine. Lots of caffeine.

With the largest mocha she'd ever seen warming her hands, she and Luke sank into the plush grey sofa in the corner.

"How are you not going to be ill drinking that thing?"

"Because I'll be insanely productive the rest of the day. Whipped cream and chocolate make me happy, not ill." He gave her a ridiculously sexy smile.

"Whipped cream and chocolate make me happy too in the right setting." She ground her teeth to keep from blushing. Or hitting him.

"You're disgusting."

"What? You're allowed to like toppings and I'm not? I think that's rather sexist."

"God, you think you're so funny," she chastised. Nevertheless, she let him kiss her cheek before returning to her beverage. The chime sounded on the door at the entrance to the shop as it had been all morning, but this time Luke's body tensed, causing her to look up. The sight she encountered was much more likely to make her ill than the 72 grams of sugar in her drink.

"Ok then, I guess this had to happen sooner or later," he muttered next to her. In line, Zack had his hands in Jess's back pockets while she ran her nails along his hairline. *Well, at least I wasn't overreacting.* Her nightmare had actually been pretty accurate.

"It's fine, we can go," she assured him, moving to stand up. Really, she just wanted to continue the morning without anyone punching anyone else.

"Under no circumstance will you or I be inconvenienced by trash like that." Luke appeared to make himself at home on the sofa and relaxed into his usual grin. His teeth were pretty. He was pretty, but she vowed not to tell him that.

It became clear by the sudden absence of giggling when Jess first spotted them. Rather, she cleared her throat several times and ordered her coffee quietly. Zack appeared to have made no such discovery, or perhaps he just didn't care.

"Luke, we can honestly just leave. Let's go to my house and watch a movie or something."

"Sure, as long as I get to pick the movie. And after I'm done enjoying this exceptional cup of coffee." *Ugh.* Much to her dismay, her hands were sweating as the new couple paid for their drinks. Zack's eyes flashed with something she couldn't name when he finally registered their presence. Gleeful anger tinged with a little bit of fear. Jess just bit her lip. "Roads! Long time dude, how've ya been?" Luke asked without faltering.

"Screw you, Miller. Better yet, go screw her, I'm sure you'll find it-" Luke was out of his seat with more speed than a human of his size should be allowed, and he was shoving Zack out the door before he finished the sentence.

"You and I need to chat," she could hear him growl on his way. Any trace of Vanessa's worry disappeared into a cloud of *I'm-with-him* when Zack's fear came to the surface of his face. She let Luke handle his business without spectating, and she instead turned her attention to the red-headed she-devil in front of her.

"Enjoying your adventure with domestic-violence?" The question was laced with as much syrupy malice as she could pour on.

Jess smiled. "You were always such a bitch. It was just funnier when you weren't bitter."

Vanessa almost spit out her coffee. *Bitter about losing out of the fun of being sexually assaulted in a parking lot?* "Yes, you're right. I'm so bitter that I'm not with an unbalanced sociopath on steroids. However will I recover? I know! With a super hot boyfriend who doesn't try to beat the shit out of me. Total bummer." Purposefully, she ended with a light smile and kept her eyes on Jess's. She tried to ignore the slight panic induced at the fact that she just called Luke her boyfriend. Hopefully he was cool with that.

"Whatever, Vanessa, I really don't have time to exchange witty insults with you in a coffee shop." This was, of course, code for *I don't have anything to best you with.* Vanessa's grin grew. "And before you hear it from Kim, or anyone else, and think you have some sort of dirt on me, I'm transferring to Troy Christian at the end of the year. You can celebrate later." Despite trying to maintain her nonchalant expression, surprise crossed Vanessa's face at this admission. She wanted to ask why, but their male counterparts reentered The Bean at that moment. Luke's face read happy and worry free. Zack's did not.

"Let's go, babe," Zack commanded, circling Jessi's wrist. They exited without further comment. Luke plopped down next to her and resumed drinking his beverage.

"Well?" Vanessa asked impatiently once they were gone.

"Well what? I won him over with my undeniable charm. He saw the light."

"Truth please?"

"Can you just trust that I handled it?"

"Oh I do, your faces were very clear about the victor and the loser, but I wanna know how." He grinned at that.

"I just let him know that the next time he opened his mouth, he should consider what it would feel like to be randomly drug tested at his next practice. Game over."

"I think I like you, Luke Miller."

"I think I like you, Vanessa Roberts."

"I may have told Jess that you were my boyfriend in one of my bitchy remarks. Just thought you'd wanna know." Her tone was light, but waiting for whatever reaction came next made her stomach drop.

"Boyfriend, lover, protector, knight in shining armor, whatever. All of it works for me." And then he winked at her. It served its purpose as she immediately pressed her lips to his and kissed him in a manner not appropriate for the only coffee shop in a town as small as theirs. And she didn't care.

Epilogue: Eight Weeks Later

Vanessa sat calmly on the edge of Luke's bed, running her fingers across the blue and gray plaid comforter, dreaming of ways to redecorate. His room was surprisingly neat, but completely in need of a makeover. His walls were a mish-mosh of posters, yes *posters,* put up with some sort of sticky nonsense. There was one area that was uncharacteristically empty, and she suspected a picture of a scantily clad girl had once hung there. At least he'd had the sense to take it down when he began dating her.

"I'm not going to yoga with you. One, I don't bend that way. Two, if I did, all of the women would be very distracted by me, and that's simply not fair. They're just trying to get a work out, and there I am, looking like this, so-"

"Put on your sweats and get in the car," she sang back happily, not dissuaded in the slightest.

"You realize you can't actually *make* me go. I'm bigger than you."

"Only physically. Mentally, I'm much bigger. And scarier."

"You *are* a bigger pain in the ass. I will not argue with you about that."

"Are you done? Because it's time to Namaste."

"Nah-Imma-Stay at *home.*"

"You read that on a t-shirt, stop trying to pretend you're that clever."

"Rahhhh!" Luke yelled as he pulled off his sweatshirt and grabbed a GCH t-shirt out of his drawer.

"Are you roaring at me?" she asked, partially amused, and partially distracted by his sudden shirtless-ness.

"Yes. You are stubborn, and I no longer have words." She chewed on her nail as he rummaged through a drawer to find appropriate yoga pants. It was unclear if she should leave the room while he changed. They'd been dating for two months, though technically they'd broken up twice. Each time, the two had just pretended not to remember about the agreement to break up and continued on as normal. Between that, a successful cheer regionals, and basketball practice, they mostly saw each other at school. There was just so much banter that they didn't really move beyond the occasional second base. It was good, she realized, that they never wanted for things to talk about. Things were *happy* with Luke, and it scared her more than she'd admit. The way her brain went fuzzy when he would finally shut up and kiss her was enough to fill up pages in her non-existent journal, but she wanted him to be the one to want more, and he seemed hesitant.

"Do you want me to close my eyes?" she questioned in a half-serious tone when he actually located acceptable workout pants.

"If you're afraid you won't be able to resist me, sure." Her eyes rolled back into their near-permanent state when they were together. He was incessant. "Sorry," he grinned sheepishly. "Sure, you can close your eyes if you want." A small grin emerged at that, as it did whenever he dropped his ego and shifted to his more serious side. Her eyelashes rested together while she waited, only peeking once, maybe twice, but she felt him standing in front of her moments later. He knelt at the edge of the bed and leaned into her, his arms pulling her in close. With difficulty, she fought the urge to open her eyes and look at him, and just let him kiss her softly. The more she was with Luke, the fainter the memories of her other relationship became. Each anxious moment from *before*, which was how she had come to refer to the whole regret-filled interlude, had slowly been replaced by funny and sweet and gentle, which were three of the last words in the English language she would have used to describe Luke Miller prior to that day in the parking lot. The little bit of scruff he kept along his jawline -after she mentioned she liked it- tickled her neck as he kissed her there.

"Are you doing your best work because you can't get enough of me? Or because you really don't wanna go to yoga?" she murmured as he continued in his journey to her collarbone.

"Obviously because I can't get enough of you," he answered seriously. He stopped what he was doing and pressed his forehead against hers. "Open your eyes." She did as he asked, feeling warm in his embrace. His green eyes were so intense at the moment, a sharp contrast to their usual jovialness. "You know how I feel about you, right?" he asked in almost a whisper. Her heart picked up at the implication he was making, and she really didn't think she could handle him making it anymore plain despite her own feelings running deeper than she originally thought they would.

"I do, yeah. Let's… can we just leave it at that? For right now?"

"Yeah," he breathed, seeming relieved. They held each other's gaze for several beats.

"I might be persuaded to stay here instead of going to the gym now," she flirted hesitantly. They were in uncharted territory, but it was more exciting than frightening. Her breaths came more quickly, not from nerves, but from needing him to stop treating her like he had to protect her from himself. He paused while his arrogant persona slipped back into view, so she took the opportunity to ruffle his hair.

"Are you sure about that? I don't wanna hear about how you missed yoga for the next three hours."

"Three hours?"

"That's when my mom gets home from work," he grinned devilishly, making her heart perform some serious acrobatics in her chest.

"Well then, I hope you have some ideas about how to entertain me. I sort of get bored easily," she teased him, wishing she were wearing something cuter than gray work out pants and a hot pink tank top.

"Bored you say? Challenge accepted," he boasted, grinning even wider now and sitting up on his knees. He tickled her sides lightly, but any laughter that began to bubble up quickly settled with the intensity of his next kiss. *He's been holding back,* she thought, returning his energy. He climbed onto the bed with her and blazed a trail with his lips from her chin to her waistband. It was more than that he was driving her insane with the scratchiness of his facial hair on her stomach; it was driving her insane that he'd found himself in a place where he could hurt her. The look on his face and the sweetness with which he traced her palm, however, told her that he didn't want to hurt her. With a renewed fire spreading through her veins, she pulled off his t-shirt to reveal a look of surprise on his face. *He should be shirtless always,* she thought with certainty, welcoming the warmth of his skin on hers.

"Hi," she whispered to him, not sure why she felt the need to say anything at all. She just needed to know they were on the same page.

"Hi," he smiled back, leaning away onto his side to gauge her expression. It wasn't necessary; she wasn't nervous. Not with him. "Everything cool?"

"Yeah, everything's cool. You smell good," she complimented randomly, wanting to hear him laugh.

"So do you," he admitted, leaning back in to kiss her neck.

"Um, so at the risk of killing the mood we have going on here, do you have protection?" She was done feeling embarrassed about talking about sex. If she'd learned anything, it was that just "going with the flow" and feeling regretful later was not something she was willing to repeat. Ever.

"Oh, ok, we're having this talk," he responded lightly. She appreciated that he took everything she threw at him in stride, never faltering. "Yes, I do. But that doesn't mean we have to do anything with it."

Vanessa sighed slightly. "I know. But do you want… that? With us? You just never say anything, so I don't… I just wanna know where your head's at, that's all." Her fingers slid between his, and their eyes met.

"V… of course I want that with you. I want everything with you. I just want to be… respectful, of where you're coming from," he explained tentatively. He kissed the tips of her fingers on her left hand, making her break out in goose bumps.

"You are so much more than I thought you were. Before, everything."

"I hope that's a compliment."

"The highest of compliments. It's not often I admit that I was wrong." He rubbed her bare arm with his free hand to chase away the shiver she experienced.

"Well in that case, go on," he joked, pulling her in even closer to him by the waist.

"Don't ruin it," she warned him jokingly. "I want that with you too." She got the words out before he captured her lips again. His playfulness had all but disappeared as his kissed every inch of her available, elbows included.

"Just tell me one more time that you're sure," he requested, his breath tickling her ear.

"I'm sure," she assured him, tracing his jaw with her nails.

"Thank god," he let out, resuming his earlier trail down her stomach. Every time he touched her, it made her feel alive, like she could remember the whole purpose for quickened heart-beats, heightened breaths, and soft lips.

* * *

"Are you ok?" he asked afterward, toying with the end of her ponytail.

"Of course. I'm with you," she replied honestly.

"That's the nicest thing I think you've ever said to me," he spoke somewhat seriously.

"Well, it's true. Now come here," she commanded lightly, drawing him back up to her lips. It didn't matter what they said or didn't say on that particular afternoon, and truthfully, she had a sincere fear of admitting her weakness for him. But she loved him. Not in the way a damsel loved her knight, though he was that for her on more than one occasion, but in the way that a fire loved oxygen. Even when she was sure it had gone out, he fed the spark that was left until she felt like herself again. He did protect her, but with the knowledge that she could take something from him too. In that moment, she let go of whatever had become of her before him. It was time to light the way to new adventures and brighter dreams.

Bonus Chapters - Luke

The Black Eye

The cold shower in the locker room had done little to quell the rage surging through his veins. The King of the Douchebags had been, as always, running his mouth while doing half the reps assigned for each rotation during weight training. *It's none of your business, it's none of your business, it's none.of.your.business,* he coached himself, pulling his t-shirt over his head. It was taking every ounce of restraint he possessed to ignore the conversation taking place one locker row over.

"I seriously can't believe you got her to give it up. She's such a princess," Rich Michaelson expressed with admiration.

"Really? I'm kind of disappointed at how easy it was. I thought she'd be a bit more of a challenge. It's amazing what a few "you make me a better man" speeches can do for a girl who wants it, I mean-"

"Does your mouth ever stop moving? Seriously, is there ever a time when absolute shit is not spewing from the hole in your face?" Apparently, he had chosen to abandon the plan of staying out of it. He was now feet away from Zack, his hands struggling to stay at his sides.

If Roads was surprised, he didn't show it. "Those are some bold words, Miller. You got a thing for Vanessa? I'm sure you can have her when I'm done. I'll try not to crush her." The smug, self-serving grin that spread across Zack's face as he looked directly into Luke's eyes was enough to snap something inside of him.

"You incredible piece of shit, I swear to-" but before he could relay the stream of expletives that had come to rest on his tongue, Rich and Mike Vlasser had him by the arms. He moved to shake them off, but they held their ground.

"Time to learn your place, sophomore," Rich murmured. Zack merely looked at him with an expression of mild amusement before he took two steps, reached back, and connected with his cheekbone. Heat and pain spread across his face like wildfire, his nerve endings screaming in protest. He managed to keep his face somewhat neutral, refusing to give the asshole the satisfaction of showing the amount of pain he was in. Rich and Mike had let him go as the punch landed, leaving him with his back against the wooden bench, his ass on the concrete floor.

"I think minding your own damn business might be the best course of action for you, Miller," Zack added, massaging his knuckles as the three of them exited the locker room.

"Shit," Luke muttered angrily to himself. He knew he could take Roads in a fight, but not three of them at once. Wincing, he touched his cheek gingerly. *Well, that escalated quickly.*

The Parking Lot

Luke checked the generic digital clock on the far side of the gym, hoping the time wasn't a mirage. Helping set up for open gym was sort of an obligation, being that he was the best player on the team- yes, that was an arrogant thought, especially as a sophomore, but there really wasn't any sense in denying it. He shot Coach Anderson a pleading glance and received a nod in return. Three point two seconds later he was out the door and on the way to his truck.

While searching for his keys in the black duffel hanging from his shoulder, he caught a glimpse of blonde hair in the distance. His eyes shot back to where Vanessa stood, looking less than comfortable with the proximity of none other than Zack Roads. Out of habit, he turned away, knowing full well she was going to have to see this asshole for what he was on her own. No amount of reason or begging had worked so far; he had no idea why it would start now. Before tearing his eyes away, he watched Zack run his thumb across Vanessa's face. It struck him at that moment that there was nothing but abject fear in her eyes.

Dammit dammit dammit. The word resounded like a shotgun blast through his head as he picked up the pace towards her Durango. *Don't kill him.* No sooner had that thought crossed his mind when the prick's hand swung forcefully at the pretty blond girl with tears in her eyes, connecting with her cheek and sending her to the ground. The world went still, and he was unable to focus on killing this creature now smiling over his victim until he saw that she was relatively ok. She was moving. Then, so was Zack. Luke felt his fist grasp the back of his shirt, and he yanked with the force of all of the adrenaline running through his veins. There was little resistance as Roads' large frame toppled towards the asphalt, landing with a satisfying grunt.

"You are so going to regret the last five minutes of your life." He stood between the pond scum and Vanessa, determined to end this by any means necessary. With effort, he shoved the flashbacks of his mom in a similar state at the hands of his father from his mind. He was a kid then, but he was not a kid now.

The dick had the audacity to laugh, as though he had no idea how much rage was about to be unleashed upon him. "Seriously Miller? Walk away before you cause yourself more trouble than she's worth."

Everything. She's worth everything. "Yeah, ok, so new rule. From this moment, you don't speak to or about her. Ever." Zack had gotten to his feet and was shooting daggers at them both.

There was only a fight response readying itself in his muscles- flight was not an option.

"Get bent, man. What do you actually think is going to happen right now?"

"I think if you take one step towards Vanessa, I'm going to deck you in the face. That's what I think is going to happen. So maybe you just walk back to your douche-mobile." It was a lie. He was going to deck him even if he had to provoke him into the altercation. Zack dropped his eyelids in doubt. It was enough.

His fist connected with Zack's jaw with one closing stride, sending him effectively back to the pavement. "Or maybe I don't actually care if you take a step. Don't.Hit.Women. You 'roided out piece of shit." Luke's voice was low and calm, but it was a barely controlled rage that came through his teeth. Zack spat blood onto the gritty parking lot surface. "Not so tough without your lackeys to hold me back, huh?" Luke asked, referencing his almost-healed cheekbone.

"You *will* regret this." Zack was up and walking away, probably more quickly than he'd admit later.

"Not even for a second," Luke shot back, shaking out his hand. It didn't matter if it was broken or sprained or anything. He'd been waiting to do that for a long time. Once he was sure Zack wouldn't return to sucker punch him, he cautiously turned around to assess Vanessa. She looked frozen, but they didn't have the luxury of waiting around until she came out of it; he needed to get her out of there. "V, get in the car." She didn't move for a moment. "V," he said more gently, touching her arm and causing her to jump slightly. "It's ok. Let me drive." He took the keys firmly from her and guided her around to the passenger side. He wanted to crush her against him, to sincerely feel that she wasn't broken, but it had to wait.

"But. Your truck?" He almost grinned at the irrelevance of her first words to him after what had transpired, but the smile wouldn't come yet.

"It's fine, let's just get you home." She allowed him to help her into the car. He could feel her shaking under his support, and he cursed inwardly at not getting there sooner. *This is your fault,* he berated himself. *You should have pushed harder to make her understand.* He placed himself in the driver's seat and pulled out of the lot slowly, looking for that ridiculous Charger.

"I, um, you were. Just…" And then she was crying. His heart was torn between wanting to pull over and hold her and wanting to get out and chase down the motherfucker that did this. The feeling of helplessness was overwhelming. She was breathing too fast.

"V. You have to take slower breaths. You're going to hyperventilate. You're ok. You're safe. Just breathe." He tried to maintain a sense of calm.

"I can't. I can't… I don't…"

"You don't owe me an explanation. You don't owe anybody anything. You're ok." She leaned out of her seatbelt and onto his shoulder, and he immediately put his arm around her and pulled her in tighter. This he could do. He could hold her and make sure she got home. A few minutes later, he was pulling into the driveway in front of the Roberts' home. He gave up trying to hold back and wrapped both arms around her, willing her to stop shaking.

"V," he almost whispered. "Let's go inside." She only nodded, but made no move to get out. Luke hurried around to the passenger door and tugged her arms slightly. "I'll carry you if you want." He was so lost as to how to treat her or what to do. She was always the strongest girl he'd ever known, sassy to a fault. This version of her was more frightening than he'd like to admit.

"I can walk," she breathed, sliding off of the seat and onto the ground.

"Is your mom home?"

"Um, I'm not sure? The other car's not here, so I guess not." *No way in hell you're leaving her alone.* He led her up the walkway, trying to give her space. Her hand found the red mark on her face, and anger swelled up inside of his chest.

"Do you want some ice?" he asked with difficulty, setting her bag on the floor. He hadn't been to her house since her birthday party in seventh grade, but it looked the same. A lot of roosters. She looked far away when she answered.

"Um, yeah, probably. I don't… will it leave a bruise?"

His fingers gently brushed her jawline, tilting her injury towards him. His breath caught in his throat thinking about Zack's hands on her. "The ice should help. It's not turning purple yet, so maybe not. You'll know in the morning." He moved into the kitchen and found a bag of frozen peas and a dishtowel, handing them to her.

"Your hand. You need ice more than me," she offered.

"Nah, I'm fine. He just had a hard face." She almost smiled as she sat tentatively on the couch in her living room. He positioned himself on the ottoman in front of her.

"Luke…Your timing was good. Today." That actually did make him chuckle. No one had ever accused him of having good timing before.

"I think it could have been a little better," he admitted, pointing at her current state.

"Maybe just a little," she agreed.

He took a breath and readied himself for an argument. "V, I think maybe we should call the police or something. I can call them, and I'll stay with you, but you need to report this."

"No. Luke, no one can know that this happened. Please." Tears started to form again, and it ate at his heart.

"If he tries to… Vanessa, I can't think about what would have happened if I had left school on time today. I was helping with open gym for new freshman, and that's the only reason I was there. No one else was there, V. He needs to pay for whatever he was going to do. What he *did* do. He put his hands on you."

He needed her to understand what could have happened. What Zack was capable of. She shook her head forcefully.

"You know how small this town is. You know who his parents are. There is very little in this situation that would go well for me." She gripped her knees tightly into her chest. "Please," she begged.

"Do you want me to kill him?" he asked. That was really the only thing he had left to offer. And he wanted to kill him.

Her eyes softened slightly. "No, but thank you for offering."

"I'll totally kill him. Seriously. Dead. People would thank me." She laughed through her nose.

"You don't have to stay and babysit me. If you need to go, you can."

"Well, no, I can't. My truck's at school. And if it's all the same to you? I'd rather not leave you alone anyway."

"I'm a big girl, Luke," she pressed, and he hated that she was pushing him away.

"Yeah, it's not really for you." She looked at him, confused. "If I leave, I'm going straight to his house. And you told me not to kill him. So it's probably better if I hang here with you for a while."

"Well, as long as it's for your benefit," she agreed. He let out a breath at her allowing him to stay.

"Oh yeah, absolutely. Nothing to do with your safety. I mean, who cares, right?"

"Right," she grinned. "Do you want to watch *The Breakfast Club* with me?"

Some of the tension left his shoulders as he saw a bit of the Vanessa he knew creep back into her face. "I don't know what that is, but ok. Is it on the Food Network?" Her mouth opened slightly in disbelief.

"Are you being for real right now?"

"Yeah, why?" She just shook her head and pulled him to his feet with his uninjured hand, leading him down the stairs to her new sanctuary.

"Whoa... this is your project? It's done?" he asked. He didn't know anything about decorating, but the room was cool. And clean, and like, put together.

"Yes!" she practically shouted at him. "*That* is the appropriate reaction to this room. Jesus. Thank you," she finished.

"Well, you clearly feel strongly about that," Luke laughed. "It looks cool in here. I mean, there are sort of a lot of pillows, but I like it."

"I do like pillows," she admitted, scouring the built-ins for her DVD. "Here we go," she announced, popping the movie into the player and turning back towards him. "Come, sit," she requested, sinking into the low-backed sofa. The couch was actually really comfortable, and he let his arm stretch out behind her, refraining from pulling her onto his lap.

"I like it. It's comfy," he declared. "Are you going to be a decorator or something?" She gave him an odd look at the question, making him wonder if he'd said something wrong.

"Like... in life?" she asked cautiously.

"Yeah, in life I guess. Do you go to school for it or do you just do it? Or intern or something. I don't know."

"There are design schools."

"Ok, are you being vague for a reason? Do you wanna go to one?"

"Who knows. Probably not. It's hard to get a job as a designer."

"Well, I would hire you," he assured her, hoping they could maintain whatever sense of calm they had going on. "So... I take it this is a movie. Is it about breakfast? Because that sounds lame."

"Just shhh. It's not lame. Don't say that." He tried to focus on the opening scenes of the film. It still looked lame. He really just wanted to know if she was ok, but he sensed that wasn't a question she would entertain at the moment. Silently, she forked over the frozen peas for his hand, and this time he didn't argue. His hand hurt. "Do you need water or anything? I have snacks..." she trailed off.

"I'm good. No worries," he assured her, nudging her shoulder slightly with his outstretched arm. She leaned back against the cushions and draped her stocking clad feet across his lap. He finally relaxed some having her closer to him. He tried not to watch her, but he couldn't help it. Less than ten minutes into the movie, she was asleep.

Luke rested his head on the back of the couch and stared up at the ceiling. *What are you doing?* He knew that he liked her more than was probably reasonable for as much as she drove him insane. Not to mention that she was now going to be dealing with the fallout from this whole Zack situation. God, he hated that guy. It didn't really matter though, he didn't think he could stay away now. When it was just an attraction, that was one thing, but now there was a whole protective instinct mixed in, and it was proving very difficult to overcome.

When he heard the garage open, he extricated himself from Vanessa's legs, hoping to meet her mom and explain *some* of what happened without waking her. He recognized that it wasn't his story to tell, but he was sure as hell going to make sure someone else was looking out for his girl, er, Vanessa.

The First Time

There was almost no way she was going to convince him to go to yoga. She was sitting on the edge of his bed wearing those damned yoga pants, which, by the way, were most certainly invented by a male because they were *amazing* and a pink tank top that didn't quite cover her belly button. They had hardly had any alone time in months besides brief moments in the car, or the one time she'd consented to let him take her to the river.

Her general anxiety while they were there made him really not want to know what when down with her and Roads, and he vowed to make her forget it if it was the last thing he did. Her blue eyes were sparkling with victory at him finally getting out gym clothes.

"Do you want me to close my eyes?" she questioned in a half-serious tone when he actually located acceptable workout pants.

"If you're afraid you won't be able to resist me, sure." Her eyes rolled back into their near-permanent state when they were to-gether. Sometimes he couldn't help himself. "Sorry," he grinned sheepishly. "Sure, you can close your eyes if you want." *Ugh, why is this so difficult?* They were *good* together, but he could see it in her eyes whenever they started to cross that threshold, that she was thinking about *him.* Purposefully, he pulled on a soft green tank top, hoping she would be mesmerized by his arms, and he could talk her out of this ridiculous yoga adventure. The only flexibility he was interested in assessing was- He stopped mid-thought as she was looking at him curiously now that he was dressed and off in his own world. *How does she do that?* he wondered. Regardless, he sauntered over to where she sat and kneeled in front of her, leaning in to nip at her neck. She would never admit how much she liked it, but he did it anyway to get her to breathe the way she did. He rubbed his thumbs along her barely exposed stomach and groaned inwardly. This girl…

"Are you doing your best work because you can't get enough of me? Or because you really don't wanna go to yoga?" she mur-mured as he continued on his journey to her collarbone.

"Obviously because I can't get enough of you," he answered seriously. He never got enough of her; how did she not under-stand this? With trepidation, he stopped what he was doing and pressed his forehead against hers. "Open your eyes." She did as he asked, and he tightened his arms all the way around her. "You know how I feel about you, right?" he asked in almost a whisper. He knew they weren't in a place to be making declarations; she was still fiercely guarding her independence, but he just needed her to know.

"I do, yeah. Let's... can we just leave it at that? For right now?"

"Yeah," he breathed, feeling like they were at least on the same chapter, if not the same page. They held each other's gaze for several beats.

"I might be persuaded to stay here instead of going to the gym now," she flirted hesitantly. *Oh thank god,* he thought. A slow smile crept over his face, and he was determined to make her enjoy that decision.

"Are you sure about that? I don't wanna hear about how you missed yoga for the next three hours."

"Three hours?"

"That's when my mom gets home from work," he grinned devilishly.

"Well then, I hope you have some ideas about how to entertain me. I sort of get bored easily," she teased him. *There's my girl.*

"Bored you say? Challenge accepted," he boasted, grinning even wider now and sitting up on his knees. He tickled her sides lightly, but captured any laughter she might have let out with his next kiss. Holding her against him tightly, he pulled her lip between his teeth. He needed to make sure she was here with him, not in her own head. Climbing onto the bed with her, he blazed a trail with his lips from her chin to her waistband. Stopping, he took in her overall demeanor and traced her palm lightly with his fingers. She paused with him, seeming to contemplate the moment. He knew that he didn't hide his surprise well when she reached for the hem of his shirt and dragged it over his head. Her hands felt good on his bare chest, and it was enough for him to shake off the uncertainty of her intentions. He needed her to be closer. Holding himself above her, he kissed her most favorite spot beneath her ear.

"Hi," she whispered to him, breaking the silence.

"Hi," he smiled back, leaning away onto his side to gauge her expression. She didn't look nervous like he'd expected. She looked...happy. "Everything cool?"

"Yeah, everything's cool. You smell good," she complimented randomly, making him laugh.

"So do you," he admitted, leaning back in to kiss her neck.

"Um, so at the risk of killing the mood we have going on here, do you have protection?" That hadn't been the next thing he expected to come out of her mouth, but her ability to shock him was sort of one of his favorite things about her.

"Oh, ok, we're having this talk," he responded lightly. He sincerely hoped this wasn't some sort of trick question. "Yes, I do. But that doesn't mean we have to do anything with it."

Vanessa sighed slightly. "I know. But do you want... that? With us? You just never say anything, so I don't... I just wanna know where your head's at, that's all." Her fingers slid between his, and their eyes met. *Jesus,* he thought.

"V... of course I want that with you. I want everything with you. I just want to be... respectful, of where you're coming from," he explained tentatively. He kissed the tips of her fingers on her left hand.

"You are so much more than I thought you were. Before, everything."

"I hope that's a compliment."

"The highest of compliments. It's not often I admit that I was wrong." He rubbed her bare arm with his free hand to chase away the shiver he'd witnessed run through her.

"Well in that case, go on," he joked, pulling her in even closer to him by the waist. She felt so good against his skin.

"Don't ruin it," she warned him jokingly. "I want that with you too." She got the words out before he captured her lips again. He wanted to kiss her everywhere, to explain what he couldn't say yet- her neck, shoulders, wrists, elbows, fingertips- everywhere he could reach.

"Just tell me one more time that you're sure," he requested, needing to hear her say it.

"I'm sure," she assured him, tracing his jaw with her nails. His brain would stop working shortly, so that answer was exactly what he needed.

"Thank god," he let out, resuming his earlier trail down her stomach. Finally, he knew she was all there, with him. There were no more ghosts of relationships past here in this moment, and he let himself be all there too, with her. Being with her, it was nothing like he'd ever experienced. She was so beautiful when she let down her walls and let him see her, let him get close to her.

* * *

"Are you ok?" he asked cautiously, toying with the end of her ponytail. He didn't know that he was ok. He was utterly infatuated with this girl. Making love to her had only shown him that he was in deep with whatever they were doing here.

"Of course. I'm with you," she replied seriously.

"That's the nicest thing I think you've ever said to me." That wasn't a joke.

"Well, it's true. Now come here," she commanded lightly, drawing him back up to her lips. He knew he was dangerously playing with fire, but there was no turning back now. He returned her kiss with everything he had, just hoping not to get burned.

Thank you so much for reading! I would love for you to leave a review and share your thoughts!

New From Nicole Campbell:

Be on the lookout for my new stand-alone:
The Tower

Also in the works is a final Gem City novel,
Where Gravel Roads Lead Home
We can finally get inside Luke's head and hear his story.

Visit NicoleCampbellBooks.com for updates and a chance to beta read or win a copy of the book!

Acknowledgements

If someone would have told me in March of last year that I would have a four books written by the following April, I would have looked at them oddly and walked away. Writing a novel just wasn't in my "right now" plan. Once I put pen to page (or fingers to keyboard), I could stop, and now I wouldn't give it up for the world.

Writing from Vanessa's point of view was eye opening. In a lot of ways, I got to re-live some of my younger years by being with these characters for the last twelve months. I want to thank all of my friends from the days of my adolescence who gave me such great inspiration to create Gem City and its residents.

My little sister has been the absolute biggest supporter of this series, having shot all of the covers and promo shots for each book (even when neither of us were too totally sure what we were doing). It has definitely been a journey, and I am so happy that she's been along for the ride.

I really wanna throw a shoutout to the whole bookstagram and Goodreads communities who have made this whole author business so much more fun. I love all of you crazy, book-obsessed, fandom-loving people, because you're my people :).

Last, but never least, my husband and my son, who still act excited when I get a new review (well, my son is four, so he's just excited about the world in general) or have a good week of sales. I love them!!!

Facebook:
https://www.facebook.com/NicoleCampbellBooks/
Instagram: @NicoleCampbellBooks
Website: NicoleCampbellBooks.com

A Note From the Author

Writing a book was sort of one of those things that I thought about and never actually intended on doing. I spoke to a seventh grader in my English class about the idea for the book one day while I was teaching a creative writing unit, and she *insisted* that I at least write it as a short story. I took that as a challenge more than anything, and I sat down that afternoon and outlined the plot in some random spiral notebook. Exactly four weeks later I had completed the draft. It became a complete obsession for me, I couldn't stop. At this point I have a hard time remembering what life was like before I started writing, and I am so thankful for that initial conversation with one of my (now favorite) students. I will publish one more book in the Gem City collection from Luke's point of view during his and Vanessa's senior year, *Where Gravel Roads Lead Home.* All in all, I can't imagine *not* writing, and I am eager to get into my next series as well to move a little bit away from just straight Contemporary/Romance. I love chatting with readers, so please comment on my blog or social media; I will totally respond!

CPSIA information can be obtained
at www.ICGtesting.com
Printed in the USA
LVHW020048190121
676853LV00022B/561/J

9 781034 243304